Cor

Cant

Literacy Festival

Suite #8
55 Canterbury Street
Saint John, NB E2L 2C6

Running Away

by

Peter H. Riddle

DREAMCATCHER PUBLISHING
Saint John • New Brunswick • Canada

The characters and events in this novel are entirely products of the author's imagination, and actual sites that exist within the Nova Scotia locale are used fictitiously.

DreamCatcher Publishing acknowledges the support of the New Brunswick Arts Council.

Canadian Cataloguing in Publication Data

Riddle, Peter H. - 1939

Running Away

ISBN - 1-894372-28-X
  I. Title.
PS8585.I4152R85 2003   C813'.6   C2003-903639-1

Editor: Yvonne Wilson

Typesetter: Chas Goguen

Cover Design: Dawn Drew, INK Graphic Design Services Corp.

Printed and bound in Canada

DREAMCATCHER PUBLISHING INC.
105 Prince William Street
Saint John, New Brunswick, Canada E2L 2B2
www.dreamcatcherbooks.ca

Dedication

For Gay, who could be Catherine…
…always there when I need her.

Acknowledgements

If I could grant one wish to aspiring authors everywhere, it would be to work with an editor as wise and helpful as Yvonne Wilson. And to Barbara Rushton, who read the manuscript first and encouraged me to continue developing it, I will forever be grateful.

Other Works by Peter H. Riddle

Fiction:

Twelfth Birthday
Thirteenth Summer
Fourteenth Concerto

Non-fiction:

The American Musical: History and Development
Wiring Your Toy Train Layout
Track Planning Ideas for Toy Trains
America's Standard Gauge Electric Trains
Easy Lionel Layouts You Can Build
Tips & Tricks for Toy Train Operators *(1ˢᵗ & 2ⁿᵈ Editions)*
Greenberg's Guide to Lionel Trains 1901-1942, Vol. III
Writing your Lionel Layout (*Three Volumes*)
Trains from Grandfather's Attic

ONE...

Highway 331 wanders along the Atlantic coast of Nova Scotia, due south of the town of Bridgewater. A few kilometres east of the tiny village of Petite Riviere, a narrow road branches off toward the southeast, skirting Green Bay on its way to the aging settlements of the LaHave Islands.

Andrew Striker leaves the highway at this intersection and manoeuvres his car down the narrow access ramp that leads to the hard sands of Crescent Beach. In the fog-shrouded promise of dawn, with the sun not yet risen above the tops of the trees on the distant islands, he backs the car up close to the weathered log pilings that separate the beach from the road. He gets out and limps toward the water's edge, the stiffness of early-morning arthritis ordering his awkward, hitching gait.

The tide is low, having left behind clumps of shiny, dark green seaweed that lie scattered in broken rows parallel to the surf line. A trio of herring gulls observes his arrival, severe sentries jealously patrolling their assigned segments of sand. Occasional discarded feathers, their wispy tendrils twitching in the gentle onshore breeze, adhere to the seaweed and cling to pieces of driftwood. Just past the tide's ebb, the water barely disturbs the stray detritus in its wash.

Andrew gazes out over the placid surface of Green Bay, where it stretches toward the far reaches of Broad Cove. He has come, as is his almost daily pattern, in *search*, although the goal remains undefined. Perhaps he longs for some sort of answer, or merely a simple lifting of his spirits. More likely it is in hope of escaping from the patient, threatening vipers that lie waiting in ambush among the jumbled, disintegrating rocks of his memory. *Alzheimer's*, he thinks. *How long before I even forget the word?*

Once he and his beloved Catherine walked hand in hand through sands like these, their children new and bright and fleeting in their graceful dance at the edge of the surf's gentle swell. How could they ever have thought that tomorrow wasn't there?

He turns to his left, finding the sands all but deserted. Despite his six-plus decades of life, his eyesight remains keen, at least at a distance. He spots just a single figure, squatting close to the water more than a mile away. No one else. He likes it that way, with nothing to disturb the fantasy of a long-gone family still at his side. As the day progresses, he will leave the beach rather than compete for space with others, the residents and summer visitors whose presence centres on recreation rather than contemplation.

The sands are cleaner than usual. The calm night and gentle waves of the receding tide have left little but the seaweed, interspersed with shards of clam and mussel shells that lie grouped as if on platters for the gulls to savour. Andrew stretches his stiff limbs and heads eastward. The ache in his right knee, the joint most ravaged by arthritic deposits, begins to recede in the face of his determined effort. The pain withdraws by half, taking with it some of the visible evidence of his lameness.

Although fine-grained and mostly devoid of gravel, the densely packed sands of Crescent Beach yield little to his footsteps. Even close to the water's edge, the rippled pattern made by his ancient Nikes barely penetrates the surface. With the tide just beginning to turn, the first tentative fingers of white-flecked brine slide noiselessly inland to erase the faint ridges left by his soles.

His attention is divided between the shore and the bay, the latter strangely empty and primitive, with not a single sail to signal human intrusion. He wanders along listlessly, his ears attuned to the tiny sounds the ripples make, awaiting in vain the peace the ocean promises but so rarely delivers. At first imperceptibly, the encroaching tide begins to gain strength, and he watches aimlessly as it progresses up the sand.

It takes him more than half an hour to come upon the solitary figure who is the only anomaly in the deserted landscape, a child absorbed in the mysteries of sand and shells. He is about to pass by, then wonders at her isolation, the absence of family or friends to see to her safety. She seems so very young. He turns toward her.

"What brings you out so early?" he asks.

The small, solemn face regards him suspiciously. "I'm not allowed to talk to strangers." The child's attention returns to the mound of seaweed on the sand between her knees.

In other words, Andrew thinks, *I should mind my own business.* "A very good rule," he comments aloud, but quietly and more to himself than to her.

She does not look up. Meticulously she separates the strands of seaweed and extracts a starfish, holding it aloft by a single arm. She places the creature into a small red plastic bucket, then peers intently at it, deliberately ignoring the tall, gaunt man who stands a half dozen yards away.

He shrugs and turns to continue on down the beach, but her presence nags at his conscience. He knows no child should be alone at such an early hour, even in the relatively safe environment of Nova Scotia's rural South Shore. *Not my concern, damn it. Still...*

He turns back to regard her. "Do you live around here?"

No response. The child fixes her concentration on the contents of the bucket, tilting it first left and then right.

He tries again. "My name is Andrew. If you tell me yours, we won't be strangers any more, and you can talk to me."

She looks up in disgust. "Yeah, and I'm supposed to fall for that one."

Andrew grins at her, but she continues to glare. He squats down, rocking back on his heels, then feels a stab of pain shoot down his leg from his arthritic knee. He pushes backward and sits down, stretching his right leg out in front of him to ease the discomfort. *Maybe I won't seem so threatening down low like this*, he thinks.

He points to her bucket. "Are you going to take that home?" Still no response, and no lessening of her distrustful glower. "It's alive, you know," he continues.

She peers down into the bucket. "No it's not."

He studies her for several long seconds. "I'll bet I can prove to you that it is. If I do, will you talk to me?"

"You don't give up, do you?"

"Is it a deal?"

The child looks back into the bucket. "It's not moving."

"That's because it's not in the water. Take it out carefully and turn it over. Don't squeeze it. If you look at the bottom, you'll see that it's all covered with little knobs."

She looks at him warily. "You stay over there." She tilts the bucket on its side, then slants it so the starfish slides out onto the palm of her hand. With one finger she gingerly levers it up and flips it over. She stares at it briefly. "It's dead."

"Nope. Look closely at the little bumps on its arms. They're like tiny thin fingers. Just keep watching them."

She brings her hand up close to her face to examine the creature. Her eyes widen in surprise as she detects tiny movements, and she peers at it even more keenly. She pokes gently at one of the arms and pushes it to one side, watching with intense concentration as it slowly creeps back again.

"Okay," she says, "so you were right."

"Now you have to tell me your name," he says.

"No I don't. I never promised to."

"Boy, you drive a hard bargain. At least tell me if you're going to take the starfish home with you."

"Why shouldn't I?"

"Because it will die."

"So what? There are a lot of starfish in the world."

"There are a lot of ten-year-old girls, too."

"I'm eleven," she says without thinking. Then she looks up, startled, suddenly grasping his meaning. "That wasn't very nice."

"I'm sorry. I just meant that I wouldn't want the world to lose anyone like you, either."

With exaggerated caution she slides the starfish off her palm and back into the bucket. Then she gets up and carries it down to the water and wades out until her bare feet and ankles are covered by the foam. She dips the bucket and fills it half way. She stands in the surf, carefully examining the now submerged animal.

"It still isn't moving."

"Maybe it got washed up on shore because it's dying," Andrew says. "There's no way to tell for sure. But it could still be okay, and if you put it back in the ocean, who knows how long it might live."

She looks down into the bucket again. "But I want to keep it."

"I'll make you a deal. Down near where I live, there's a gift shop. They have dried starfish for sale, already dead ones. If you let this one go, I'll bring you one of those."

She considers his offer carefully. Andrew draws his knees up and wraps his arms around them, smiling in her direction. She makes her decision, wades out until the water reaches her knees, and upends the bucket. She stands there for several seconds, looking down at the spot where the creature has disappeared into the greenish froth. Then she wades back to shore and sits down again, carefully maintaining the distance between them.

"I'll bring you your starfish tomorrow morning," he says.

She looks down at the sand and toys with a half clamshell. "I don't want it."

"Why not?"

Her head snaps up, her eyes flashing but sad with resignation. "Because if you buy one, then the store will need more to sell, and somebody will have to kill another one to replace it. So it's the same as if I let one die myself."

He regards her with a mixture of wonder and admiration, and she shrinks in discomfort from his gaze. For several long minutes they sit in silence. Occasionally she steals a glance in his direction, seeing him first smiling at her, then looking out to sea.

"Jennie," she says softly.

"What?"

"My name is Jennie."

"Jennie what?"

"Don't push it!" She turns to stare out over the bay.

"Okay, Jennie Don't-push-it, and my name is Andrew Striker. It's very nice to meet you."

She turns her face back toward him. This time her smile is more relaxed and friendly. "Jennie Horton. And no donut shop jokes, please."

"I wouldn't think of it. Do you come out here often, all by yourself?"

"This is the first time. My mom started her new job today, at McDonald's in Bridgewater. She had to be there by six. She dropped my little sister off at day care, but I get to stay home alone." She pauses, stirring little whorls into the sand. "I guess she'd be mad if she knew I was out here."

"How come?"

" 'Jennie, don't talk to strangers. Jennie, don't go out after dark. Jennie, don't go to the beach alone.' It's always something with her."

"That doesn't sound like such bad advice to me," Andrew says.

She bristles. "I'm not a little kid. I can figure things out for myself. Like for instance, I know *you* wouldn't do anything bad to me." Suddenly alarmed, she looks at him uncertainly, her eyes widening.

He laughs gently. "But you're not absolutely sure, are you?"

She drops her eyes, her finger idly tracing loops in the sand.

"How about your dad?" he continues. "What does he do?"

"He drinks," she says in disgust. "At least, that's about all he ever did until he left."

Andrew backs off. "I'm sorry. That's none of my business."

"It's none of mine either, not any more. I was seven the last time I saw him. He came out of the kitchen with a bottle in his hand, and my mom was crying, and he threw the bottle at the wall and it broke all over the place. Some of the glass flew into my sister's playpen. Mom started screaming at him, and ran over to pick her up."

"Was she hurt?"

"No. The glass missed her. I remember the look on my dad's face, though. His eyes got real wide, and he looked down at his hands and turned them over and just stared at them. Then he looked at my sister, and he backed up and went out the door. Mom said he came back the next day and got his clothes and stuff, but I didn't see him. And I haven't seen him since."

Andrew sits silently, not quite sure how to respond to such candour. Presently Jennie gets up and takes a few steps toward him. She measures the distance between them with her eyes, then sits down a careful two feet out of his reach. She draws her knees up in imitation of his posture. She puts her bucket down between her feet and begins sifting the sand for small shells. Each time she finds one, she drops it into the bucket.

He looks west toward his parked car. Three more have joined it, and he can just make out the tiny figures of the day's first vacationers, some sitting on blankets and some wading in the bay. "Company coming," he says absently. "I usually leave when anyone else gets here." He starts to rise.

"I hate him!" she says softly but vehemently, her head down and her eyes fixed on the bucket.

He sinks down again. "Your dad?"

"Uh, huh."

"Does it help?"

She looks up, confused by his question.

"I mean, does it make you feel better to hate him?"

She considers briefly. "I don't know. I never thought about it before. I guess it does, though."

He decides to pursue it a little further. "Does he know you hate him?"

"You'd think he could figure it out!" she says hotly. "But why would he care? He never cared about me when he was home!"

"So being mad at him doesn't do him any harm, does it?"

She sighs deeply and extracts another shell from the sand. "Nope."

"What does it do to you?"

"Makes me feel better, I guess."

"Maybe," Andrew says. "But you don't sound so sure. Maybe it really makes you feel worse. Hate does that, you know. It does the most damage to the person who does the hating."

Jennie compresses her lips tightly, unconvinced.

"Do you have any idea why he left you and your sister and your mom?"

"Because he drinks..."

"And why does he drink?"

"I don't *know!*" she says angrily. "But he wasn't *supposed* to. He was supposed to take *care* of us. And now Mom has to go to work, and I get left alone."

Andrew finds a tiny perfect limpet shell and stretches out his hand to give it to her, being careful not to come too close. She turns and looks at it, then cautiously reaches out. He drops the shell into her palm. She examines it and places it in the bucket.

"Some day," he says quietly, "you're going to discover that people *can't* always do what they're supposed to do. Sometimes it's their fault, and sometimes it isn't. But the result is the same, either way." He finds another shell and holds it out.

This time she slides over a couple of feet so he won't have to stretch so far, and takes it from his fingers. He smiles at her and she smiles back, the traces of her suspicion almost gone. For the next ten minutes they both scour the sand, trying to find every shell within reach, until her small bucket is a quarter full. He names them all for her, the periwinkles and moon snails, and one that makes her laugh aloud, a dogwinkle.

The far end of the beach has begun to fill up. Andrew stiffly regains his feet and brushes the sand off the seat of his jeans. "Time I moved on, before any more people get here."

Jennie stands up too, forgetting to stay at arm's length. "Don't you like people?"

"I've had my fill of them, I guess. And they of me. That's why I only come out here when it's early. Are you going home now?"

"I guess so. Mom said she'd call me, and I'd better be home when she does. She said she takes a break at nine."

"I don't suppose you'd pay any attention to me if I said you shouldn't come out here all alone," he says.

Defiance sparkles in her eyes again. "Nope." Then sudden alarm replaces her bravado. "You won't tell my mom, will you?"

"You know, that's a problem. What we call an ethical dilemma. I don't know your mom, and it's none of my business whether you do what she says. But suppose, for example, you knew that your little sister was going to do something that wasn't safe, and you didn't tell anyone, and then something happened to her. How would you feel?"

She looks up at him seriously. "It won't be your fault if something happens to me."

"No? Even if I knew you were disobeying your mom, and I didn't do anything about it?"

"I'm not your responsibility."

Andrew gazes out over the water, it's surface suddenly pierced by dozens of black triangular fins, circling ever closer to shore. He blinks, and they're gone. Suddenly unnerved, he feels pairs of malevolent, feral eyes staring out from the distant forest, intent on the child's vulnerability.

Sometimes I wonder what my responsibilities really are any more, he thinks. *For example, why am I bothering to worry about this kid, when what I really want is to be left alone?*

He sighs. "The world isn't as safe as you think it is," he says aloud.

Jennie scuffs her toes in the sand. "Do you come out here every morning?"

"Most days." *What else do I have to do?* he thinks.

"Are you coming tomorrow?"

"Uh, huh."

"So nothing will happen to me if you're here, right?"

"Are you training to be a Philadelphia lawyer or something?" he says, laughing gently.

"What does that mean?"

"Never mind. Let's leave it at this. If you come out to the beach after your mom goes to work tomorrow, I'll be here, and we'll talk some more. But sooner or later your mom needs to know what you're up to. And if you and I are going to be friends, she needs to meet me, too. All right?"

"Do you really want to?" she asks.

"Do I want to what?"

"Be friends with me. And meet my mom. I thought you didn't like people."

Talk about perceptive. "I'll make an exception in your case. Now suppose you promise to stop coming out here alone."

"You said you'd be here tomorrow," Jennie says defiantly, "so I won't *be* alone. And I want to learn more about starfish and shells and stuff.

"All right, we've got a deal. At least for tomorrow."

"Promise you'll come?"

"I promise."

"Good." She turns to go, heading west toward the houses that lie hidden among the trees on the islands. After half a dozen steps, she stops. "Andrew?"

"What?"

"Do you think it's still alive?"

He knows she means the starfish. He considers the glib response: *I'm sure it is.* But instead he says, "I don't know. But that doesn't matter. The important thing is that whatever happens to it, it isn't our responsibility. But if we'd kept it, it would be."

Jennie stares at him for a long moment. Then she grins. "I get it!" She whirls and starts running along the beach. "Bye!"

"Goodbye."

He watches her light and agile step with the envy of age for youth, all the way to the glacial rocks that rise at the far end of the sand. She places her bucket carefully on the sand and climbs the nearest rock. She reaches the very top, then turns to wave gaily back at him. The fingers of her tiny hand are spread wide like the arms of the creature she set free. She clambers down, retrieves her treasures, and disappears among the trees that line the narrow roadway leading to the homes on the island.

He turns stiffly and starts back toward his car. *Now*, he thinks with an unsettling mixture of regret and anticipation, *I have something*

to do tomorrow. How the hell did that happen?
He tries to recall the contours of her face, already shifting and fading in the recesses of his defective memory. *So I promised. But when tomorrow morning comes, will I even remember that I met her?*

Lectures

The first time Andrew suspected something unusual was happening to him, he was lecturing to his Monday morning Comparative Popular Literature class. The topic concerned parallels between the word images created by Edgar Allan Poe and Stephen King. Step by step he quoted from each author, analysing their powerful use of language to paint not just pictures but vivid emotions that insinuated themselves into the minds of their readers. And suddenly, as he reached for a thought, a fusion, an analogy to drive the point home, his mind wandered into a confused, chaotic landscape. The correlation he was charting vanished, the meaning escaped him, and he groped for words and stuttered to a stop.

Alarmed, he scanned the lecture hall in panic, seeing his own bewilderment reflected in the students' eyes. Expecting at any moment to feel the text come flooding back, he hammered futilely on grey mental walls, tall, opaque.

Since the earliest years of his university career, he had been blessed with a flawless memory and seemingly infinite organizational skills. He could maintain direct eye contact with his classes for a full period, never having to look down at his lecture notes. As if extemporaneously, he erected the structures of his theses brick by figurative brick, ultimately creating for the alert listener an unambiguous, symmetrical cathedral of understanding.

But on this day he struggled to recall the concluding synthesis of meaning that was the culmination of all the examples he had just quoted so accurately from memory, only to find it not just vague but entirely absent from his mind.

He fumbled for his binder, taking far too long to locate the page and paragraph that corresponded to the moment where he had floundered. The hall fell deathly silent as he ran his finger down the text, which he had printed single spaced in a tiny font that was never intended for reading in public.

The words blurred before his eyes, and he thrust his hand into his jacket pocket for his reading glasses and jammed them onto his nose. Finally finding the relevant passage, he began to read from the notes and regained the thrust of his argument. Among the students, however, the silence gave way to stirring and shuffling. He had lost their attention.

At the end of the hour he gathered his books and papers at an unnecessarily slow pace while the class filed out. Only when the last of the students had gone did he leave the room and make his way to his third-floor office. He entered quickly, tossed his materials on the desk, and collapsed into his swivel chair.

He was sweating profusely, he who had never suffered from academic stage fright, never endured even the slightest uncertainty when speaking before groups large and small. Anxiety prodded his heartbeat to a gallop and rattled the breath in his throat. He couldn't seem to get enough oxygen. The walls buckled and swayed around him, and he closed his eyes and dragged huge draughts of air into his lungs. Gradually the panic subsided.

For more than half an hour he sat with his eyes closed, his mind thrashing about in narrow jumbled corridors where at one time broad avenues of thought had unfolded before him in geometric precision. Finally, by pure force of will, he turned once more to the day's lecture and sought to replay it. Rapidly and with accustomed ease, it began to unreel point by point, until at last he reached the spot where his concentration had deserted him the previous hour. This time the engine of his intellect chugged on, missing not a beat.

Instead of giving him reassurance, his success sparked new dread, shattering his confidence. It had been so clear in his mind just now, every word and nuance well within his grasp. How could his mental hard disk have crashed so disastrously, only to reconstitute itself again when it no longer mattered?

He picked up the phone, punched in the number for the departmental secretary, and got her voice mail instead. Twelve fifteen, her lunch hour. He left a message that he was cancelling his afternoon classes, not telling her why, although he knew it would occasion speculation. In nearly four decades of university teaching, the number of lectures he had missed could be counted on the fingers of one hand. He put his binder in his briefcase along with the computer disk that held backup copies of his class notes, and headed out the door. An unfamiliar feeling of weakness and disorientation plagued him, and he paused in front of the elevator instead of going to the stairs as was his habit. While waiting for the car to arrive, he reflected on the morning's debacle. *Anomaly or an omen? And how can I be sure which it is?*

* * *

Andrew struggled to subdue his growing anxiety as he drove the short distance to his home on the outskirts of town. The house was silent when he entered the kitchen from the garage. With his wife still at the hospital in Kentville where she volunteered three times a week, he knew he could count on several uninterrupted hours to try to sort out what had happened. He moved immediately to their combination den and office and turned on the computer.

As soon as it booted up, he opened the file containing the notes for his next Comparative Popular Literature class and printed it out in a font large enough to be read easily from a distance. He stood at his desk as if behind a lectern and placed the sheets of paper before him on its surface. He stared down at the first paragraph and, reassuringly, the familiar opening words were as present in his mind as on the page.

As he had done so many times in his classroom, he launched into the lecture aloud. The quotations from Poe and King unreeled rapidly behind his eyes, finding their way unerringly to his lips. The pages of text lay forgotten. His thoughts flowed like burning lava, relentless, directed and resolute. Fifty minutes later he concluded with a cogent, forceful summation of the congruence between the old and new styles of horror fiction, and suddenly realized that he had not had to consult his notes, not even once.

He collapsed into his chair, his forehead damp with sweat and his heart racing. *It was a fluke!* he thought. *A goddamn accident, that's all. I'm fine. Fine!*

He sat still for several long minutes, letting the tension drain out of his system. Despite his success, however, the memory of his momentary disorientation that morning nagged at him, filling him with uncertainty. Reluctantly he arose and went back to the computer screen, calling up the files for the next two lectures.

Won't hurt to have a little insurance, he thought. He converted the text to larger type and printed it out. Doing the same for a week's worth of lectures in his other courses, he punched holes in the pages and assembled them all in orderly fashion in the appropriate sections of his binder. As he finished the task he heard the garage door open, signalling Catherine's return from the hospital.

He hastily repacked his briefcase and shut off the computer. He left the office and was seated in the living room with the newspaper open on his lap when his wife entered the kitchen from the back hall, calling out to him.

"Andrew? You home?"

"In here," he answered.

"Everything okay, sweetheart?" she asked as she reached the living room. "You're home early." She looked at her watch, puzzled and somewhat concerned. "Don't you have a Lit class this hour?"

He ignored her question. "What did the slave drivers have you doing today?"

She sank onto the sofa beside him, her enthusiasm for her work surfacing in a rush. "I had a great time. They had a flood of deliveries over the weekend, and the nursery is full, so they put me there. The children's ward is short staffed, and they pulled some of the nurses out of obstetrics. I've been feeding, diapering and cuddling ever since breakfast. And why didn't you answer me?"

"It's nothing serious," he dismissed. "I just needed a break, that's all." He got up and started out of the room.

Catherine rose beside him. "You aren't sick, are you?"

"I told you, I'm fine!" He pushed past her brusquely, leaving her open-mouthed as he stomped down the hall to the kitchen. He entered the back hall, closing the door a little too loudly, and headed down into the basement.

Once alone in the confines of his workshop, he found himself without purpose. He stood in front of his cluttered bench trying to control his irritation, his pulse pounding in his temples and his face flushed and damp. *That was smart*, he thought. *Jumped all over her for no reason. One lecture, damn it! One lousy lecture goes a little bit wrong, and you can't even hide it from your wife.*

He paced around the workshop, idly picking up various tools and putting them down again. Gradually his breathing and heart rate slowed, and he sat on a stool to gather his thoughts. A kind of lethargy settled over him as the tension drained out, leaving him sad and regretful. Twenty minutes later, his emotions finally under close control, he returned upstairs and walked into the living room and sat down on the sofa.

Catherine looked up from her book. "What would taste good to you for supper?"

He gazed at her balefully. "I'm sorry for biting your head off."

"I know… It's okay."

"No it's not. You deserve better than my bad temper. How about a meal out, to make up for it?"

"I'll never turn that down. But are you sure you don't want to talk about it?"

"It's really nothing," he said. "I'll shake it off. Let's go into New Minas and eat somewhere cheap and greasy."

"You've got a deal. Give me a few minutes to get put together." She got to her feet and left the room to change clothes, while Andrew sat and brooded over the day's embarrassment.

It won't happen again, he insisted to himself. *Next time I'll be prepared.*

* * *

Andrew spent the following day, Tuesday, conducting tutorials with his creative writing students, a part of his work that he especially loved. As he coaxed the fledgling authors from banality to incisiveness, and the more clever ones from glibness to insight, he had little time to dwell on the previous day's troubles. Monday's class seemed to take on an air of unreality as it receded far back into his memory.

On Wednesday morning he arrived at the lecture hall well ahead of the class, feeling unnaturally alert if a bit apprehensive. With almost compulsive precision he squared the corners of his notes on the lectern and rehearsed the opening paragraphs, once again feeling no need to look down at the page. The entire address seemed to display itself across his mental landscape, as accessible and clear as if painted on canvas. But his confidence ebbed when the students began to enter, and an unaccustomed insecurity fluttered in his gut like a living thing.

His palms grew damp, and when he greeted the class to start the hour his voice quavered, his words hesitant and unsure. He saw in their faces, or thought he saw, apprehension and even derision, an expectation of failure and the possibility of a rare glimpse of clay feet beneath the marble.

Once into the topic, however, his thoughts surged forth in measured precision, as flowing water disciplined by the banks of an intellectual canal. The students' pens raced to keep up, capturing the clever analogies and similes in his comparisons and unassailable arguments. The hour raced by and, uncommonly, he drew to a close with five minutes to spare. His notes remained open to the first page, unheeded and unneeded.

"This concludes our comparison of Poe and King, parallel voices from two different centuries. On Friday we will begin our examination of two separate and distinct voices within a single body, the works of Evan Hunter and Ed McBain. I'll see you then."

As he gathered his possessions and prepared to leave the podium, a tentative spatter of applause arose somewhere near the back of the room. It was quickly picked up by those closer to him, then gradually built into a warm and appreciative approval that said to him, *They recognize the worth of what I've given them.* He paused at the door to nod in acceptance of their praise. *Or maybe, after the mess I made of things the last time, they're just saying, "Welcome back."*

His two afternoon classes were similarly successful, and Andrew arrived home in uncommonly good spirits. He and Catherine wasted the evening in the indulgence of an old movie, too much popcorn, and the easy companionship that four decades of marriage affords. By the time they went to bed, his unease had receded to a minor cloud on the horizon, one which he was certain would soon blow far offshore.

*   *   *

Andrew entertained a particular fascination with authors who wrote under two or more names. When compiling his required reading list at the beginning of the term, he had briefly considered including one of the books by Stephen King that the author wrote under the pseudonym of Richard Bachmann. However, a much more compelling dichotomy existed in the works of Evan Hunter, the topic of his lecture on Friday morning.

What intrigued him most was the consistency of style throughout the police procedural novels that Hunter wrote under the pseudonym Ed McBain, and especially how that style differed from Hunter's works under his own name. To Andrew's discernment, Hunter and McBain wrote as if they were two separate and unrelated persons, or at the very least distant cousins. He saw in that author's large body of work the chance to explore for his students this most unusual and exacting aspect of a novelist's craft.

Friday's class marked the beginning of his analysis, a series of lectures that would consume two full weeks of the term. With caution bred by the previous Monday's aberration, he began the lecture with his notes spread out before him, but after passing the first few paragraphs without needing to look at them, he forgot to turn the pages.

In clipped, precise language he delivered a brief introductory overview of the extensive nature of Hunter's output, which included not only novels but also screenplays, children's books and television scripts. Then he turned to the core of his presentation, Hunter's early and evocative musical analogy, *Second Ending*.

"In a novel or a symphony," he began, "as in a more concrete and physical creation such as a building, form and function are two sides of a single coin. Nowhere is this more apparent in literature than in works that borrow from the other arts. The discipline of music, like literature, depends in most incarnations upon a logical structure to achieve coherence. The balanced development of short motives in a Mozart sonata, for example, like the symmetry of a Bach fugue, serves to build a balanced edifice not unlike the proportions of a beautiful work of architecture. The form serves the function and vice versa, and in the intellectual arts, form and function both serve comprehension."

As was his pattern, Andrew had loaded his introductory thesis with a complexity that defied easy assimilation, at least on a single hearing, and many of the students wore puzzled looks. However, those who were familiar with his teaching techniques knew of his skill at subdividing his arguments into neat, comprehensible units, all of which would eventually come together like the pieces of a finely cut jigsaw puzzle.

"To appreciate how Hunter used the organization of musical elements in the story line when writing *Amanda's Passage*, consider the heroine's first encounter with…"

He stopped short. Momentarily confused, he reviewed what he had just said. *To appreciate how Hunter used the organization of musical elements in the story line when writing "Second Ending"… That is what I said, isn't it?* He looked down at his notes, but since he had not been turning the pages, he could not quickly orient himself to the paragraph in question.

"Excuse me for a moment," he said. The students looked up expectantly, not quite sure what was happening. Only a few had read their professor's early novel, and the reference to *Amanda's Passage* meant nothing to the rest of them.

Andrew leafed forward through the pages and finally spotted the correct reference. He read the paragraph quickly to himself, then looked up and began again. "To appreciate how Hunter used the organization of musical elements in the story line when writing *Second Ending*, consider how the problem of Amanda's pregnancy at age fourteen drives the…"

What the hell?

"Consider how the problem of… the *inclusion* of each character's leitmotif within the…"

He stumbled to a halt. Frantically he searched his notes, trying to bring reason and order out of the printed page, and found the sentence he had already begun. Sweat poured from his face, and the students stared at him in wonder, their pens stilled, their faces etched with concern. "Consider how the problem of the inclusion of each character's... each character's..."

The words swam out of focus, replaced by whole paragraphs of dialogue from his own work that danced across his mind: Amanda, her grieving father, her mother's stern refusal to accept or even to recognize the inevitable consequences of the events her daughter's pregnancy had set in motion. Or the role, and the ultimate responsibility, that belonged to her mother alone.

He wiped his forehead and tried to clear his mind. *Evan Hunter! Second Ending! Musical analogy...* Coherence eluded him. He glanced around the hall, struck by every eye, every stilled hand, every expectant indrawn breath that hung on his next words. Words that would not come.

Leaving his notes on the lectern, he fled the room for the sanctuary and secrecy of his office.

* * *

Andrew sat trembling at his desk, unable to focus on any task or to rouse himself to any sort of action. Presently he heard a tentative tapping on the door, but he ignored it. After a second knock the knob turned, and the door swung inward cautiously.

"Dr. Striker?"

He turned to face his visitor, trying to gather his thoughts and erase the signs of distress he knew must be sketched across his face. He recognized one of his students. "Yes, Paul?"

"I brought you your binder." The young man eased into the room and placed the notebook on the corner of the desk.

"Thank you," Andrew said vaguely, turning to look out the window.

"Dr. Striker, are you okay? Is there something I can do for you?"

He turned back to face the young man. "I'm fine, Paul, just a momentary lapse of some sort."

"The rest of the class is still there, waiting for you. Are you coming back?"

Panic welled in his chest. *Go back?* He took several harsh breaths, then regained control. "Paul, could you please go and tell them we'll resume on Monday? And tell them I wish them a pleasant weekend," he added as an afterthought, hoping to strike a note of normalcy.

"Would you like me to call someone for you?"

"I'm okay." He realized that wasn't enough to allay the students' concerns. "I had a very late night," he continued, "some problems at home kept me up. I shouldn't have tried to have class today."

"Well, if you're sure…"

"Really, I'm fine. Just please tell the class for me, all right?"

Not fully reassured but anxious to leave, the boy headed toward the door. "Have a nice weekend," he said as he stepped into the corridor and disappeared.

Have a nice weekend… Sure. Sure.

TWO...

After seeing Jennie Horton vanish into the depths of the closest of the LaHave Islands, Andrew turns and heads west along the boulders and pilings that line the back edge of Crescent Beach. It takes him more than fifteen minutes to reach the row of cars that have joined his own near the narrow mouth of the access road. He plans his route to pass well away from the early visitors who are claiming their share of the sand, anticipating the warmth of the climbing sun.

He reaches his car and unlocks the door. His knee still throbs from the exercise and from the unaccustomed position he sat in while talking to the child, and he has to grasp his thigh with both hands and lift it to get clear of the door sill. He sinks gratefully into the driver's seat and shuts the door.

Another vehicle descends the steep ramp at the end of the beach, an ugly sport utility model with ungainly tires and too much bumper. The driver weaves around the nose of Andrew's car and threads his way among the bathers who cluster in groups on the hard-packed sand. *Two miles of beach, and they all have to hang around in the same damn place. Lemmings...*

With the inertia of having nowhere to go, he stares through the windshield at a group of small children, squealing and dancing backward as the chilly water laps their toes. Three teenage girls parade past in their bikinis, looking in vain for males to take an interest, and young mothers unfold their deck chairs and settle down to socialize while watching over their charges. The aimless rhythms of life...

Another car arrives, and another: crowds. Andrew sighs and inserts his key in the ignition. He starts the engine and eases the car carefully out of its slot and up the ramp. Reaching the highway, he turns and drives off northeast toward the village of LaHave.

The day is spectacularly beautiful. Traces of morning mist linger near the horizon, but with the low humidity and calm winds, visibility is otherwise unlimited. The rich green hills of the peninsulas and offshore islands shimmer in the rising heat, etched in sharp contrast against the soft powder blue of the summer sky.

He passes West Dublin and then Dublin Shore where, off to his right, the mouth of the LaHave River joins the sea at Ships Channel. A low-slung coupe roars up behind him, and he hugs the right shoulder, not wishing to impede anyone else's progress, but unwilling to be bullied into hurrying. The coupe pulls out to pass and speeds off around the next bend and out of sight. The line on the bottom of the license plate reads "Je Me Souviens"; another Quebec tourist.

I remember, too. Sometimes, anyway.

Following the curve of the road as it winds northwest, he enters the village of LaHave. Quaint and little more than a wide spot in the road, it clings to the river bank with the undeniable nineteenth century charm and serenity that travel brochures tout with blatant exaggeration. By noon, he knows, oversized cars with American and Upper Canadian license plates will crowd the shoulders of the road and the small parking lots that front the shoreline. But for now, visitors are few.

He passes by the bakery and pulls off into a wide gravel lot adjacent to a small pier, where two men listlessly scrape rust from the steel flanks of a small coastal freighter. The once-white letters of her name, the "Aimee LeBlanc", are now a smeared and faded yellow, and her topside shouts of years of neglect in the shabbiness of her fittings.

Like to have seen her when she was new...

He climbs out stiffly and locks the car, then starts back toward the bakery. Two elderly travellers seated on the porch outside raise their coffee mugs in greeting as he climbs the rough plank steps. Everything about them, from their mode of dress and shoulder-slung tote bags to the gleaming Lexus at the curb, shouts "American tourist". Andrew doesn't mind. Nova Scotia's rare, rugged beauty conceals an economy ravaged by decades of political ineptitude and corruption, and every US dollar that comes in has to help a little. He acknowledges the couple with a smile and a brief lifting of his hand, and opens the wooden screen door to enter.

Housed in a riverside loft building, the interior of the bakery resembles a general store of a century past. Dark-stained tongue-and-groove walls and elaborate carved woodwork generate an antique atmosphere. A massive radiator dominates the centre of the floor, now thankfully idle in the gathering heat of the August day. A young couple stands by the display case on the left, trying to choose from among the immense scones, muffins and cookies for which the LaHave Bakery is famous. He steps up to the counter.

Ramona Billings comes through the door that separates the shop from the back hall. "Morning, Dr. Striker. Coffee?"

"My dear Ms. Billings," he says formally, "am I never to convince you that my name is Andrew?"

"I know your name all right. And I reckon it's my choice whether I use it. Besides, I don't know too many professors and such, and I've always been taught to be respectful."

He smiles inwardly at the word "reckon" and at the foolishness of her little speech. He knows Ramona Billings to be a transplanted New Englander, less than ten years in the Maritimes and still blessed with more than a trace of Boston's vowels in her speech. The folksy manner she affects for the tourists is wasted on him. "You know damn well I'm no professor, not any longer," he says irritably.

She looks him over sadly, then turns gruff again. "Feeling sorry for ourselves, are we?"

"Just give me the damn coffee!"

"There's the mugs on the shelf, as usual. You know I don't do the pourin'."

"What would the Cabots and the Lowells think if they heard

you leaving the g's off your words like that?"

She laughs delightedly and turns to the row of baked goods. "I'm just a poor, uneducated South Shore lady, you know that. The muffins are fresh, by the way. Not twenty minutes out of the oven."

"All right. One of the blueberry ones." She takes a paper plate from the stack beside the cash register, adds a plastic knife and two tiny tubs of butter, and picks up a pair of tongs to handle the muffin. He reaches for a mug and places it under the spout of the urn. The coffee splashes out, broadcasting its rich, dark aroma throughout the room. He turns and takes the plate from her hand, then heads toward the door.

"Ain't too many people yet," she says. "Feel like a little conversation?"

He pauses with his hand on the screen door pull. "I don't converse with proper Bostonian ladies who say 'ain't' to me."

Ramona laughs again. "Come on, don't deny me the pleasure of playing a role. And talk to me a little. I'm between jobs here, and when the Yanks start coming later, I'll get run off my feet."

"Thanks," he says, "but I'm poor company. Not much in my head to make conversation with." He opens the door and walks outside.

The American couple is gone and the porch is empty. The sun has just reached the front of the building, and he walks around the side to find some shade beneath the trees. He slides onto the bench of a picnic table and sits gazing out at the water.

The narrow dock plays host to a couple of skiffs and a sleek vintage wooden yacht, gleaming in white paint and mahogany: thirty feet of expensive maintenance costs. Its bowline tugs gently on a piling, on top of which a gull poses with stiff dignity, inviting tourists' cameras. Between the gull and the line, a poster emblazoned with a drawing of an endangered sea turtle flutters slightly in the weak breeze off the water. *Have you seen this turtle…?*

A softly rounded pea green Morris Minor squats next to the building, decades old and mute testimony to the formerly ubiquitous British influence in Nova Scotia. The distinctive Austins and Vauxhalls and little Triumph sedans that once plied the coastal roads have given way to anonymous Japanese boxes and egg-shaped Fords and

Chevrolets, barely distinguishable from each other except by their nameplates. Elderly though she may be, the little Morris has undeniable class.

He knows that Ramona drives it to work every day. It is just one of her affectations, a protective cloak she draws around herself to hide her Yankee roots. He wonders at the expense of keeping such an old relic on the road, the need to search international salvage yards whenever a part wears out. But these old cars are simple, he thinks, and the members of car clubs who lavish their love on old machinery take great pride in their ingenuity. Fix up, substitute, make do...

Would that spare parts for me might be so easily found. He shakes his head. *Ramona's right. Self-pity is an embarrassment to everyone.*

He finishes his coffee and puts the mug down on the table. The muffin lies before him untasted, and he stares at it morosely. Then he rises and takes the plate to the nearest trash can and dumps it in. He turns and walks out onto the dock, inspecting the clean, well-kept lines of the yacht and noting minor chores the owner has yet to do: a frayed sail cover, salt corrosion just beginning to pit a cleat, a spot worn through the varnish where the jib sheet rubs the woodwork. A boat never leaves you alone.

A small ketch tacks downstream, making slow headway against the light breeze. Andrew hears the helmsman cajoling his crew, two young teenagers, one cranking in the jib on the starboard winch while the other looks on. The mainsail luffs, and the helmsman spins the wheel. Andrew leans with the shift of the deck, catching his balance and reaching for the winch handle.

"Coming about!" Charlie Grant shouts. Andrew lets go the port sheet as the big boom starts to come over. He hauls in the jib on the opposite side and wraps the line around the winch. The forward sail snaps in the wind, and the *Mary Bee* dips her bow and tacks toward the distant coastline. Catherine laughs her pleasure, revelling as she always does in the pleasure of being at sea, and of having her husband and his closest friend to do all the work.

Andrew cranks the winch tight and shouts to his friend, "Pinching!"

"The hell you say," Charlie laughs. He glances up the mast, where the ticklers are plastered flat against the canvas. "Just close to the wind, that's all."

"Bull. Haul her back a little, and you'll get an extra half knot out of her."

"Who taught you to sail, big shot?"

"You did, remember? And you're still pinching."

The mainsail flutters, and Charlie eases off on the helm. The canvas snaps taut again, and the boat cants to starboard. "Don't say it!" Charlie warns.

"What?"

" 'I told you so.' "

Andrew grins at his friend and sinks down on the port locker. He reaches for his drink where it hangs on the rope railing, and his hand strikes the top of the piling. A splinter cuts his finger.

He shakes his head and looks down to see a drop of blood oozing out, then out at the ketch, now on the opposite tack and two dozen yards past the dock. *Charlie?* The man at the helm is about thirty-five, stocky and dark haired. Charlie was freckled, his hair reddish and tinged with the first signs of grey, when he and Andrew sailed every weekend from the Northwest Arm out of Halifax around to St. Margaret's Bay. Charlie was gone, frozen forever at forty-six.

"Who taught you to sail, big shot?"

Andrew hears Charlie's voice, clear and impossibly young on the morning air, and he looks in confusion at the receding ketch. The sunlight on the water flares unnaturally bright, the waves crest and break, and storm clouds roil on the horizon, bearing down on their bow.

"Go back!" Catherine shouts. "I'm afraid!"

Andrew faces the wind. "It's only a squall. We can weather it."

"Go back, I'm afraid! Go back, go back…"

He turns and sees his wife's figure behind him, waving from the shore. "What?"

"Go back!"

What?

"I said, are you through with the mug?"

He blinks in the harsh light, shielding his eyes against the sun. Catherine stands with one hand on her hip, the other pointing to the surface of the picnic table. He blinks again. Ramona Billings waits for his answer.

Catherine. God, I miss you so.

He takes a deep, rasping breath and rotates his neck against the stiffness of his calcified joints. Gradually the present returns. He starts forward off the dock.

"Are you okay, Dr. Striker?" Ramona calls out.

"I'm just plain Andrew, goddamnit!" he mutters under his breath. "I'm fine," he says more loudly.

"You finished with the mug, or you want some more coffee?"

"I'm done. You can take it." He reaches the gravel driveway and continues on unsteadily. He glances back and sees Ramona's sad eyes regarding him. He grimaces in frustration. "I'm fine, I said. It's just this damned arthritis. Quit looking at me like I'm a sick puppy."

He glares at her, taking in her hurt expression but unwilling to apologize. In the year since he has been coming to the bakery she has tried to offer him friendship, but he has rebuffed any but her most impersonal overtures. The wall he has built around himself has no gate for her to find.

He treads heavily past her, and she turns and begins to follow in his wake. He reaches the road and stops, momentarily bewildered as he tries to locate his car. Then he remembers where he left it and heads west without looking back.

*   *   *

Ramona Billings comes to a stop and stands near the foot of the bakery steps, sadly watching his departure. In the months she has known him she has watched with concern his slow deterioration, both physical and mental. Once robust and vital, he now appears to her somewhat shrunken, his step hesitant where once it was firm and precise.

The memory lapses like the one she has just witnessed are

now more frequent, as he has become gradually more confused and less aware of his surroundings. Even more disturbing to her is his change in personality, from an affable and talkative customer to a reclusive, irritable and unfriendly loner. She longs to reach out to him, somehow to help him adjust to the inevitability of his decline, but her kindness seems only to drive him further away.

She watches him fumble with the key to his car door and climb painfully into the driver's seat. A moment later the engine comes to life.

"Goodbye, Andrew," she says softly to herself. "Somehow I don't think I'll see you very much from now on." She shrugs in resignation and begins to climb the steps of the bakery.

*   *   *

Andrew unlocks his car and climbs inside, again favouring his weakened right leg. The two crewmen are still lazily scraping the freighter's hull, but to Andrew's eye, they have made little or no progress. *Maybe the damn thing's rusted all the way through. They'll scrape and scrape until there's nothing left. Nothing left...*

He sticks the key in the ignition and starts the car. After waiting for an ungainly motor home to pass by he pulls out onto the road to head for home, but turns right and heads northwest instead. He passes the ramp where the cable ferry is discharging a dozen cars, and puzzles over it. *Where am I?* His brow furrows as he follows the motor home's slow progress, but he cannot figure out what's wrong.

Several kilometres down the road, the sign for Pentz appears on the shoulder. In confusion he begins to look for the turnoff to his cottage, searching every lane and driveway on the left side of the road. He passes a small Baptist church, a used bookstore, a convenience store with a single gas pump out front.

The motor home has outdistanced him, and the road ahead is empty. A dark sedan crowds his rear bumper. He remembers that his cottage lies on the Green Bay road that branches off from Route 331 at Petite Riviere, just after crossing the old iron one-lane bridge. He slows the car and strains to see ahead, expecting the bridge to come into view. The driver behind him sounds his horn, and Andrew glances at the mirror in irritation. He pulls over to the right, and the follower passes him in a rush.

A pickup truck pulls up close behind him, and several vehicles behind that. Andrew scans the roadside, and another sign comes into view: West LaHave. *Jesus Christ, I'm headed for Bridgewater!* He slams on the brakes, and the pickup slews to avoid him and crunches onto the gravel of the shoulder. The driver punches his horn in frustration, and Andrew pulls completely off the road and stops, the nose of his car buried in a hedge. He turns off the ignition and slumps back in the seat.

Outside his window the traffic continues to pass him in either direction, but he barely sees it. He stares in frustration at the West LaHave sign, then pounds his fist on the steering wheel. He opens his mouth, but no sound comes out. Hot tears begin to fall from his eyes.

Creative Writing

Thanks to an unexpected late-winter thaw the afternoon sun warmed the classroom, and Andrew Striker found his attention waning, lulled by a filling lunch and the boredom of his class. Normally energized by the enthusiasm of this year's crop of aspiring novelists, he had found the week's assignments to be dull and pedestrian, and he stared listlessly out the window as Alan Baker read from his latest effort.

The student droned on, and through his torpor Andrew detected a common failing among beginners, a concentration upon clever language that served only to obscure the meaning of the prose. After a particularly offensive string of sibilant syllables, he was about to interrupt when another class member saved him the trouble.

"Have you been watching Sesame Street again, Alan?" Cassandra Walker jibed. "Got a crush on the letter 's', I bet."

Alan Baker flushed and stammered a cutting retort, but Andrew cut him short. He promoted constructive criticism and discouraged the students' attacks upon each others' work by turning the tables on them. Cassie Walker knew this, but had counted on his apparent inattention to allow her to get away with it.

"Despite the rudeness of her delivery," Andrew said mildly and with exaggerated formality, "Miss Walker's point is well taken. Alliteration must serve the text, not just exist for its own sake. And it must never attract so much attention to itself that it disrupts the course of the narrative." Then he turned the tables on Cassie. "How would you rewrite that sentence, Miss Walker?"

She sighed. "Read it back to me."

Alan reluctantly consulted the sheets in front of him and repeated the offending passage. Andrew heard only half of it, then missed entirely the correction that Cassie Walker offered. As he struggled to think of a comment, another student offered an alternative, and a brief argument ensued over the difference between alliteration and onomatopoeia. Several others joined in, and the discussion became heated. Finally they turned to Andrew for an explanation, and were puzzled by his blank gaze.

He searched each pair of eyes in turn, trying vainly to remember what any of them had said. Their faces blurred and shifted, and a phantom sheet of paper danced behind his eyes, filled with scribbles that crawled and writhed like snakes in a parody of cursive English letters. They held no meaning. He blinked furiously to drive them away.

The class waited expectantly as he struggled to refocus his concentration. "I think we're off the point. Alliteration deals with similar sounds, most often in the repetition of the initial consonant, the overuse of which Alan is certainly guilty. Onomatopoeia involves..."

He stuttered to a halt. He knew the meaning of the word, had known it ever since his elementary school days, when he had first discovered the power of words to describe, to move, and ultimately to influence. He had delighted in choosing those sounds of language that described and reflected the essence of objects and actions themselves. But now he could not call up the definition to explain how it worked.

The class waited politely, and he started again. "Alan's sentence has characteristics of onomatopoeia in the word... the word..."

" 'Hiss' is the one Cassie complained about," Alan offered.

"Yes, exactly. The alliteration proceeds from following that word immediately by the initial 's' in…" Again his mind went blank, as if Alan Baker's sentence had never been read at all in his presence. *When you don't know the answer, ask a question.*

"Can anyone give me another illustration of alliteration and onomatopoeia used in combination? Remember that the language must be made to serve the meaning, not the reverse."

The students turned to their task, and within a few minutes two of them gathered the courage to offer their examples. As Andrew listened this time, the shades of meaning paraded in orderly single file, and stuck to him like post-it notes. He engaged the students in dissecting their phrases and reworking the syntax until each sentence became not just words but poetic language.

As the hour drew toward its close they returned to Alan Baker's offending passage, and tried again to repair it. When their efforts failed, Cassie Walker finally said, this time with considerably more humour and not unkindly, "Alan, you just have to get your 's' out of there."

On that note the class dispersed, but Andrew remained in the classroom after everyone had departed. He sat motionless, his eyes turned unseeing toward the windows in the far wall, focused inward instead. He visualized a crowded mental courtyard in which words, once his beloved friends, jostled him and each other like bullies on a playground.

Today had been the worst. Ever since his initial lapses in memory, several weeks earlier in the Comparative Lit course, he had redoubled his efforts at preparation. Every lecture was honed and practiced until he felt secure, and he never mounted the podium without his notes spread before him. On those days when the words flowed with ease, he nevertheless kept the pages turning, alert to his place within the text in case his mind should go blank once more. And when the haze of confusion stood between him and his memory, he read from the page, word for word, fiercely intent upon maintaining the flow and rhythm of the thoughts that he found he could not comprehend.

Student presentations posed a different problem, especially in the Creative Writing course. Although he required all submissions to be handed in well in advance, giving him time to study them and to prepare corrections and suggestions, he could not anticipate the direction that classroom discussions would take. And this year's class was especially bright and eager. Their questions often ranged far afield, and their experiments in technique provoked frequent arguments that Andrew was called upon to mediate.

He felt himself no longer up to the task. In the heat of spirited give and take, he could no longer be sure of calling to mind just the right example, just the perfect turn of phrase, that had made his reputation as a teacher and a novelist secure for more than a quarter century.

What will I do if I can't write? If I can't teach?

The light outside began to fade, and he looked with surprise at his watch. Although the sun was but a month from the equinox, promising the eventual return of the wonderfully long summer days that made it possible to endure February in Nova Scotia, drab winter still ruled, and darkness still preceded the evening meal. Catherine would be expecting him.

Reluctantly he gathered his belongings and left the classroom. The halls were nearly deserted. He climbed the stairs to his office, retrieved his coat and gloves, then stared around vaguely, unsure of where he was. The room seemed unfamiliar to him, and he wandered out into the corridor and stood in its centre, trying to orient himself.

The sound of voices penetrated his trance, and as he approached the conference room at the end of the third floor corridor, memory and responsibility flooded back: the weekly departmental meeting. Despite the notation on his calendar, and the reminder from his secretary just before his class, he had forgotten it completely.

He pushed open the door and edged in, seating himself at the nearest end of the long table. The Dean of Arts was speaking to the question of enrolment and recruitment, and paused only briefly to acknowledge him with a smile of welcome. Andrew murmured an apology.

The Dean concluded her remarks and thanked those present for their attention. Andrew sat in growing confusion as the other members of the English Department stood and reached for their coats.

He checked the wall clock and was alarmed to discover that it was already time for adjournment. He had lost an hour somewhere.

Confusion overwhelmed him. His colleagues spoke to him in passing, people he had worked with for years, and he returned their greetings but could recall only one or two of their names. Frightened and feeling very much alone, he watched them all as they disappeared through the door, and still he sat, not knowing what to do next.

The building custodian came down the hall twenty minutes later, and noticing the light still on in the conference room, he reached inside for the wall switch. Then he spotted Andrew sitting alone.

"Sorry, professor, I didn't know anyone was here. You going to be long?" Andrew looked up vaguely, unable to comprehend the question. "Sorry to rush you," the man said, " but I'm supposed to lock everything up before I go."

"Lock up?"

"You know, the new security rules. Ever since some of those data projectors walked out the door…"

Andrew rallied a bit. "Someone stole them?"

"Yup, out of three of the first floor classrooms. Unbolted them right off the ceiling mounts. Took the VCRs, too. Didn't you hear about it?"

"I guess." Andrew vaguely remembered a Student Union bulletin, and a directive from the Head of Security.

"So except for evening classes, I have to check all the doors. If any of them are open, the night guy'll write me up."

"Of course." Andrew got wearily to his feet. He shuffled to the door and stood uncertainly in the corridor, unable to decide which way to go. The custodian shut off the lights and secured the door behind him. As the man walked off in the opposite direction, Andrew spotted the exit sign and entered the stairwell.

The night air was cold on his face as he left the building, but with little wind, it was not uncomfortable. He walked indecisively up the hill to the parking lot and wandered among the few cars that remained at that late hour. He passed his own vehicle without recognizing it. He reached the sidewalk again and turned south, climbing up Highland Avenue away from the centre of town.

* * *

The lights of Wolfville shimmered weakly through the ground fog that lay low in the north, stretching across the Minas Basin off toward Cape Blomidon. Andrew puzzled over his surroundings, trying to determine where he could be and how he had come there. To his back, the wooded slope that fell away from Stile Park lay dark and forbidding. A sudden gust chilled him, and he looked around for shelter, finding only an open-sided gazebo and a few picnic tables scattered about the clearing.

Vague shadows caused him unease, some cast by the clouds that rushed past the quarter moon and some asserting themselves from within his unreliable memory. As he looked around, he discerned a solitary vehicle, a rusted and elderly Toyota almost hidden beneath the trees at the far edge of the meadow, its lights out and seemingly deserted. He started toward it, intent on getting out of the wind.

He reached for the handle on the passenger side and depressed the lever, finding the door locked. At his touch, a head appeared in the window, the outline of a coed's face, her features indistinct in the gloom. A second head appeared behind her.

"Beat it, pervert!"

He recoiled from the car and stumbled backwards. He retraced his steps and made his way to the gazebo. He looked back over his shoulder at the car, its headlights now glowing and its engine idling. As he sank down onto the rough wooden planks, the car reversed and headed toward the main road, spewing slush-soaked gravel behind it.

Andrew clutched his coat around him and huddled behind the gazebo's railing. His consciousness wavered, and he found himself once again in his classroom, his notes spread before him in a meaningless muddle of indecipherable dots and slashes. Thinking he was lecturing, he struggled to form his sentences, and from the sea of faces before him raucous laughter poured forth, burying his words.

The students began hurling questions at him, shouting them, and before he could answer one, another assaulted his ears, disrespectful and meaningless. He struggled to understand what they said.

"Dr. Striker?"

What?

"Are you all right, sir?"

Something gripped his shoulder gently, and he forced his eyes to focus on the concerned face of the police officer who stood over him. The man's mouth seemed to be forming words, but Andrew couldn't comprehend them. He tried weakly to shake off his hand.

The officer turned his head, and Andrew became aware of a second figure, also in uniform, and the lights of a patrol car pulled up next to the grass. The two men spoke in quiet tones, and he frowned in concentration, trying to understand them.

"This guy matches the lady's description," the first voice said. "Suit and tie, looks like a professor."

"Not the ones who taught me," the second one said. "Jeans and beards, all of them."

"You must have had mostly the young ones. Old guys like this still go formal sometimes." He turned back to address Andrew again. "Can you hear me, sir?"

"Of course I can hear you!" he said in irritation. "Let go of me!"

"We just want to help you, sir. Your wife called nine-one-one when you didn't go home tonight, and we've been out looking for you. You left your car in the university parking lot. Do you know it's past eleven o'clock?"

Andrew drew his legs up under him and tried to rise, but his body spasmed in uncontrollable shivering. His strength failed and he fell heavily against the railing. The officer reached out to steady him.

"We better get him down to the clinic," the officer suggested to his partner in an undertone. "And call it in, so the wife will stop worrying. She can meet him there. Give me a hand."

Together they helped Andrew to his feet and led him to the squad car. When he was safely inside, he slumped against the door pillar, his eyes unfocused and his hearing muted. He was aware of the two policemen talking as they started the car and drove out of the clearing, but nothing they said made any sense to him. He closed his eyes and drifted off.

*   *   *

Andrew was sitting fully dressed on the examining table with his legs dangling over the edge, the paper sheet crinkled and bunched up beneath him, when Catherine burst through the door. He looked at her balefully, barely reacting when she grabbed him around the neck and hugged him tightly.

"Where have you been?"

At first he didn't respond. Catherine backed up to arm's length, her palms still resting on his shoulders, and stared at his downcast eyes. Slowly he looked up. "I was just out walking…"

"Walking where? Why didn't you call me?"

"Damn it, I don't have to report in to you!"

Andrew watched her recoil and saw the hurt in her eyes. Never before had he made her the target of his tension and irritability, no matter his mood or state of mind. Nor had he ever snapped at her so harshly. He felt instant remorse, but turned away from her without apology and glared at the tall, tired-looking doctor who stood next to the table.

"When can I get out of here?" he grumbled.

Bob Melanson draped a stethoscope around his neck and picked up a blood pressure cuff. He smiled reassuringly at Catherine and reached out to lift Andrew's arm. "Let's check your pressure once more," he said affably. He wrapped the cuff around Andrew's upper arm and began to squeeze the bulb.

"That's more like it," the doctor said as he completed the test. He folded the apparatus and placed it on a nearby table, then sat down in a swivel chair and looked up at his patient. "Andrew, my friend, you gave everybody a hell of a scare, and you're not helping yourself at all. If you don't tell us what happened, we can't do anything for you."

"Nothing happened. I don't need any help," he muttered.

"Don't tell me that," Melanson continued. "The police found you lying on the floor of the Stile Park gazebo in the middle of the night, and you couldn't even tell them your name. You haven't been drinking, and I've never known you to use drugs. Are you on any kind of medication that I don't know about?"

"I don't even take aspirin, you know that."

"Your pulse was double what it should be when they brought you in here, and your blood pressure was practically nonexistent. It's okay now, but I'm going to order a series of tests. We'll check your chemistry and see if…"

"Forget it," Andrew said. He slid forward off the table and rolled down his sleeve, then reached for his coat.

"Please, Andrew. Listen to him." Catherine tried to take his arm, and he shook her off.

"I said forget it! There's nothing wrong with me. I just decided to take the long way home and got cold, that's all. Now leave me alone!" He struggled into his coat and stamped through the door and out into the corridor. His knees trembled and he slumped against the wall, his mind clouded and his senses dulled.

He shook his head to clear it, and was about to push off down the passageway when his wife's voice drifted out to him through the examination room door. "What's wrong with him, Bob?"

"I can only guess," he heard Melanson reply. "Either something happened today that disturbed him deeply and set him off, or there's some organic reason."

"What can it be? Oh God, not a brain tumour…"

"Don't borrow trouble. It could be any number of things. But if he won't let me do the tests, I can't find out for sure."

"Leave that to me," Catherine said. "Once he calms down some, I'll talk him into it. He's always been so reasonable…"

I'm still reasonable, damn it, Andrew thought. *Shit! If you really want to help, why don't all of you just leave me the hell alone!*

"I'd back off if I were you," Melanson continued, "at least for a little while. Humour him. See if you can get him to sleep more, maybe take tomorrow off. When you're sure he's calmed down, get in touch with me, and I'll schedule a thorough workup."

"When?" she asked.

"There isn't any rush. He needs to settle down first. If he's okay by morning we can go ahead, but if he's still irritable, let it go, at least until the weekend."

"He's never done anything like this before."

"Don't worry, we'll find out why. It's important that you keep cool, though. Try to act like nothing out of the ordinary has happened."

"He isn't crazy, is he?"

"No more than usual. It's probably something that happened at the university that's got him stirred up. You know all the infighting that goes on with that crowd. If he wants to talk about it, just listen. But I wouldn't push him right now. And look, you have my home number. Call me if you think there's anything you can't handle by yourself."

"I wouldn't bother you like that."

"You'd better," Melanson said. "This is your friend Bob talking, not your doctor."

"Thank you."

"Forget it," the doctor replied. "Now get him home."

Their voices seemed louder, and Andrew realized they were approaching the door. Feeling momentarily dizzy, he struggled to maintain his balance and started toward the exit. He shoved through the outer door and shuffled over to the edge of the parking lot. He stood there stiffly, his hands stuffed in his coat pockets, as his wife came outside to join him. Avoiding her eyes, he stared down at the dormant beds where perennial flowers would flourish again as spring crept back up the North American coast, but which now looked as bleak as his future.

She walked up beside him and slipped her hand into the crook of his elbow. "Ready to go home?"

He turned his head and looked down at her, feeling confused and miserable. Without speaking he turned and gathered her into his arms. A soft shudder passed through him and he held her tightly, as if to draw comfort and support from her presence. Very softly, he wept.

Once the spasm had passed he released her and began walking toward the car, and she followed along. He reached it first and got in the passenger side, and Catherine got behind the wheel. "Do you want to pick up your car, or shall we leave it until morning?"

"Better get it," he said. "It's behind the Student Union building."

She started the car and wheeled out of the lot onto Earnscliff Avenue, and coasted down the gentle hill to Main Street. Turning right, she drove to the intersection of Highland Avenue and headed for the parking lot. She pulled up beside his car, and he got out in silence and unlocked it. He started the engine and backed out of the slot.

Catherine followed along as he drove slowly home and pulled into the garage. When they both were inside the house, he paced to the living room and collapsed into his recliner without removing his coat. He stared across the room at the drapes that were drawn across the windows, barely aware of where he was.

Catherine called to him from the kitchen. "Some coffee?" He didn't answer her. She looked in at him, then walked over and stood behind his chair. She reached over his shoulders to unbutton his coat and folded back the lapels. She leaned forward and rested her cheek against his.

He stirred. He placed his hand gently over hers, then edged out of her embrace and stood up to remove his coat. He tossed it over the arm of the recliner and started out of the room. He shuffled out into the hall and headed toward the bedroom, his stiff posture conveying his desire to be left alone, but Catherine started to follow him. Catching sight of her over his shoulder, he entered the bedroom and closed the door behind him a little too forcefully, shutting her out.

Uncertain what to do next, he moved to the window on the opposite side of the bed and stared out at the evergreen trees that bordered the back of their lot. Faint moonlight reflected off the thin and scattered layer of snow that was all that remained after a recent thaw. Spring was not far off, the time he looked forward to so much each year, the world coming alive again. But all he could foresee now was despair.

Faintly through the door, he could hear the rattle of dishes in the kitchen, and he realized that Catherine would soon complete her chores. He couldn't exclude her from their bedroom after that. Without undressing he lay down on top of the covers and faced toward the wall. When Catherine entered the room a few minutes later he feigned sleep, keeping still until she had climbed into bed and drifted off.

In the silence of the room he lay staring up at the ceiling. It was a long time before he too fell into a shallow, troubled sleep.

THREE...

A light tapping on the window rouses Andrew from his misery. The first thing he sees is the small silhouette of a horse and rider, then primary-coloured stripes on a white background. Gradually the form of an RCMP car swims into focus through the windshield.

He turns to face the side window and sees the concerned face of a young officer staring in at him. He presses the button to lower the window, but nothing happens. Momentarily bewildered, he looks back at the officer, who raises his hand and makes a motion like the turning of a key.

Andrew reaches for his ignition key and twists it. He punches the window control again, and the glass slides downward into the door.

"Good afternoon, sir," the policeman begins. "Is everything all right?"

Andrew breathes deeply and passes the back of his hand across his eyes. He pulls himself half upright. "I'm okay, officer."

"May I see your license and registration, please?"

Trying to process the request, Andrew stares at him, perplexed. He reaches for his wallet and thumbs through it, finally locating a laminated card that bears his photo. He hands it to the officer.

"This is a university identification card, sir," the Mountie says.

"I need your driver's license."

He searches again, finally finding the card issued to him by the Province of Nova Scotia. He hands it over.

"And your registration, please."

He fumbles in the glove compartment and locates the certificate. The officer takes it from him. "Please remain here, sir." He walks to the patrol car and sits behind the wheel. Andrew watches as the officer uses the radio, reading into the microphone from the license and registration. Several minutes pass.

The Mountie opens his door again and returns to Andrew's car. He leans down beside the window. "Dr. Striker, I stopped because the back of your car is sticking out very close to the pavement, and the front is in this hedge. Did you have an accident?"

"I don't think so."

"Have you been drinking, sir?"

"I don't drink," he answers vaguely. "Never have." He frowns and shies away as the policeman leans in close to see if there is any smell of alcohol on his breath. He rubs away the stiffness of dried tears on his cheeks.

"Are you ill, sir? Or diabetic, perhaps?"

"No… I'm just tired, I think. I was trying to find my way home."

"You live in Wolfville, sir?"

"Yes," Andrew answers. Then he frowns. "I mean, no. I used to, I mean. I moved down here last summer. To Green Bay."

"That's in the opposite direction."

"I know. I got confused."

The officer searches Andrew's creased, bewildered face, as if uncertain of how to proceed. "I'd like to help you, sir. According to the Detachment, you have a clean driving record. You haven't done any damage here, either to your car or to anyone's property. Do you feel well enough now to drive?"

Andrew's irritation begins to mount. "Of course I do! I was just resting, that's all." He sits up straight and fumbles for the key, finally managing to grasp and turn it. The engine comes to life.

"Where in Green Bay do you live?" the Mountie asks.

"I've rented a cottage. It's just off the paved road, after you pass the restaurant."

"Do you want to go home now, sir? Perhaps I could call your wife to come and get you."

"My wife…" Andrew pauses and stares out the windshield.

"Sir?"

He snaps his head around. His head has cleared, and his memory of the road to his cottage comes flooding back. He doesn't want anyone in an official capacity prying into his affairs.

"I'm perfectly fine, officer. Thank you for your concern. May I go now?"

The Mountie hesitates, searching Andrew's face. Finally he says, "I'll go back that way with you, sir. I'd like to be sure you get home safely." He backs away from the window and returns to the patrol car. He gets in and waits for a break in the traffic, then makes a U turn and pulls up on the opposite shoulder.

Andrew sighs and puts his car in gear. He backs it carefully out of the hedge and reverses direction. As he pulls up behind the patrol car, the officer edges out onto the road and drives off. Andrew follows.

They reach LaHave and turn south, going past the road that leads to the Fort Point historic site and down the coastline toward Dublin Shore. The Mountie drives conservatively, and Andrew keeps well back. Other motorists begin to collect behind them but are reluctant to pass the police car, and by the time they reach Petite Riviere, a small caravan trails them.

The Mountie crosses the bridge and signals a left turn, and Andrew follows him onto the slender road that is the primary approach to Green Bay. They pass the shingled community hall on the left, then the Mariner Gift Shop on the right, and as the road narrows further they slow to negotiate the sharp bends and uneven, potholed pavement.

The bay appears ahead of them between the trees, and they follow the right hand bend that takes them along the shoreline, dipping down almost to water level. The sunlight scatters brightly from the tips of the minuscule waves and the surface of the almost white sand. Andrew lowers the visor to shield his eyes and glances out toward the water. Half a dozen children dig along the surf's edge, watched over by casual young parents who lounge above the tide line, idly conversing among themselves. He feels unreasonable envy for their relaxed contentment.

Carefully avoiding a couple of ungainly recreational vehicles on the constricted roadway, he reluctantly follows his concerned shepherd like a wayward and irritated sheep, and they make their way slowly until they pass the small canteen on the right. The Mountie pulls off next to the restaurant to let Andrew go by, and watches as he drives past and steers in among the trees, and then into his driveway.

Andrew gets out and starts up the path to his shabby cottage. He notes with annoyance that the RCMP car has followed him again and has pulled up close behind his back bumper. He ignores the officer, who has lowered the window of his car and is leaning out. As he climbs the porch and reaches the door, the Mountie calls to him. "Is there anything else I can do for you, sir?"

Andrew turns to stare, as if seeing the police car for the first time. He shakes his head to clear it, then forces down his growing irritation. *No sense in antagonizing him. Just so he'll go away...* He waves half-heartedly, mounts the steps and goes inside.

He tosses his keys on the end of the sofa and heads to the kitchen for a glass of water. He downs it in a single gulp, then returns to the living room and looks out toward the driveway. The patrol car still sits idling at the end of the driveway. The officer appears to be writing in a notebook. *Damn nosy bastard*, Andrew thinks.

As he continues to stare, he sees the policeman glance at his license plate, then down again at his notes. Finally the patrol car backs out and reverses direction, and Andrew watches until it is completely out of sight. Then he turns and stumbles down the hallway toward his bedroom.

What if he calls Catherine? What if he tells her where I am, and she comes out here?

*   *   *

Agitated and disturbed, Andrew lies on his bed trying to sort through the jumbled images and unrecognized faces that mingle behind his eyelids. A rumbling of cellos echoes in his head, and he covers his ears as if to shut them out. His temples throb and his bowels cramp alarmingly. Bile rises in his throat, driving him to the bathroom where he sinks to the floor beside the toilet and retches dryly above the bowl. Gradually the convulsions subside.

He raises his head, unable to identify his surroundings. He gets up and stumbles down the hall, heading for the front door. As he crosses the living room, nausea sweeps over him, and he falls to his knees and drops his head between his hands. He sways back and forth and his balance fails, tumbling him onto his side. Oblivion...

Several hours later he stirs and opens his eyes. His muscles are stiff and sore, and his back aches from the hard floor. He pushes himself into a sitting position and looks around. The sun is low in the sky, filtered through the pines and etching tangled, flickering shadows on the far inside wall. He stands shakily and is surprised to find his mind sharp and clear, except that the day's events have vanished from his memory.

He walks gingerly down the hall to the bathroom and looks in the mirror. His face is a ruin. He turns the tap and splashes water in his eyes, then pumps liquid soap from the bottle beside the sink and begins to wash. He dries his hands, then takes a comb from his back pocket and runs it through his hair. He looks down at his clothes.

His pants are rumpled, and several unidentified stains trail down the front of his shirt. He undresses in disgust, leaving the clothing on the bathroom floor, and pads out to the bedroom to find something more presentable.

Old Cat looks up at him from her place on the windowsill. He can't remember her being there when he arrived home, but she probably was. At her age, sleeping is her main preoccupation, and she rarely stirs from her favourite spot except when he is home to pay attention to her.

He walks over and strokes her soft fur, noting her sleek, healthy appearance. He remembers combing her that morning. He remembers feeling good then, making a small breakfast of cereal and milk instead of just his usual cup of coffee. His trip to Crescent Beach...

More memories creep back. The beauty of the morning, the sands vacant but for pushy seagulls guarding their clamshell meals. A starfish...

Jennie Horton's tiny heart-shaped face flows back to him, and he hears her voice again: "I'm not allowed to talk to strangers... Yeah, and I'm supposed to fall for that..." He smiles.

Then Ramona Billings. *God, why does she bother to talk to me, the way I treat her? Why can't she see I just want to be left alone?*

He sits on the edge of the bed and Old Cat sidles over to join him, butting her head against his arm. He pets her distractedly as fragmented memories of the day play out in hazy detail, up until his misdirected journey toward Bridgewater. But after that, the rest of what happened remains stubbornly confused and indistinct.

How did I get here?

Anxiety wells up inside him, the fear of someone or something that threatens him, menaces his privacy or even his safety, but he can't recall what brought it about. His mind now feels orderly and his thoughts are precise, a college professor's intellect resurfacing, but the recent past stays obstinately vague. He feels exhausted and frightened, never knowing when the clouds will gather again to carry him off to an empty terrain where nothing ever seems familiar, and where he can find no one he knows.

His stomach feels hollow, and he remembers tossing the muffin away behind the bakery. Surprisingly he feels hunger, a rare condition these days. He leaves the bedroom and makes his way to the kitchen, followed closely by Old Cat. The animal twines herself between his legs as he stands before the refrigerator, and he locates a half-empty can of tuna and carries it over to the counter. He spoons some into a bowl and sets it down on the floor.

Old Cat sniffs it and looks up at him questioningly.

"What's the matter, day-old tuna's not good enough for you? You want something fresh?" The cat opens her mouth and utters a queer, high-pitched interrogatory, more of a squeak than a meow. Andrew laughs and picks up the bowl again. He scoops the tuna back into the can. "You'll get this the next time." *If I don't eat it myself...* He puts it back in the refrigerator.

He goes to the cupboard and searches among the cat food cans on the bottom shelf. "What is your pleasure, your highness? Chicken? Beef? Ocean whitefish, perhaps?" Comically, Old Cat licks her chops.

"Ocean whitefish it is," he tells her, and takes out the can opener. Old Cat rubs against his leg as he fills her bowl with the fresh food, and she begins to eat immediately when he sets it down on the floor. "Spoiled damn cat," he mutters good-naturedly. "Oh well, at your age you're entitled to be fussy."

He smiles inwardly, amused at his habit of talking to the cat as if she were a person. He straightens up and tries to decide what to eat himself. Nothing in the near-empty fridge appeals to him, and except for the cat food, the cupboard shelves are bare. He retrieves his wallet and keys and goes out the door, heading for the canteen.

To his right, swarms of children play on the sand between the road and the waters of Green Bay. He pauses to watch them as they chase among the rocks, squealing in delight as they splash after each other through the shallows. They provoke a host of memories within him: two long ago children, Catherine's and his, and their summer holidays spent at Maritime beaches.

He puzzles at the strange workings of his mind. *How can I feel so normal now, when a short time ago I couldn't even find my way home?* He grimaces in disgust and heads off for the restaurant.

* * *

The little canteen is almost deserted. Five teenagers crowd into a corner booth, eating fries and drinking colas, but the other two booths and all four tables are empty. Through the screen door, happy sounds float into the room from a steady stream of little ones as they come to the takeout window for fast food and ice cream. Nadia Marshall looks up from wiping a table and watches Andrew enter and take a seat beside the window. She picks up a menu and heads toward him.

"Hi, Doc," she greets him cheerfully. "Need to see a menu?"

"Just fish chowder," he says with a smile. "And watch what

you call me, you fresh kid."

"You don't scare me. Anything to drink?"

"Started a new coffee bean yet today?" he kids her. His complaint about the canteen's weak coffee is a running gag between them.

"I'll chase a fresh one through your cup, just for you." She leaves the dining room and enters the kitchen area where Josh Watson stands behind the grill, flipping a burger for a customer at the takeout window.

"Doc's here," she says as she takes a soup bowl, bread plate and coffee mug from a shelf.

"How is he today?" Josh asks.

"Seems great," she answers. "I wish I knew what it is that makes the difference. Some days when he comes in here, it's like he doesn't even know me. Other times, he teases the hell out of me."

"Got the hots for teenagers, I bet."

"Stuff it. He's just nice, that's all."

"How old do you think he is?"

"I can't tell. He looks a lot older now than when he came last summer. He's lost a bunch of weight, and his hair looks sort of brittle, you know? Dull, like old steel wool. Half the time he doesn't eat what he orders, just sort of picks at it. Maybe he's sick."

Nadia ladles chowder into a bowl, absently watching as Josh flips the burger into a bun, expertly adding tomato and lettuce and wrapping it in waxed paper. She steps out of his way in the narrow kitchen as he turns from the grill toward the takeout window in the wall behind him. He hands the burger to the nine-year-old outside and collects her money.

"Where's he from, anyway?" Josh asks as he rings the sale up on the register.

"Wolfville," she replies. "He told me he used to teach English at Acadia. I gave him a hard time, told him I was going to a *good* school, St. Mary's or Dalhousie, but he knew I was kidding. Mom says he used to write books. Novels."

"Nothing I ever read, I guess."

"Me either," she says. "I asked him if I could borrow one of his books, and he promised to bring me one, but he never did." She places the bowl on a tray alongside a plate containing a fresh biscuit and butter. She pours a mug of coffee. "You watch, I'll be bringing most of this back when he leaves. A little soup, maybe one bite out of the biscuit is all he ever takes."

"Maybe he's got an ulcer or something. Or stomach cancer."

"God, I hope not!" Nadia puzzles over the meal as Josh turns back toward the grill. "I've got an idea," she mutters to herself. She adds a second biscuit to the plate, and more butter. Then she leaves the kitchen and returns to the dining room.

The teenagers have left their booth and are crowding around the register. "Josh, can you get the cash?" she calls out. She carries the tray to Andrew's table and sets it down. She places the chowder and biscuits before him, along with the coffee.

"How come the extra biscuit?" he asks.

"That's mine," she says. "I'll be right back." She flees to the kitchen. "Josh, if anybody else comes in, can you give them the menus? Take their order too?"

"You owe me."

"Don't I always? But thanks." She picks up an extra plate and knife and goes back into the dining room. She sits down opposite Andrew. "Want some company?" She plucks one of the biscuits off his plate and transfers it to her own.

"Won't you get fired, fraternizing with the customers?" he jokes. "Besides, why would you want to spend time with an antique like me?"

"Hoping to learn something, I guess," she says brightly, splitting open the biscuit. "Just how long did it take you and Noah to build that ark anyway?"

"You're rude!" he laughs.

"And you love it," she counters. "Eat your chowder. I made it myself, and I get really insulted if somebody doesn't finish it."

He picks up the spoon and samples it. "It's terrible!" he teases. "Tastes like you boiled a shoe. And how come they let a spoiled brat like you work here? What are you, eight? Nine?"

Nadia realizes he knows little about her, and finds herself eager to share her plans with her new friend. "Seventeen last month," she answers, "and going into Grade Twelve in September. My mom and dad own this place, and I've worked here every summer for six years." She grins at him. "That's why I'm so good at it." She butters her biscuit and adds some strawberry jam from a small prepackaged tub.

Andrew follows suit and takes a bite. "Whatever happened to child labour laws?"

"Family businesses don't count, Mom says. Besides, it's not so bad. I kind of like it. And some days I get out on the beach in the morning, and between lunch and dinner, too. Mom pays me a salary and puts it in my education fund. Tips go there, too."

"So who buys your clothes and CDs and who knows what? My kids cost me a fortune at your age."

"I get an allowance. I make out okay. Dad works in Bridgewater, so the canteen is an extra, and the overhead's low. We don't have much staff to pay, just Josh and a guy who cleans the place every Monday night. Mom and I both cook, so we all take turns at the grill. That way everything I make goes for university."

"Good for you!" he says approvingly. "I worked my way through college too, and it wasn't easy, so you're smart to get a head start. What are you going to study?"

"I'm going to be a doctor," she says proudly.

Andrew eats more of the chowder and tries the coffee. "That's a lot of years of study. Going to specialize in something?"

"Babies, I think. Or maybe heart surgery. Who knows?" She notes with pleasure that all of his meal is gone. "Want another biscuit?"

"No, I'm okay."

"Come on, I'm going to have one." She bounces up and heads for the kitchen. An elderly couple comes in the door, and she whirls and plucks a pair of menus from the rack on the wall. She hands them to the new arrivals. "Sit anyplace you like. Someone'll be right with you." She heads for the kitchen.

"Josh, can you take the dining room? I'm busy with Doc."

"Busy how?" he says with a leer.

"I'm making sure he eats, jerk." She scoops up two more biscuits and fills another bowl with chowder. She carries them out to the table and sets them down.

"Hang on," she says to Andrew, and goes back for the coffee pot as Josh comes out to take the order from the elderly couple. She returns from the kitchen and empties the pot into Andrew's mug. She hands the pot to Josh as he heads back to the kitchen, and he glares at her. She sticks her tongue out at him, then sits down again.

"Okay," Andrew says, "what are you up to?"

"Who, me?"

" 'Who, me?' " he mimics. "I ordered a simple bowl of chowder, and you come on like the banquet scene in Beauty and the Beast."

She laughs. "I just like talking to you," she says. "You listen to me. Really listen, not just like being polite. And besides, you owe me."

"Owe you how?"

"You promised me I could borrow one of your books."

"You're a pest, you know that?"

"And you're a welcher. You promised."

"Fine. You can borrow my dictionary, then."

She pretends disgust. "That's not what I meant, and you know it. One of *your* books, the ones you wrote."

He sighs. "You wouldn't like them." He lifts his spoon and tries the new bowl of chowder. She stares at him with concern but stays silent as he takes several mouthfuls, then lowers the spoon. "To tell the truth," he says, "I barely remember what they're about any more. It was a long time ago that I wrote them."

Nadia breaks open another biscuit and pushes it toward him. "Mom says she read them once, all of them. Library copies, so we don't have them around the house. She says they were good."

He focuses on the chowder. "I have to admit, this soup is all right."

"I'm glad you like it, and don't try to change the subject. When can I borrow your books?"

"You can't. Some of the words in them have more than one syllable. You wouldn't be able to handle them."

She bursts out laughing. "I bet I know what your problem is.

You write dirty books, and you're ashamed of them."

He throws up his hands helplessly. "I give up. Read the damn things, if you want to."

"When?"

"I'll bring you one next time I come."

"Oh, no. That's what you said the last time. I'm coming to get it myself, soon as we close."

"You're worse than a pest, you're a leech! Give me the check so I can get out of here."

"You haven't finished your chowder. I'm insulted."

"Jesus Christ." He scoops the last few spoonfuls into his mouth and sits back. "Satisfied?"

She grins at him in triumph. "I'll be right back." She goes into the kitchen and writes up the bill: one bowl of chowder, one biscuit and coffee. She takes it out and drops it on the table. "See you later, Doc."

He looks at the slip of paper. "Half of this is missing."

"On the house," she says as she walks away. "I want to be able to laugh at you when you get fat."

Andrew smiles ruefully and digs into his pocket for change for a tip, then pauses. He takes out his wallet and extracts a large bill instead, and slides it under the edge of his plate. *No matter how much she saves for med school, it won't be enough.* He heads for the register.

Josh Watson comes out and rings up the sale. "Everything okay, Dr. Striker?"

"No, everything is not okay. Your waitress is rude, incompetent and bossy."

"She's also *my* boss," he laughs. "Come again." He disappears back into the kitchen.

Andrew goes outside and heads for the beach. The air is turning chill and the children are gone. He has the sand to himself. He pulls himself up onto one of the rocks that were left by the last ice age glaciers. The sun has set behind him, turning the sky over the bay into a palette of pinks and blues.

He remembers sadly how much he always enjoyed the repartee with his students, not unlike the banter and mock insults during the meal just past. *Godspeed, Nadia Marshall. I bet you'll make that medical school sit up and take notice.*

Once more he puzzles over the clouds growing within his mind, and the fact that there seems to be no pattern to it, except that the periods of lucidity are becoming fewer and farther apart. Most disturbing, on several occasions he has awakened from a daze to find he does not know where he is, nor how he has come to be there. He knows the disease is progressing at a rapid rate.

Feeling energized by his first good meal in days, he stirs himself and looks across toward Cape LaHave Island. Then he starts back toward his cottage, but upon reaching the driveway, he decides to continue a little farther. He walks to the end of the pavement and then follows a narrow gravel path as it curves back toward the water. He emerges from among the trees onto the remnants of the old coast road, once a major thoroughfare but now mostly overgrown and no longer passable by vehicles.

He threads his way carefully through a stand of rushes and climbs a low dune that rises between the sea and the shallow remains of ponds that once served a commercial fishery in the nineteenth century. The wind has dropped. The evening light clings to the earth, as if reluctant to leave these northern latitudes that now, for just a few brief months, tilt hungrily toward the summer sun. Evenings can seem endless at this lovely time of the year.

Like a silent stalker, another memory from earlier that day assaults him, suddenly and without warning: his hallucinatory vision of Catherine on the boat that afternoon. He sinks down on the sand, and the misery of loneliness tears like a clawed hand at his gut. He tries to imagine her, still living in their home in Wolfville or perhaps visiting Penny and the grandchildren in Ottawa.

She might even be with Donald in Calgary. He longed to see his son once more, and to meet the lovely young woman who would soon be Donald's wife. And now, cut off from them by his own choice, she was a girl he would no doubt never get to know.

Catherine...

He has no regrets. Once he was sure of what was happening to his mind, he knew he could never subject those he loved to the spectacle of his eventual decline. The pain of separation, however sharp, was pale compared with his current situation, the relentless deterioration within him that left him never knowing whether a day would be lucid or lost.

Wearily he stands and brushes the sand from his pants. He continues on down the path, stepping carefully over a narrow stream that bisects the old roadway. He stops beneath a weather-worn pine that stands sentinel on Green Point, overlooking the bay. The last of the sun's reflected light fades away as he lingers. He finds himself unwilling to leave the consolation of the sea he loves so much.

* * *

Andrew picks his way carefully along the broken pavement and turns into the driveway of his silent cottage. It is full dark now, and he has not left a light on inside. He climbs the sagging steps, opens the screen door, and inserts his key in the lock.

"Can I come in?"

The voice startles him. He turns and makes out a barely visible figure at the end of the porch, seated with legs hanging over the edge. He strains to see who it is.

Nadia Marshall levers herself up and walks toward him. "You owe me a book, remember?"

"Does your mother know you're out, little girl?"

"Uh, huh, and she knows where I am, so you better watch your step."

He laughs. "All right, you've cornered me. Come in and get your damn book." He opens the door and holds it for her, first reaching inside to flip the wall switch. A weak bulb comes on overhead, accentuating the dreariness of the run-down cottage.

"The Dennises used to come here every summer," she says as she steps inside. "Until the kids got big, anyway. Then Mrs. Dennis got sick, and now she's in a wheelchair."

"Multiple sclerosis," Andrew says as he switches on a table lamp, driving the shadows back into the far corners of the small room. "Harold Dennis told me she's too weak to enjoy being out here any more. He said they might try to come out for a weekend or two before the summer's over, but I haven't heard from him."

Nadia stands in front of a tall bookcase, running her eyes over the titles. "You rent this place from them?"

"Summer and winter both. It's small, so it's not too hard to heat or keep clean. Which book do you want? Mine are all on the top row."

Nadia stretches to read the spines and slides one volume out from between the others. "This one. Mom says *Amanda's Passage* is your best one, and that every teenage girl ought to read it."

A smart remark jumps unbidden to his lips, but he looks at the young woman's earnest expression and stifles it. "I wrote it for Penny."

"Who's that?" She crosses to the faded sofa and sinks down on one end, cradling the volume in her lap. Andrew moves to his battered easy chair.

"My daughter. She lives in Ottawa now. Her husband works for the government, but I forgave him for that." Nadia smiles at his humour. "When she was little, she scared me to death. All I ever thought about were all the awful things that could happen to her, and I wrote the book to try to head off at least some of them."

"Did it work?"

"Probably not. She didn't get into any of the trouble I was expecting, but she went out and invented her own."

"Mom says the story is beautiful, and full of hope."

"I suppose so. Like all fairy tales…"

"I thought you said you didn't remember it."

Andrew gets up and paces over to the bookcase. He runs his fingers over the dust jackets, surprised as always to see his own name associated with titles he most often can no longer bring to mind. But *Amanda's Passage* seems different somehow. More personal, and therefore more easily recalled.

Nadia lingers by the bookcase, the slim volume cradled against her forearm, making no move to leave. "Hadn't you better be going?" Andrew says.

"Can I see your cat?"

He reacts with surprise. "How do you know I've got a cat?"

"I've seen her sitting in the window. Is she here?"

"Someplace. She never goes out. She's old…" He leaves the room and finds Old Cat in her normal spot on the bedroom windowsill. He picks her up, and she stretches and sinks her claws into the fabric of his shirt. He carries her into the living room and sits down, letting her arrange herself on his lap.

Nadia gets up and walks over to stand beside him. She offers her hand tentatively, and Old Cat sniffs it, then stretches her head out to be scratched. "She's cute. Where did you get her?"

"From a vet. She'd been abandoned."

Nadia finds Old Cat's favourite under-the-chin petting spot, and the animal stretches luxuriantly and purrs like a stoked furnace. "She's lucky she found you."

Found me? Was thrust upon me, is more like it.

"Is there a Mrs. Dr. Striker?"

Andrew's head snaps up abruptly, startling the cat. He looks at the girl suspiciously, wondering just how much he dares to reveal. "Yes. She lives in Wolfville."

"Divorced?" she asks tentatively.

"No. Not exactly." He feels momentary irritation as she probes into personal territory.

"Does she come out to visit you much?"

Andrew lifts Old Cat down to the floor and stands up. "I hope you enjoy the book. You'll have to excuse me now." He strides to the door and opens it, expecting her to go through it, but she remains standing by his chair.

"I didn't mean to pry."

"Good night, Nadia."

She crosses the floor slowly and steps over the threshold. Before he can close the door, she turns to him and smiles sadly. "Even when you're nasty to me, I still like you."

Conflicting emotions threaten to overwhelm him. With his own family abandoned, he has determined not to let anyone get close to him again. "Go home, you dopey kid."

"When I finish this one, can I borrow another?"

"You won't finish it."

"Want to bet?" She doesn't wait for a response. She skips down off the porch and heads back toward the canteen, now closed for the night, and her home beyond it.

He watches her go. At the bend in the road she whirls and waves to him, all in one motion, as if knowing he would still be standing there. He is instantly reminded of Jennie Horton, climbing the rock at the end of the beach that morning, her tiny starfish of a hand carving arcs in the air. He lets the screen door swing shut and retreats inside.

Tests

On the morning after his confused ramble on the outskirts of Wolfville, a Wednesday, Andrew awoke before the alarm, still exhausted but clear-headed. Brushing off Catherine's tentative expressions of concern, he drove to the university and prepared to deliver his morning lecture. It went fairly smoothly, although after a few stumbles in the first fifteen minutes of the period, he resorted to reading much of the remainder from his notes.

At noon he sat alone in his office. Where once he had spent most lunch hours in the Student Union building, enjoying the company of many of the young people who considered him not just a teacher but a friend, now he avoided most such contact. He never knew when he would forget a name, lose track of a conversation, utter an inexplicable gaff.

The afternoon sessions were similarly successful, although less than inspiring. Andrew felt removed from his classes, as if a wall had grown up between him and the students. His lack of spontaneity and awkward reliance on his notes hung like a gauze curtain before him, allowing light to pass but obscuring the details. They had a right to expect his best, and he knew he could no longer deliver it. He was cheating them.

Fatigued and depressed, he headed home at the end of the day to find Catherine waiting for him at the door to the garage. She stepped forward and hugged him as he got out of the car. Distracted and somewhat annoyed at her solicitous attitude, he brushed past her and headed for the living room.

He read the newspaper while Catherine finished making supper, and they filled their plates and sat before the television set while the evening news played out on the CTV network. He picked at his food, leaving most of it untouched. Even after they had finished eating, his mood remained dark and distant, as if daring his wife to disturb him. She sat in silence.

When the weather report concluded, Andrew decided to try to clear the air between them. He muted the TV sound with the remote control and strove to inject a calming normalcy into his voice. "Anything new at the hospital?"

He tried to concentrate as Catherine launched into a description of her day and details about the coming and going of the new helicopter ambulance service. He asked occasional questions, although he felt distracted and knew he was unable to hide it.

At a lull in the conversation, Catherine again broached the subject of the medical tests. "Bob stopped by the ward while I was helping to bathe patients," she said.

"I bet I know what he wanted," Andrew grumbled.

"All he said was, how were you feeling this morning, and I told him fine."

"Uh, huh." He picked up the newspaper again and folded back a section of the classified ads to address the daily crossword.

"Andrew, what are you afraid of?"

"Don't start."

She sat in silence for several minutes. He continued to ignore her, concentrating on the puzzle.

"I love you," she said quietly. He looked up in surprise. "And I'm frightened. I've been married to you for almost forty years, and all of a sudden you're someone else, and I don't know why."

"That's foolish."

"No it's not, and you know it. Something's going on with you, and you won't tell me. That's what hurts me the most."

"There isn't anything wrong with me."

"There is, and you're trying to ignore it, but you can't. Is there something happening at Acadia that I don't know about?"

"Just the usual bullshit. Territorial skirmishes between the faculties, under-the-table funding grabs… You know the score. None of it affects me any more, and hasn't since I gave up the department chairmanship."

"Then there's no reason not to let Bob check you out."

"Only that it's a waste of time. There's nothing to find."

"So then what's the harm?"

"Damn it, Catherine, leave me alone!"

She didn't back down. "That's another thing. In all the years we've been married, you've never said anything like that to me before. And now twice in less than a day…"

He sighed. "I'm sorry. It isn't anything you've done. It's just that…" He stuttered to a halt. Catherine looked at him helplessly as his eyes darted around the room in desperation. Gradually he regained control, collected himself and went back to the crossword puzzle, refusing to meet her gaze.

"Please?"

He lowered the paper in exasperation. "If I agree, will you drop it?"

"Yes."

"Fine. But you'll have to set it up. I'd feel like a damned fool, asking for tests when I know nothing's wrong with me." He dropped the paper beside his chair and punched a button on the remote. The television set blared, but he stared at the screen unseeing and unhearing.

* * *

Entering his office shortly before noon the next day, Andrew listened to his voice mail with mounting irritation. Catherine's voice, filled with forced cheer, passed on the time of his appointment at the hospital. Briefly he considered not going, but knowing Catherine's stubbornness, he was sure that would not be the end of it. Reluctantly he called the departmental secretary and asked her to cancel his afternoon engagements.

Annoyed at having to skip the noon meal so as not to affect the blood test results, he shuffled through a stack of assignments and began to read, making corrections in the margins and sometimes rewriting whole paragraphs to show the students how to shape their language more effectively. Immersed in the work, he was surprised to find almost two hours had elapsed, and that the stack of unread papers had shrunk by more than half.

He felt satisfied with the work he had accomplished, and with the quality of his corrections to the students' papers. *Maybe I'm already better,* he thought. *Maybe I can beat this thing on my own.* But uncertainty nagged at him, and he realized that his reluctance to go to the hospital lay mostly in the fear of what the tests might show. *Better not to know...*

He got his coat and checked in with the secretary before leaving, then drove the twelve or so kilometres to the regional hospital. He arrived only a few minutes late, and the volunteer at the desk directed him to the laboratory on the lower level. He walked to the stairway at the back of the lobby and went down, then turned left and followed the signs to the lab.

He checked in at the long counter where a receptionist took his personal information and asked him to wait. He took a seat and picked up a magazine, thumbing through it without interest. In less than ten minutes, a technician came out and beckoned for him to follow. He got up and went through a door at the end of the room. *Here we go...*

* * *

Late the following Monday morning, Andrew was correcting essays when the phone rang. He picked it up and heard his wife's voice on the opposite end. "Hi, sweetheart. How's today going?"

"All right," he answered glumly. "What's up?"

"Bob called. He wants to see you this afternoon at four."

"What did he say about the tests?"

He heard her hesitate, and sharp anxiety gripped him. "Well?"

"You need more potassium, and you need to gain back the weight you've lost. Other than that, you're fine."

"So I'll eat some bananas or something. Why do I have to go

see him?"

"He just wants to talk to you, I guess."

"Damn it, I've got too much to do! Tell him no!"

"I can't do that," Catherine said. "He said you have to go."

"What for, if I'm okay?"

Again she hesitated. "Maybe he didn't tell me everything…"

"Listen," he said angrily, "I'm sick of this whole damned thing. I took the tests the way you wanted, so now leave me alone. You and Bob both."

"Call him," she said quietly. "Please."

"Damn it, Catherine…"

"Please?"

Shit! "All right!" He slammed the receiver into its cradle and sat in angry but frightened silence. *Something's wrong with me. I've got a tumour or something, and Catherine knows and won't tell me.*

He got up from his desk and paced restlessly around the office. He stopped in front of the window and looked out across the campus, bleak and bare with its leafless trees under overcast skies matching his state of mind. He turned and stared at the phone for several long seconds. Then he snatched up his coat and slammed out the door, heading for downtown and a cup of coffee. And some peace and quiet.

*   *   *

Later, following his afternoon class, Andrew sat at his desk with a pile of student assignments centred on his blotter. Despite his efforts to concentrate, the words and sentences blurred on the page, and he had to reread them several times before the meaning sank in. His mind kept returning to Catherine's call, and to the possibility that he was seriously ill.

Forcing himself to focus, he ploughed through the papers, but as the shadows lengthened outside the window, he realized he would probably have to reread them all again later. Finally he set everything aside and reached for the phone. He punched the key for an outside line and called the medical centre. Dr. Melanson's receptionist put him on hold, but it was only a short time before the doctor's familiar voice came over the line.

"Andrew, good to hear from you. Did Catherine call you?"

"What's going on, Bob?" Andrew began heatedly. "She said the tests didn't show anything wrong, but that you still want to see me."

"That's only half right. Look, are you done for the day? This will be a lot easier if you come down here. I'll lay it all out for you then."

"The hell you say!" Andrew exploded. "What have I got, cancer or something? Don't leave me hanging like this."

"Calm down," Melanson said reasonably. "It's just like I told Catherine, there's nothing physically wrong with you, except you have to start watching what you eat. Catherine says your appetite isn't so good lately."

"Nothing tastes good any more," Andrew conceded.

"That's not uncommon at your age, and we can fix that. You need a couple of supplements to get your chemistry straightened out. I'll write out a prescription, and you can pick it up when you come in."

"Put it in the mail," Andrew said testily.

"I can't do that. You know that."

"Listen, Bob, just tell me what to get, and I'll do it. And I'll start eating more, if that's what it takes to get you and Catherine off my back."

"That may not be enough," Melanson continued patiently. "Even if we get your diet straightened out, that doesn't mean you're out of the woods. Look, this will be a lot easier face to face."

"Bob…"

"I just want to run some more tests."

"What kind of tests? You've already stabbed me and poked me and run me through every damn machine in the hospital."

"We need to bring someone else in on this," the doctor said in a calm, reassuring tone. "Someone with a little more expertise than I. There's a psychologist who's had a lot of success with…"

"A goddamn shrink? Forget it!"

"Andrew…"

"There's nothing wrong with my head!"

"Listen, clinical depression is a fairly common…"

"No, *you* listen. I've gone along with you and Catherine up to now, but this is way off base. Just butt out, will you?"

Andrew dropped the receiver and stamped over to the window, shaking with a mixture of fear and anger. *What the hell is wrong with me? Hanging up on people, shouting at my friends…* He struggled to regain control, and suddenly felt drained and exhausted. He collapsed into his chair and cradled his head in his hands. *I have to fight this on my own. I have to…*

FOUR...

Andrew Striker lies staring up at the ceiling. The digital clock turns from four fifty-nine to five. He has been awake for over an hour. He throws back the blanket and disturbs Old Cat at the foot of the bed. As he makes his way out of the room, she turns around once and settles down to go back to sleep.

He measures out some coffee into the brewing basket and turns the unit on. Outside the window, the birds are setting up a pre-dawn racket. He sits down and stares at the first few brown drops that fall into the carafe.

Nothing to do today. As usual.

Grey light begins to penetrate the room, but he isn't aware of it until the sunlight shows through the tops of the trees. He looks up in surprise. The coffee has finished brewing, he doesn't know how long ago, and in front of him his empty mug shows traces of grounds in the bottom. He doesn't remember drinking any.

He stands up and goes to the refrigerator out of habit. A carton of milk less than half full sits on the upper right hand shelf, and a single egg lies in the door keeper. Wilted lettuce and a single shrivelled orange rest on the lowest level. He opens the meat drawer, thinking there might be some bacon left, but there is none.

He returns to the table and pours more coffee. The sun is gaining strength, and as the room begins to warm, he recalls the previous evening's walk among the dunes, and his return to find Nadia Marshall waiting to borrow *Amanda's Passage*.

Andrew's passage, he thinks. *Who is there to write that book?*

Then he remembers his confused departure from the LaHave bakery, and a vague memory of an RCMP officer following (leading?) him home. He wonders if he dares to drive again.

He wanders aimlessly throughout the cottage, mug in hand, forcing himself to identify every one of his few belongings, to call them to mind and place them in a proper perspective in his past. He comes upon Old Cat, still curled up and sleeping at the foot of the bed. She won't move to the windowsill until the sun comes around the corner. He goes back to the kitchen and checks her dishes, then replenishes the water and adds another layer of dried pellets to the other bowl.

He thinks of walking down by the shore again. Then, *What the hell, if I drive slow, I won't hurt anyone if I forget what I'm doing.* He locates his keys and wallet and goes out to the car, surprised that he remembers to lock the cottage. He backs out of the driveway and starts down the Green Bay road.

At the first bend, where the road curls around a narrow stretch of white, rock-free sand that hugs the shoreline, an elderly woman sits in a folding aluminum chair. She wears a shapeless cardigan and baggy slacks, and a broad-brimmed hat shields her eyes as she reads from a hard-cover novel. Despite the early morning warmth, she huddles within herself, as small and shrivelled as Andrew's thoughts.

Older than I am. I wonder if she remembers what she reads.

He drives on, manoeuvring cautiously over cracked and crumbling asphalt. Once past the cottage area the surface improves, and he soon comes abreast of the gift shop. He considers turning left; he has never explored the country lane that wanders off to the southwest. He seems to remember that it must lead to Broad Cove, but he isn't sure. Fearful of getting lost again, he continues on into Petite Riviere, and turns right to cross the bridge.

A few minutes later he spots the wooden boardwalk at the

western end of the provincial park at Risser's Beach. Several couples are exploring the salt marsh that it traverses, keeping watch on their eager children as they spy on the varieties of birds that nest there. He lifts his foot from the accelerator and considers stopping, then is reminded of the numbers of people that probably already crowd the sands, the sort of horde that he would do anything to avoid. He continues onward.

The Crescent Beach turnoff appears on his right, and almost without conscious decision he turns in. It is later in the day than he thought. The small mobile canteen has already arrived, and several children are lined up at the window to buy drinks and cones. Down on the sand more than a dozen cars are drawn up beside the fence, and the tide is higher than when he left the previous day.

He coasts to a stop at the top of the ramp. As usual most of the bathers are clustered here at the western end of the beach, and the far end is nearly deserted. Later in the day they will spread out more, but there is still some hope of solitude further along, at least for an hour or so.

Instead of driving onto the sand, he parks along the upper roadway, diagonally across from the canteen. He gets out and locks the car. A crowd of noisy children comes boiling up the ramp, and in order to avoid them he starts off down the road behind the fence instead of descending to the beach. Before long he finds a spot where dunes reach the top of the upright fence pilings, their sand held in place by the roots of substantial broad-leafed grasses. He makes his way to the top, crosses the line of pilings, and picks his way down over the rocks onto the sand.

He has come far enough to avoid the morning visitors, most of whom are more than two hundred yards to his right. In the opposite direction, toward the LaHave Islands, only a couple of joggers and a handful of solitary figures can be seen. He turns and starts off that way, angling down toward the water's edge.

He reaches the high tide line and steps over a clump of stringy seaweed. Out of the corner of his eye, he sees a figure running toward him. He looks up without recognition, then back down at his feet, careful to avoid stepping on anything sharp or slippery.

The child skids to a stop next to him. "I was afraid you weren't going to come!"

He looks up, puzzled. She seems somehow familiar, and he smiles at her politely, then is surprised when she grabs his hand and tugs at it. "Come and see!"

He lets her lead him a few steps, and she drops his hand and begins to run again. After a few yards, she spins around and looks back impatiently. "Hurry up! The tide's gonna get them!" She whirls and runs off again.

Andrew picks up his pace, still trying to understand who she might be, and why she thinks she knows him. Ahead, she has fallen to her knees close to the water's edge. She scoops handfuls of sand and pats them into a low wall, making a barrier between the gentle waves and whatever she wants him to see.

He comes up to her. She has scooped a shallow bowl out of the sand and has filled it halfway with water. "See, I found six of them, all stuck to the seaweed." She points down into the depression. Among the strands of kelp he sees several starfish.

She pokes the kelp aside, revealing two more on the sand beneath it. "What kind are they?"

The sight of the starfish prods his memory. "Jennie…?"

"Huh?" She looks up at him, puzzled by his vagueness.

He screws his eyes shut and shakes his head to clear it. Slowly he recalls pieces of the previous day's encounter. He hears her voice inside his head: *"Yeah, and I'm supposed to fall for that one."*

He opens his eyes. "What?"

"I said, are you okay?" Her enthusiasm over her catches washes away in the wake of her concern.

He smiles at her. "I'm fine." He squats down beside the miniature pond to inspect the creatures. "Where did you find them?"

"I told you, on the seaweed. They were all alive, like you said, and I dug them a pool. The tide's gonna wash it out pretty soon. So do you know?"

"Do I know what?"

"What kind they are! Aren't you listening to me?"

"I'm sorry. I guess I'm not really awake yet. Let's see." He peers closely, and reaches down to flip one of the creatures over to examine its underside. A Latin name teases the rim of his thoughts, then skitters away beyond his grasp.

"I used to know," he tells her, "but I've forgotten. But I know how we can find out."

"How?" A wash of tide laps the dam, and a plug of sand slides out. "Uh, oh, here we go!" She grabs a handful and slaps it into the breach, but the next wave takes it out again. She moves from her knees into a squat and watches the water's inexorable approach. "Guess it's time to let them go."

Andrew smiles as he watches her, the rhythm of the waves seeming to fascinate her. The next two are gentler, barely reaching the base of her makeshift dam. Then the third washes over the top and cascades down into the bowl, roiling the water. Two more weak ones arrive, and then a third that splits the dam in two.

She laughs and looks up into his face. "Guess they'll get to go home now, won't they? So how?"

"How what?"

"How can we find out what they're called?"

"I've got a book. When I moved down here last summer, I brought some of my library with me. I'll bring the one on marine life tomorrow morning, and we can look it up."

"You've got a whole library?" she asks in wonder.

He laughs. "Not a building! Just a collection of books in my house. Quite a few, too, but I left most of them with my wife."

"Where is she?"

"Back in Wolfville."

"So how come she isn't here with you?"

"Anyway," he sidesteps her question, "next time I see you I'll bring the book. It has pictures of all kinds of starfish, and we'll pick out the right one. Did you know there's a kind that can open up a clamshell with its arms?"

She stares at him seriously. "Is it because you drink, too?"

"What?"

"Are you like my dad? Did you have to go away because you drink?"

His knee begins to throb, and he sits down on the sand. "No, my dear, I most definitely do not drink. And I didn't *have* to go away. It was just better that I did."

"How come?"

"How come you're so nosy?" he asks. She looks at him sadly. "Okay, it's like this. I've been sick for a while, so I moved out here to see if I can get better."

"And are you?"

"Sure I am," he lies.

She scoots over and sits beside him. "I'm glad. Where do you live?"

"Over there." He points vaguely southwest across the broad expanse of Green Bay. "Do you know where the bridge is in Petite Riviere?"

"Sure."

"There's a road on the other side that goes down to the beach, and there's a bunch of cottages at the end. I'm renting one of those."

"I know where that is. There's an old restaurant there, right?" He nods. Her eyes are shining with excitement. "Let's go get that book now."

"Not without your mom's permission." His memory stirs again; this child seems to have a positive effect on him. "Which reminds me, did you ask her if it's okay for you to come out here in the morning?"

"Not yet."

"I thought we had a deal."

"That wasn't part of it. You just said you'd come so I wouldn't be here alone."

"You ought to tell her."

She thinks this over. "I want to see your book. I want to see where you live, too."

"Fine. When your mom gets home from work, you tell her about coming out to the beach, and you tell her about me. And this is very important. You have to tell her I said you should. Okay?"

She looks at him dubiously. "Why?"

"Because I'm a stranger."

"No you're not."

"As far as she's concerned, I am."

"Shit!"

"I beg your pardon?"

"I mean shoot."

He smiles. "The only way you're going to see my book is if you come clean with your mom." He turns serious. "Look, Jennie, the world isn't always a safe place. For all you know, I'm a Texas chainsaw serial killer."

"Neat! Do you cut up the bodies and put them in your freezer?"

"Kids! You're dumb as a brick!"

"I'm smart enough to know I can trust you." She grins.

"So you think. It's the smart ones like you that get eaten by the big bad wolf."

The teasing has turned serious, and her face grows sorrowful and somewhat apprehensive. He looks at her and grimaces at her expression, then reaches out and squeezes her hand gently. "I'm sorry. I didn't mean to scare you. I just worry about you, that's all."

"I'll be okay."

"Not if you keep lying to your mother like this."

"I don't lie to her."

"What do you call it, then? You come out here alone when she tells you not to. It's the same thing." She sits in silence, running her fingers through the sand. "Hadn't you better go home now? You said your mom calls you on her break." *How did I remember that?*

She gets up and brushes off the seat of her shorts. She frowns at him. "You spoiled it."

"What did I spoil?"

"Showing you the starfish." She looks off toward the eastern end of the beach but makes no move to leave. She turns over a mussel shell with her toes.

He regards her sadly. "I had a little girl once."

She looks up. "What happened to her?"

"She grew up."

Jennie cocks her head, waiting for him to go on. When he doesn't, she leans down and puts her arms gently around his neck. He feels her cheek, soft against his own. She straightens and turns to walk off down the beach. She goes slowly, turning every so often to see if he is watching her. Finally she reaches the rocks and disappears among the trees. He waits to see if she will reappear and climb the rock to wave. He waits…

*   *   *

After his customary stop at the LaHave bakery, and another uneaten muffin, Andrew gets into his car and starts back the way he came. He turns off at Fort Point and follows the one-lane road out toward the modest museum that commemorates the early settlements along the shore. He pulls into the old cemetery on the right, just before the museum grounds, and gets out to stretch his legs.

Several of the headstones bear the names and epitaphs of sea captains, and Andrew wonders whether it makes any difference to eternity that they are buried so close to the Atlantic they once sailed. *Probably not. Dead is dead.* He gazes out across the strait toward the distant peninsula and watches a cabin cruiser come around the point, heading for Riverport on the opposite shore.

He walks down to the water. A slight breeze disturbs the grasses along the channel, and although the sun does not feel as warm as the day before, it is pleasant to be beside the gently flowing stream, and quiet. He sits, then lies back and puts his hands behind his head, a cushion against the scratchy undergrowth. He closes his eyes.

Jennie's words drift back to him. "So how come she isn't here with you?"

Catherine. He cannot bear the thought of having her beside him now, witness to the deterioration of his mind. Would he even recognize her? Today, yes, but tomorrow? But only slightly less sorrowful is the lack of her.

Am I selfish? Does she grieve at my absence, as I do at hers? Do I spare her pain by being here, when some days I might be the man she once knew, even if only for a few hours at a time?

He knows, however, that he could not tolerate her concern, her love, and much worse her pity, when strained through the gauze of his weakness. Better to be apart, where she cannot see his final failure. He drifts off to sleep.

*   *   *

According to the sun, it is just a little past noon when he awakes. He stretches to relieve his aches and makes his way back to the car. Soon he is on Route 331 again, driving slowly and carefully down the coast to Petite Riviere, then on to Green Bay and his cottage. He pulls into the driveway and nearly strikes a small bicycle lying on its side where the path to the front door begins.

He gets out and looks around, but no one is in sight. He stares down at the bicycle, then reaches out for it and moves it over onto the bed of pine needles beneath the trees that overhang the driveway. He starts toward the cottage.

"Hi."

He turns. Jennie Horton is coming across the road from the beach, swinging her red plastic pail. "I heard you drive in. I found another one. See?"

She comes up to him and holds the bucket out. A tiny starfish sits on the bottom. "This one's dead for sure. It's all stiff. I found it in between the rocks. Can we go look it up?"

"How did you know which cottage is mine?"

"They told me at the canteen. Can we?"

"Did you ride your bike all the way out here?" he asks incredulously.

"Sure."

"How long did it take you?"

"I don't know. The phone was ringing when I got back to the house, and I just made it inside before it stopped. Mom sounded mad, but I told her I was in the bathroom."

"Another lie, then."

"I'm sorry. Anyway, as soon as she hung up, I got my bike. And here I am!"

"You could have been killed. People drive like hell on that road, and there's practically no shoulder."

"Tell me about it! You should have seen this one guy, he had this red pickup with a Tasmanian Devil on the hood, and he came around a curve on the wrong side of the road, practically right at me. Scared him a lot more than me, I bet. He slewed all over the place trying to miss me."

"Jennie..."

"Come on, let's go get the starfish book." She starts toward the porch, unconcerned at her narrow escape on the road. "Hey, there's a cat in there!" She runs up to the wall and stretches up to the window, laying her palm flat against the screen. Old Cat paws the glass from the inside.

Andrew comes up behind her. "When does your mother get home?"

"About quarter to four. She works until three, and then she has to get my sister from day care. What's your cat's name?"

"Then we have to get you back before then. If she finds you gone, she'll be scared out of her wits."

"I've got lots of time to ride back."

"No! You're not going out on that highway again."

"How will I get home, then?"

"I'll take you. Right now, in fact."

"I don't want to go yet. You have to show me the book, and I want to see your cat."

He stares at her in exasperation. "All right, come and sit on the porch and wait for me." He climbs the steps and unlocks the door, then goes inside and shuts it behind him. He walks toward the bookcase to look for the book on marine life, and Old Cat jumps down off the windowsill and comes over to greet him. He bends down to scratch her ears.

"Come on, old girl. Someone wants to meet you." He picks her up and carries her outside, where Jennie is sitting on the top step. The bucket lies beside her, on her left. He levers himself down carefully to her right, holding Old Cat on his lap.

"Oh, she's so pretty. You didn't tell me her name," she says, reaching out to pet the long, silky grey fur.

"Old Cat," he replies.

Jennie laughs out loud. "That's not a name."

"She thinks so."

"I'll bet she's got another name. Something nobody but her knows about. Where'd you find her?"

"She found me, I guess. Sort of."

"You're lucky."

I'm lucky? What did Nadia say to me last night? "She's lucky she found you." Which one of them is right?

Old Cat

A ragged sob escaped his throat as he crossed over from sleep to awareness. His hand rose to the corner of one eye and found it wet with tears. The remnant of his dream echoed with traces of a song (something painful from *Les Miserables*, he thought), then faded beyond recollection, lacking both meaning and context and leaving only a residue of impenetrable sadness.

He wiped his eyes and shook his head to clear it, then tried vainly to recall whatever the spectre was that now scuttled crablike into the recesses of his subconscious. Like all his dreams of late, it vanished completely, but the lingering grief did not.

The cottage squatted in sullen, vacant silence. Reluctantly he rose and pulled on his threadbare robe, then shuffled barefoot into the cramped bathroom and relieved himself. He splashed water on his face, consciously avoiding a glance in the mirror, and towelled himself dry. Then he made his way down the hall to the drab and featureless kitchen.

A weak sun barely penetrated the thin layer of clouds off to the east, suggesting the presence of fog over Green Bay. He glanced out the window and guessed the time as something after ten by its position in the sky. There was no clock in the kitchen. The entire cottage contained but one timepiece, a cheap digital device in the bedroom that he pointedly ignored.

More from habit than from need, he measured ground beans into a paper filter and stuffed it into the basket of his coffee maker. He poured enough water for two cups and started the brewing process, then eased his arthritic frame onto one of the two battered chairs beside the old pine table. He gazed through the window at the dull, muted colours of the landscape, seeing but not really aware of the birches that clung tenaciously to the last of their brownish, fall-withered leaves.

Relentless as time itself, the coffee dripped into the carafe. When the last of the water had run its course, the coffee maker hissed its emptiness and roused Andrew from his lethargy. He sighed and reached across the table to pour the black brew into an ancient, crazed mug. Adding neither milk nor sugar, he tasted it and found it curiously flat and without character. *Nothing tastes good any more.*

Another day…

He rose from the chair and picked up the mug. Carrying it through into the small square living room, he made his way to the front door and opened it to retrieve the morning paper.

No sign of the damn thing, as usual. I don't know why I bother with the subscription, anyway. Never anything but bad news in it. He scanned the surface of the narrow wooden porch, then looked out over his dormant, patchy lawn, starved by neglect and gone mostly to weeds. A dozen yards out, the newspaper lay half hidden beneath a forsythia bush where the bike-riding teenager had flung it.

Andrew bent to retrieve his shabby Nikes from the tray beside the door, and stuffed his bare feet into them. Clutching his robe more tightly around him, he shuffled off the porch and crossed the yard. He pushed the lower branches of the forsythia aside and extracted the paper from beneath them.

As he made his way back, he caught sight of a dishevelled mound of black and white fur, lying on its side and pressed into the corner where the rough wooden steps were nailed to the porch. *Dead skunk*, he thought. *At least it seems to have passed on without leaving its signature.* He started to mount the steps, then noted that the matted white fur seemed to be on its belly instead of its back. *Not a skunk…*

He peered more closely and made out the unmistakable shape of a cat's head, the ears bitten and ragged, the eyes half open and cloudy. He was about to turn toward the door when he detected a minute rise and fall in the animal's sunken chest. He leaned over to look more closely, spilling a few drops from his mug. One splattered near the cat's muzzle, and its whiskers twitched.

Goddamnit, why did you have to come here to die?

Andrew climbed the last of the steps and went back inside. Puzzled by the anger he felt, he shucked his Nikes and made his way into the kitchen. He collapsed into the chair and opened the paper. He scanned the front page, took a few deep gulps from his mug, and began to read about the latest carnage on the province's highways.

After three paragraphs he realized he hadn't absorbed a single word. He slapped the paper down on the table, drained his mug, and headed back to the porch. Without concern for his bare feet, he stepped outside and looked over the side.

The cat hadn't moved. It's eyes were now closed, and its breath came in shallow, rapid gasps, barely disturbing the filthy, tangled fur. Its mouth was open just enough to reveal long yellow teeth, pointed and encrusted with tartar. A patch of fur had been torn from its flank just forward of its tail, which was bent at the end as if broken.

Shit!

Andrew went back inside and padded to the closet next to the bathroom. He dug to the back of an upper shelf and found an old grey terrycloth towel, frayed at the edges and soft from many washings. He carried it outside and spread it out on the porch.

He reached back inside to get his Nikes and put them on again, then went down the steps into the yard and approached the corner where the cat lay. Its battered appearance repelled him. He paused to see if it was still breathing, and when he was sure it lived, he slid both hands gingerly under the small body and lifted it carefully, placing it in the centre of the towel. The cat's eyes remained closed, its breath laboured and uneven.

Andrew gathered the towel's edges around the cat's body and lifted the entire package, then carried it inside the cottage and placed it on the floor. He closed the door, removed his shoes, and stood looking at the bedraggled creature. Then he grimaced and returned to the kitchen.

The telephone directory, a battered remnant from a former tenant, lay in a corner of an overhead cupboard. It took him several minutes to locate it, reminding him of how seldom he sought any sort of human contact outside of his retreat. He thumbed to the back of the yellow pages and found the section for veterinarians.

He checked the addresses in the listings and found one for the nearest animal hospital. The Riverview Animal Clinic was probably a marginal operation, he thought, with neither bold face type nor a display ad to call attention to it. *What the hell. It doesn't take an expert to put an animal down.* He picked up the receiver and punched in the numbers.

A pleasant young female voice came over the line: "Riverview Animal Clinic, good morning. How can we help you?"

Andrew struggled to find his voice. "Uh, I've got a cat."

"Yes, sir?"

"A sick cat. I need it put down."

"How old is your cat, sir?"

"I have no idea."

"How long have you had it, then?"

"About five minutes!" Andrew said in exasperation. "Look, this isn't my cat. It crawled up next to my house to die, and I can't just leave it there."

The young woman began to understand. "You should know, sir, we have to charge for what you want done."

"How much?"

"Our normal fee for euthanasia is sixty dollars."

Jesus H. Christ, Andrew muttered under his breath. Aloud he said, "How soon can you do it?"

"I can make an appointment for you."

"Look, this animal is probably suffering." Andrew's voice rose. "It's going to die anyway, sooner probably than later. If I'm going to spend sixty bucks, the least I should get for my money is to help the damn thing go *sooner.*"

"Please wait a moment," she answered formally. "I'll have to ask the doctor if he can accommodate you this morning." Her voice was replaced by innocuous music as she placed him on hold.

Andrew fidgeted impatiently. *That was bright. Ask her for help, then antagonize her.*

The phone line clicked and the music stopped abruptly, replaced by a frosty voice. "Dr. McKinley will see you as soon as you can get here," she said brusquely.

Andrew considered making an apology, then abandoned the idea. He was in a hurry and out of practice with that sort of social nicety. "Where is your clinic?" He received the directions and hung up the receiver.

The cat was still breathing when he knelt down beside the towel. "Couldn't make it easy on either of us, could you?" he said aloud, and was surprised when the cat stirred. It's eyes opened, and it managed to raise its head briefly from the towel, trying to locate his voice.

"Well, I'll be damned. You like it in here where it's warm, do you?"

The cat tried to stretch and pawed the air slightly. Its head flopped back down on the towel, but its eyes locked onto his. It opened its mouth and tried to mew, but no sound came out.

"Okay, old boy. Or girl, whatever. Let me get dressed and we'll get you some relief." He stood up and headed toward the bedroom. *Talking to a cat, now. How crazy can you get?* He pulled on some old clothes and located his wallet and keys, then went out the back door to start the car, letting it run to take the chill off the interior.

He went back inside and found the cat trying to get to its feet. It was pawing the towel, and had managed to move forward a foot or so, but its back legs were dragging. *Broken spine maybe*, Andrew thought. He bent and gathered the towel in again, then carefully supported the cat's hindquarters and lifted it gently, expecting it to cry out. The animal arched its back and tensed, but didn't seem to be in pain.

"What happened to you, anyway?" he said, as he headed toward the back door and opened it. He flipped the end of the towel over the cat's head, stepped outside, closed the door, and started toward the car. He opened the passenger side and placed his burden gently on the seat, then closed the door again and got in behind the wheel.

Traffic was light, and Andrew drove slowly and carefully, trying not to jostle his passenger. With only one wrong turn, he found the clinic in less than fifteen minutes, parked, and went inside, cradling the cat carefully in front of him.

The outer office was dominated by a short, high counter, behind which a desk, a computer console and two filing cabinets competed for the meagre floor space. Andrew stepped up to the counter. A young woman in her early twenties looked up brightly, wearing a warm smile, and rose from behind the desk.

"I called about a cat…"

At the sound of his voice her face turned neutral, reflecting neither greeting nor disapproval as she walked toward him. She picked up a pen and clipboard from a tray on the counter.

"Name?" she asked curtly.

"Andrew Striker. Look, I'm sorry if I was rude on the phone."

She ignored his attempt at apology. "Phone?" He gave her the number.

"Your pet's name?"

Andrew looked at her disbelievingly. Hadn't she been listening to him before? "It's not my pet. I told you on the phone. I just want it put down."

"I have to put something on the form, sir."

Jesus Christ, this is ridiculous! "Cat! It's name is Cat. Look, can't I set it down somewhere while we do this?" The cat had begun to stir in his arms, and had poked its head out from under the towel.

"Sex?"

"What?"

"Is it a male or a female?"

"I have no idea. What difference does it make? Look, I don't know anything about cats. This poor beast just ended up in my yard somehow. I don't know its name, or what's wrong with it, or anything else."

The receptionist made a note on her clipboard and turned away from the counter. "Please take a seat," she said coldly. She passed through a door at the far right in the wall behind her desk.

Andrew sank wearily onto a chair and arranged the cat on his lap. *She must be new*, he thought, trying to be charitable. Several minutes passed, and the young woman emerged again and sat down at her console. "The doctor will be with you in just a few minutes."

"Can't I just pay you and leave it here, or something? I told you, it's not my cat."

"The doctor will see you soon, sir."

I give up!

Andrew was gazing out the window when a small noise startled him, something between a croak and a cry. He looked down at the cat, just as it opened its mouth and the strangled sound emerged again.

"You can talk, can you? Look, cat, I'm doing the best I can for you, okay? I'm sorry it's taking so long." Absently he reached out and stroked the creature's head just behind the ears. Amazingly, it began to purr.

The door in the back wall opened again. A stout woman emerged carrying the smallest dog Andrew had ever seen. With its tufted ears and huge alert eyes, it looked like something out of Jim Henson's quirky imagination. The woman thanked the doctor and headed toward the door, and Andrew appraised the white-coated figure that followed her into the outer office. The man stuck out his hand.

"Mr. Striker? I'm Brian McKinley."

Awkwardly, Andrew tried to rise and take his hand at the same time, nearly losing his grip on the cat. McKinley steadied him, then relieved him of the animal.

"My granddaughter tells me you found an injured cat. Come this way, please."

Granddaughter! Andrew glanced at the receptionist, who was busy at her computer and steadfastly ignoring him. *He needs to teach her how to deal with the public.*

Andrew followed him into the back room of the clinic, and the doctor placed the cat in the centre of a stainless steel examining table. He began to probe the animal's body, his fingers gently raising each limb, prying back lips and eyelids, and exploring the spine. Andrew examined the man more closely.

Brian McKinley was at least seventy-five, Andrew thought. The man's abundant hair was almost white, and his thin face and long jaw reminded Andrew of the actor Dick Van Dyke, with the same air of youthful vitality in an aged countenance. His flesh was deeply tanned and seamed. *Probably spends his spare time out on the water.* His posture was erect and his touch sure and steady, belying his years. His dark brown eyes, while surrounded by veined whites and crinkled skin, glittered with intelligence and energy.

With expert precision the veterinarian levered the cat's mouth open and flicked bits of tartar off of several teeth. He examined the gums, then let the animal close its jaw again. He peered closely into each eye. He rotated it onto its side, glanced briefly at the genitals and rectum, then placed it upright again. He fingered the bent tail. The cat seemed to have little control of its hindquarters, and when McKinley lifted it to probe the area of the kidneys, its back legs flopped loosely.

When he finished the examination, he stroked the cat's head gently and turned to Andrew. "Very sick cat, I'm afraid. Badly dehydrated, probably full of parasites, worms anyway. And see these lesions on its skin?" McKinley pointed to the missing area of fur near the tail, and to another on the cat's left side. "Allergy, probably, and malnutrition. And the fleas aren't helping things, either."

Idly the old vet scratched the cat's ears, then ran his hand down its back, roughing up the fur just above the base of its tail. "On the plus side, her kidneys are a bit small, but still functioning. That's sometimes a problem with older cats. No tumours either that I can find. Can't be sure there's nothing else wrong without a blood test, but I suspect it's just neglect that's put her in this shape. Any idea who she belongs to?"

At least now I know what sex it is, Andrew thought, *just in case somebody asks me again.* "I found her outside the house this morning. I thought she was suffering, and ought to be put down."

McKinley looked back at the cat, considering. "That's the owner's say-so, if we knew who that was. But she's been on her own for some time, I think. Hasn't had any care lately, probably eating nothing but rodents. And maybe birds, although she's not likely fast or strong enough to catch them. She's not young, either."

Neither am I, and not getting any younger, standing here listening to you.

"We see a lot of this," the vet said. "She was somebody's pet once. Been spayed, probably a long time ago. More than likely they just got tired of her. The kids wanted a new kitten, or maybe a dog. Or maybe she started messing outside the litter box or something. So they turfed her out."

What's this got to do with me?

"So there's two options here," the doctor continued. "We can euthanize her, like you say." The old man turned his intense gaze upon Andrew's face. "Or we could try to put her back on her feet."

"What for?" Andrew said in amazement. "She's suffering, isn't she?"

"Probably no more than you are," McKinley said shrewdly. "I'm sure she feels lousy, but most of us old timers do a lot of the time, right? We might be able to make her feel a lot better. Couple of injections, steroids to clear up that skin problem, and get rid of the worms and fleas. Most important, some good food."

"She can't walk," Andrew persisted. "And her tail's broken."

"The tail's an old injury that healed on its own, but crooked. As for not walking, I'm fairly sure she's just weak. Some nourishment, and I think you'd be surprised."

Nothing surprises me any more. "She's not my cat."

"I know…"

"Look, nobody wants her, right? I just didn't want her to suffer. I'm willing to pay your fee to give her some relief, and that's probably all she wants, anyway. What's the point of prolonging things?"

"Your decision, Mr. Striker." McKinley looked back at the emaciated animal, now stretching its chin to take advantage of his caressing fingers.

Nobody wants her… There's a lot of that going around.

"So if you try to fix her up, then what? Where could she go? Who'd want an old cat like this?"

McKinley's eyes rose slowly from the table and fixed on Andrew's face, but he said nothing.

"How much?" Andrew asked.

"You want it straight out, or the song and dance?"

Andrew grimaced. "Not cheap, I take it."

"Blood test, steroids, get the skin cleared up, get rid of whatever's eating her insides, put some weight back on her… Figure five hundred at the outside, to start."

"Christ on a crutch! For a *cat?*" McKinley just looked at him.

"Let me get this straight. For sixty bucks she's out of her misery, but for five bills we end up with an old cat nobody wants. Right?"

"That's if she lives. I think there's hope, with treatment, but there's no guarantee she'll make it until morning. Her heart's a little irregular, but once we get her chemistry straightened out, that may clear up. And like I say, I think her kidneys are still sound, but she's pretty weak."

"Five hundred bucks, and she'll likely be just as dead as if we do it now," Andrew muttered.

McKinley's eyes softened. "Might come in a little under that, but you wanted it straight. For what it's worth, it's my guess that if she had any say in the matter, this old lady would want to live. Just the same as you or I would."

"Don't make assumptions," Andrew said brusquely. "At least not for me."

McKinley searched Andrew's face for several long seconds. "Ever read any Travis McGee?" he asked finally.

"John D. MacDonald's fictional hero," Andrew answered. "Or alter ego, depending upon your point of view."

"You have some appreciation for popular literature, then."

"I'm a retired English prof, Doctor, although I'm not sure I'd list my respect for MacDonald among the credits in my resume. My former colleagues were somewhat stuffy. But yes, I know the colourful McGee chronicles. They contain some rather piercing philosophy, mixed in with all that adventure and mayhem."

"Then perhaps you'll remember one of his more insightful lines. In one of the later novels, I think, when John D. was himself getting old. Something about, when the time finally comes, we'll all, each and every one of us, be saying, 'No, not yet, just a little more time.' I think he was right. No matter when the grim reaper calls, it's too soon."

"You're entitled to your opinion, doctor."

McKinley shook his head once and turned back to the table. "I can take it from here," he said dispassionately. "If you'll see my granddaughter, she'll make up your bill for the disposal."

Andrew turned to leave, then paused with his hand on the

door handle and looked back at the aging vet. The doctor was stroking the cat's back gently.

"How the hell can you do this sort of thing, day after day?" Andrew asked. McKinley raised his head and stared back at him sadly, saying nothing. "All right, I give up. Shoot the beast full of vitamins or whatever, and we'll see what happens."

"Mr. Striker… Or is it Dr. Striker?"

"Just plain Andrew. Dr. Striker, the learned professor, was another lifetime ago."

"Andrew, then. You realize there are no guarantees. She may not last the night."

"Look, I've made up my mind. Just do it!"

"All right, then. My granddaughter will give you the bill. Call us back in about three days, and we'll let you know what the results are."

Andrew considered the situation. "No. Do what's necessary, and I'll take her with me now."

McKinley frowned. "She'll be better off here where I can keep an eye on her. She's going to need more care and treatment…"

"She chose my place to die. If she's going to do it, I don't want it to be in a cage." Andrew sighed. "Just tell me what I have to do. And write it down. My memory isn't worth a damn any more."

"She'll need a warm place to sleep, and you'll probably have to feed her by hand. And if she…"

"Write it down, I told you," Andrew said angrily. "How long's this going to take?"

"Why don't you wait outside? I'll do what I can, as quickly as I can, and my granddaughter will type up some instructions for you."

"Fine!" Andrew flung the door open and strode angrily out into the reception area. The young woman behind the counter looked up, startled by his sudden reappearance. McKinley followed him.

"Emily, Dr. Striker will need our standard set of instructions for caring for his cat. And you'll have to set him up with a few things. You know the drill. He'll be taking her with him after I'm through. And make an appointment for him for tomorrow morning, about eleven. If the cat makes it through the night, I want to see her again."

Emily McKinley looked back and forth in surprise between her grandfather and the angry visage of the man on the opposite side of the counter. She seemed about to ask a question, then held back. "Yes, Grandpa."

"I won't be too long," the vet said to Andrew as he turned back toward the inner office. He disappeared behind the door.

Andrew glowered at the young woman, expecting more of her sullen disapproval, but instead she gave him a dazzling smile. "Do you have a litter pan, Dr. Striker?"

"I don't have anything. I've never had a cat."

"We can let you borrow one, at least until we see how your cat makes out. Or you can buy one. They're cheaper in Bridgewater than here. And we've got bags of litter."

"That'll be fine. Borrowing, I mean."

"We have a special diet formula to feed her. And if Grandfather wants her to take pills, you'll have to learn how to give them to her."

"Whatever. Just write down exactly what I have to do." Andrew sank wearily onto a chair. *How the hell did I get into this?*

"Would you like some coffee while you wait?"

He looked up in surprise. Emily McKinley was still smiling at him, waiting for his answer.

"What's with the change of heart?" he asked sarcastically. "When I came in here, I was dirt under your shoe."

She cocked her head slightly, and the warm smile stayed in place. "What is your cat's name, sir?" she asked.

He searched her eyes. "*My* cat..." *Shit!*

Abruptly she turned away from the counter and walked back to her desk. "Cream and sugar?"

"Just black, please. And thank you."

"My pleasure." She poured from the coffee maker that sat on the corner of her desk, and took him the steaming mug. Then she returned to her seat and began to type.

Andrew stirred restlessly. He scanned the shelves of pet products and the posters on the walls: a display of dog breeds, an anatomical cutaway of a cat listing all the consequences of feline leukemia, a Purina pet food ad. Then he gazed listlessly out the window.

"I've read *Amanda's Passage*. Twice."

Her voice surprised him. He turned from the window and found her looking at him over the counter top. "Ancient history, I'm afraid," he replied.

"I'd say 'timeless' instead. It's a beautiful story."

"Thank you."

"I also read *Running In Place*. I discovered it in a bookshop just a few months ago."

"You're among a very small minority, I'm afraid. That one attracted about as much attention as a snowflake in the middle of the Atlantic."

"That doesn't mean it isn't good."

"Miss McKinley, you're very kind. Have you made up my bill yet?"

"Right here. I'll get your supplies." She placed a small sheet of paper on the counter, and left through another door in the back wall. Andrew levered himself up and walked over to look at the bad news. Grimacing at the total, he withdrew his credit card and placed it on top. *Sweet little racket they've got going here. Con me into letting them pick my own pocket.*

Emily McKinley returned presently with a litter pan, a bag of litter, several cans of moist food and a small bag of dry pellets. "She probably won't be able to manage the hard stuff yet, not for a few days. And she may not even want to eat the wet food, but we won't want to force feed her unless we have to. To start with, try putting some on your fingers and see if she'll lick it off. And this eyedropper is for water. She may not be able to drink on her own at first."

Andrew scanned the items she placed on the counter. "This is all probably a waste of time, isn't it?"

She regarded him carefully. "Maybe," she said candidly. "So why are you doing it, then?"

Damned if I know. He slid the bill across to her. "Here's my credit card. You do take them, don't you?"

"Of course. And you didn't answer my question. Why are you doing this?"

"So you won't get mad at me any more, I guess."

"Oh, sure." She smiled.

"Okay, let's just say the cat and I have something in common, and let it go at that." This time she frowned at him. He knew she didn't understand, and was glad that she decided to let it drop.

The door opened again, and Brian McKinley came out carrying Andrew's towel, the cat carefully wrapped inside with just its head visible. It's eyes were fully open, and seemed to Andrew to have regained some bit of lustre. "Are you sure you don't want to leave her here with us?" the vet asked.

The cat opened her mouth and uttered her distinctive croak, and Andrew laughed in spite of his depression. "I think that was a 'no'." He turned back to the counter and signed the charge slip that Emily handed him, then took the cat from the vet's arms.

"Eleven tomorrow," McKinley said. "Or if there's any change, call me. Our number is answered around the clock."

"What kind of change?"

"If she seems to be in pain, or if she isn't responsive."

"And if she simply dies?"

"Think positive, Dr. Striker. And give her a little credit for courage. She managed to find you, didn't she?"

"Sentimental bullshit," Andrew muttered. He turned toward the door, and Emily stepped out from behind the counter to help him with the food and litter. They went outside, and he opened the car door and placed the cat on the seat. She managed to lift her head up and to look around inquisitively.

"It's not, you know," Emily said as he turned to take the parcels from her.

"What?"

"It's not sentimental bullshit. Life is precious. At least I think so, and apparently you do, too, or you wouldn't be doing this."

"Miss McKinley, you're very young, and you have a lot to learn yet."

"Maybe so." She grinned back at him. "But you're the one who just paid me almost half a thousand bucks because of an old cat."

"And that simply speaks to my own stupidity," he said, getting into the driver's seat.

"I don't think so," she said softly. He grimaced and closed the door a little too hard. He started the engine, and as he backed out onto the road, he looked in the mirror. She was watching him, and she waved as he drove off.

Andrew drove slowly, keeping close to the shoulder of the road to allow others to pass. He arrived at the cottage and took the cat inside, and laid her gently on the floor of the living room. Then he went to the closet and retrieved an old woollen blanket. He folded it twice in half and then lengthwise, making a soft foundation, and placed it on the floor beside the cat. Then he transferred her, still inside the towel, onto the centre of the blanket. He slid it across the rough boards until it lay next to his old overstuffed chair.

When he unfolded the towel, he hardly recognized the animal. Her coat had been combed free of tangles and appeared almost sleek, and the fur around the lesions had been carefully clipped, leaving large patches of bare skin. She lay limply on her side, her rapid breathing almost impossibly shallow, but her eyes were open.

"You'll win no beauty contests today," he said aloud. Favouring his arthritic knee, he rose from beside her and went into the kitchen. He unfolded Emily McKinley's list of instructions and sat down to read them. After going through them three times, he thought he had the basic procedures committed to memory, but he left the list on the table for future reference, held down by the saltshaker.

He went outside to the car and took the sack of litter, the pan, and the bag of supplies from where he had placed them on the back seat. Once back in the kitchen, he opened the bag and took out the cans of cat food, the dry pellets and the eyedropper. He opened the litter and poured an inch-thick layer into the pan, then carried it back into the living room.

The cat had not moved. Her eyes remained open but unfocused, although her breathing had steadied into a slower and deeper rhythm. Andrew stroked her back, but she didn't move.

Sighing, he returned to the kitchen and got his old hand-operated can opener out of the drawer beside the sink. He fitted it onto the rim of a can and cranked it until the lid came free. Then he carried the can into the living room and sat down in his chair next to the cat.

He scooped out a small portion of the fishy-smelling mixture and leaned over the arm of the chair, bringing it close to the cat's nose. At first she didn't respond, but then he saw her whiskers twitch. Her eyes came into focus, and she lifted her head slightly, then stretched forward to sniff his finger. Tentatively she licked the food into her mouth.

"No accounting for taste," Andrew muttered, but he smiled. He scooped out a bit more food and offered it to the cat, and she licked his finger clean again. Twice more he repeated the gesture, but the cat seemed to tire, and left half of the last offering untouched.

"That's okay. Get that inside you, and maybe you'll feel like more a little later." He wiped his finger on the edge of the can. *Jesus Christ, now I'm talking to her!* He took the can back to the kitchen and put it inside the refrigerator. Then he filled a small bowl with water and took it back to her.

He placed the bowl in front of her, but she didn't seem to notice. He filled the eyedropper and inserted it between her teeth. When he squeezed the bulb, most of the liquid dribbled out on the towel, but the cat roused and licked her mouth. She drew her front paws back under her and stretched to sniff the bowl. Tentatively she tried to lap the water with her tongue, but couldn't hold her head steady and gave up the effort.

Andrew refilled the eyedropper and offered it to her again. This time most of the water trickled down her throat, but when he tried again, she turned her head away. *Well, what else can we do here?* He tried to recall the list of instructions, but they blurred and ran together in his memory. Dejectedly, he rose from the chair and went back to the kitchen to reread them, but found nothing else that he should be doing for her.

When he went back into the living room, the cat was asleep. He sat down again and picked up the novel he had been reading. After a few pages, he was surprised and pleased to discover he still remembered most of the characters, and the main elements of the plot so far. He read several chapters while the cat slept on, stopping only when he felt his attention wandering.

About mid afternoon he went to his CD player and selected an early Mozart symphony. As the gentle strings and pairs of soft woodwinds filled the room with their mathematical precision and order, he sank back in the chair and closed his eyes. Soon he too was asleep.

A soft scratching sound invaded his dreams. He roused himself to find the music no longer playing and looked around, searching for the source of the sound. The cat had managed to get to her feet, and was standing with her front paws inside the litter box. She was trying without success to lift her back feet over the rim of the pan.

Andrew stood up and bent to help her. He gently lifted her hindquarters and eased her forward until she was completely inside the pan, then watched as she squatted unsteadily and voided her bladder. She turned stiffly and pawed ineffectually at the litter, trying to cover what she had done. Andrew lifted her again and returned her to her bed.

The rest of the afternoon passed quietly. Andrew offered the cat more food, and was pleased that she showed some interest in it. He had no idea how much she should be eating, but she seemed to know her own limits. As the light outside started to fail he ate his solitary supper at the kitchen table, then returned to the living room, once more picking up his book.

When he estimated the time to be about ten thirty, he again offered the cat more water and something to eat. As nearly as he could tell, she felt no discomfort, and after eating a little she went back to sleep. This time she curled up into what in his limited experience he thought to be a more cat-like position. He picked up his book, but it no longer captured his attention, and he left the room and went to bed.

Sometime later he came awake abruptly in the darkened room, unable to discern what had disturbed him. The small digital clock read one fourteen, and he lay there straining to hear any unusual sounds that might have penetrated his sleep. The now familiar croaking cry floated into the room.

He got up and pulled on his robe, then walked out into the hall and switched on the overhead light. The cat had made it halfway out of the living room. She was perched precariously on all four legs and cautiously placing one in front of the other, one at a time. Seeing him in the sudden brightness, she let out another, more piercing cry.

"Where do you think you're going?" Andrew said aloud to her. He picked her up carefully and returned her to the living room, feeling her begin to purr. "Well, that's a good sign, I think." *Shit, I'm talking to her again.*

He placed her on her bed and went to the kitchen to get the can of cat food from the refrigerator, but this time she refused to eat any. He offered her more water and she took a few swallows from the eyedropper, but made no effort to drink from the bowl. She lowered her head and tucked her paws beneath her.

Andrew sat in the chair for a few minutes. He reached over and began stroking her back, and she made feeble stretching motions and rolled over partially onto her side. She stretched her chin out onto her front paws and closed her eyes.

After a few minutes, he got up and retraced his steps toward the bedroom, but before he was halfway down the hall he heard the cat's choked cry again. Returning to the living room, he found her struggling to follow him, so he sat down in the chair again and petted her behind the ears. This time she refused to settle down. She managed to get all four feet under her, and butted her head against his bare leg.

"Now what do you want?" he said. The cat raised her head and looked directly into his face. Her mouth opened and a more gentle mew came out, almost free of the coarse croaking quality that had been her only communication up to that time.

Sighing, he reached down beside the chair and plucked the towel from the blanket. He arranged it over his robe, then bent forward and lifted the cat onto his lap. Her front paws made weak kneading motions on the towel, and he again began the gentle stroking motions that had seemed to soothe her before. Once she was satisfied with the shape of her nest, she curled up and began to purr.

Great! Now I'm a cat's mattress.

Carefully avoiding the lesions in the shaved areas, he petted her lightly. The feel of her fur was somehow comforting to him, and his head lolled against the back of the chair. He drifted off to sleep.

Early sunlight roused him, and as he came awake, Andrew felt a painful stiffness in his neck. He craned it left and right, then up and down, working out the tension. Briefly he wondered why he had fallen asleep in the chair, and then memory flooded back.

He looked down at his lap and discovered the cat, still in the same curled-up position. He reached out and scratched her behind the ears, and her head rolled loosely to one side. Alarmed, he placed his fingers under her chin and lifted gently, but encountered no resistance. He touched her limp front paws, then stroked her back, and realized she felt cold to his touch. He slid his hand under her small body and felt for her heart, but wasn't even sure where to find it. The cat lay still, lifeless.

God DAMN it!

Sudden tears flowed from his eyes. He stroked her soft fur mindlessly. Her eyes were closed, and she seemed not to have moved from when he had picked her up in the night. Sometime before morning, she had just slipped quietly away.

He didn't know how long he sat there. The morning light strengthened, and eventually he roused himself and folded the towel carefully around the animal's body, covering her head. He lifted her off his lap and placed her on the blanket.

He padded to the bathroom and splashed cold water on his face and into his reddened eyes. He entered the bedroom and dressed with a slow, methodical lethargy, then went back to the kitchen and sat down at the table. The coffee maker sat unnoticed on the counter.

Anguished sobs wracked his frame. He didn't know for what he cried: the cat; himself; the career that now floated in his memory with its great missing pages, like rents in the sails of a foundering ship… His wife…

Finally drained and stilled, he turned his attention to what to do next. Wearily he left the cottage and retrieved his shovel from the shed out back, then moved to the front yard and started to dig a hole next to the forsythia bush. Just below the surface he encountered twisted roots, small ones from the bush and larger ones that radiated from a nearby pine tree. Unable to sever them with the blade of the shovel, he went back for his axe. Once he had cleared a rectangle in the woody mass, he continued removing soil until the hole was sufficiently wide and deep.

He returned to the cottage and found a second terry cloth towel in the closet. He wrapped it around the first one, sadly feeling the limp and lifeless body within. He could not bring himself to unwrap it to look at her again. He carried the cat out into the yard and placed her in the hole, arranging her carefully on her side, just as she had fallen asleep on his lap. Then he filled in the hole and raked needles from the pine tree across the surface.

He stood there for many minutes gazing down at the ground, waiting for the tears to start again. When they didn't, he returned the tools to the storage shed and went back inside. He sat in silence at the kitchen table, looking out through the window but seeing little as a shrouded sun climbed into a grey and sombre sky.

The morning passed and Andrew barely moved, lost in curiously undefined corridors of his consciousness. Images of people, events, possessions, all lay around the twisted corners, always out of reach, familiar but at the same time strange to him. And the cat; always the cat. Each vision evoked a terrible and numbing sadness within him.

The telephone brought him back. For several long rings he simply stared at it, then, from force of habit, he lifted the receiver.

"Yes?"

"Dr. Striker? This is the Riverview Animal Clinic." When he didn't reply, Emily McKinley continued, "Did you forget your appointment this morning?"

Several seconds passed before he could respond. He cleared his throat, not trusting his voice, and took a deep breath. "The cat died."

Emily was briefly silent. Then, "I'm so sorry."

"I should have left her with you," Andrew said.

"I'm sure it wouldn't have mattered."

Andrew was suddenly overcome with the need to talk, to explain what had happened. "She seemed so good, she ate some food, and she used her litter, and during the night she wanted to be close to me." Emily kept silent. "She died right on my lap, right…" He couldn't go on.

Emily waited a respectful interval, then spoke to him in a

quiet, professional voice. "If she had been here, she would have died alone, in a cage. You did exactly the right thing."

"I let her die."

"No. You helped her to die. That's not the same thing. You helped her."

"It doesn't feel that way."

"I know. But after a while, I think you'll see it more clearly."

He sighed and gathered his thoughts, embarrassed at how much of himself he had revealed to this young stranger. "It was just a cat. Anyway, thank you for calling."

He had begun to replace the receiver when her voice came back over the line. "Dr. Striker... Could you do me a favour?"

"I suppose."

"We have another old cat here. One of the summer people got her from us, and then just abandoned her when they went back to Ontario. Some neighbours dropped her off here. We haven't been able to find anyone to take care of her."

"I'm sorry, but I'm not interested."

"She's a beautiful animal, and in perfect health. We think she's about fifteen, and very calm and affectionate. She's had her shots, too. She's long haired, so you'd have to comb her, but..."

"I don't get it. I thought you people destroyed unwanted animals. How come you kept her?"

"I can see you don't know my grandfather very well," she said.

"Miss McKinley, I can't take care of a cat. I tried once, and it didn't work out."

"I think it worked out fine."

"Sure."

"Dr. Striker, this is none of my business, but after reading your books, and especially after meeting you yesterday, I feel I know you, even if only a little bit."

"So?"

"So I think you need something to take care of. Maybe something that will take care of you a little bit, too."

"More sentimental bullshit," he muttered.

"Will you at least think about it?"

"Will you leave me alone if I do?"

Emily McKinley laughed gently. "I can't promise."

Andrew found himself strangely cheered. "All right. I'll *think* about it."

"That's all I ask."

"Good-bye, Miss McKinley." He hung up the phone without waiting for her reply.

He considered making some lunch, but nothing appealed to him. He left the cottage and walked around the perimeter of the property, finally coming to stand beside the small grave. He stood there for several minutes, then went back inside to get his wallet and keys. He got in the car and backed out onto the road, then headed in the direction of Crescent Beach.

The sands were nearly deserted. In the far distance, almost at the mouth of the narrow road that led to the LaHave islands, he saw two solitary joggers, bundled in sweats against the chill of the breeze coming across Green Bay. Otherwise, there were only herring gulls. He picked his way along the shoreline, absently poking at the mounds of seaweed that the tide had left behind. He flipped one over, and a tiny crab scuttled away, leaving a strange geometric pattern in the wet sand.

Life everywhere, he thought. *And I couldn't even save one poor old cat.*

He kicked at the weed, then thrust his hands deep into his pockets and continued along the water's edge. An officious gull, raising its head from the innards of a broken clamshell, challenged him with aggressive bravado. He skirted around the bird, not wanting to drive it from its meal.

A hundred yards farther on he discovered a starfish buried among strands of kelp. The creature lay on its back, the intricate pattern of tiny nodules on the underside of its arms fully exposed to the pale sunlight. He had seen many such creatures, dried and stiff, for sale in souvenir shops. This one, by contrast, was still soft and pliable. Scooping up the seaweed beneath it, he raised the starfish to examine it, and was surprised to see tiny movements in the countless little foot-like protuberances on its arms.

He stared at it for several minutes, then looked out over the bay. He wondered whether such a creature could be sentient, then remembered that starfish were predators, and that some species could even pry open shellfish for their meals. *Instinct? Intelligence?* Not for the first time, he marvelled at the incredible variety and persistence of life, and at the unfathomable complexity of its interdependence.

Dependence...

Unmindful of the frigid water seeping into his shoes and soaking his socks, he walked out several yards and lowered the kelp and starfish into the surf. He had no idea whether the creature could still survive, but it seemed the right thing to do. Then he backed out of the water and walked on.

Andrew reached the far end of Crescent Beach. The joggers had disappeared, either into the woods of the islands or back along the road that paralleled the sand behind the log pilings. Once more he stared out across the bay, its waters impersonal in their wind-blown crests and foam, yet home to countless creatures for which living was not just an accident but a treasure to be preserved; a gift to be given in some measure to all the other living things with which they shared existence.

He sighed deeply and strode off down the sand, back toward where he had parked his car. He took out his keys and started the engine. Then he drove up onto the road and turned in the direction of the Riverside Animal Clinic.

FIVE...

"So how did she get her name?" Jennie asks as she fondles the animal's fur. Old Cat is lapping up the attention.

"Well, it's what she is," Andrew answers.

"Not when she was little. You didn't call her 'Old Cat' when she was a kitten, did you?"

"I didn't have her then. I only got her last fall."

"Where?"

"From the vet. Actually, the vet practically forced her on me."

Jennie looks at him questioningly, waiting to hear the rest. He sighs. "It's kind of a sad story."

"So tell me."

"I found a sick cat in my yard one morning, and I took her to the vet. He tried to save her, and I took her home with me, but she was too sick, and she died that night." *Why am I telling her this?* "Anyway, the vet had this other one that needed a home, and conned me into taking her."

"I don't get it. Why didn't you get a kitten instead?" she asks. "They're more fun."

I don't get it either. Why did I end up with a cat at all? He shrugs off her question. She turns her attention back to Old Cat, who is almost beside herself with pleasure, turning her head this way and that to expose every inch of her chin to the child's caressing fingers.

"What did you do with the first one?" she asks finally.

Andrew's thoughts have wandered. "What?"

"Did you bury her or something?"

"Oh. Yes, out there." He waves his hand in the direction of the forsythia bush, now lushly green in the fullness of August.

"That's a pretty spot."

"Yes…" *For all that it matters…*

Jennie's hand has stopped petting, and Old Cat mews her displeasure, butting her head against the child's forearm. They both laugh, and she scratches the animal behind the ears. "You like cats. Why don't you like people? You said you'd tell me."

"*I* didn't say I don't like people. *You* did."

"So how come you won't stay at the beach when people are there, and how come you live out here all alone?"

He gazes out across the yard, and his eyes linger on the cat's grave. "Shall we take a look at the starfish book now?"

She turns a solemn face up to him, and he smiles gently. "I'll go get it." He rises stiffly to his feet, cradling Old Cat in the crook of his elbow, and Jennie jumps up beside him, then follows him toward the door.

"Can I come in?"

"No."

"Why not?"

He turns and considers her, his hand on the screen door latch. He remembers the vet's frank candour, and quotes him. "You want it straight out, or the song and dance?"

She cocks her head, puzzled.

"Look, Jennie, you're an eleven-year-old girl and I'm an old coot that nobody down here knows. You're out here where you shouldn't be, and your mom doesn't even know it. You've been going off half-cocked, down to the beach and riding your bike to hell and gone without permission. Sooner or later something's going to happen to you, and when it does, I don't want anyone saying they saw you going into my place."

Jennie takes a half step back, her eyes huge and the corners of her mouth trembling. Her eyes fill.

"Jesus Christ! Now I'm scaring you again. But it's for your own good, damn it. You have to start playing by the rules."

"You wouldn't hurt me. I know it."

"No, I wouldn't, but nobody else knows that. And someone else might. You don't have any idea what kinds of things can happen to you. Hasn't your mother warned you?"

" 'Jennie, don't talk to strangers. Jennie, don't go out after dark. Jennie, don't go to the…' "

"Stop it! She's right! You have to start acting more responsibly. It isn't just your safety that's important. How will she feel if she loses you? And how about your little sister? She needs you. Do you want to hurt them, too?"

The child stares at him gravely. "How about you?"

He draws a deep breath. "What do you mean?"

"I bet your wife misses *you*, too."

Shit!

He gives up trying to reason with her. He sighs deeply, and his shoulders slump in resignation. "Stay here. I'll get the book." He opens the door and sets Old Cat down gently on the floor. The animal looks up at him expectantly, perhaps hoping for more petting, but he is already crossing the room toward the bookcase. She wanders out of the room and down the hall to the bedroom.

Andrew finds the marine life book and takes it out onto the porch. They sit on the top step and leaf through it, easily finding the common North Atlantic species of starfish, as well as pictures of the more exotic ones from southern climates. Their mood lightens as they explore farther afield, looking up the periwinkles and limpet shells that she collected in her bucket the previous day.

Jennie comes upon a picture of a large moon snail. "We found some of these, right? But ours are little. This one looks pretty big."

"The little ones get washed up on the beach more easily," Andrew says, "but once in a while a bigger one comes ashore." A vague memory teases the back of his mind. "Hang on a minute."

He gets painfully to his feet and re-enters the cottage. He

remembers seeing a pile of shells in one of the drawers in the kitchen, left behind by the children of the owners. He opens it and searches among them, then selects two and takes them back outside again.

He sits down beside Jennie, favouring his aching knee. "How about this one?" he says to her, giving her a substantial, inch-and-a-half moon snail shell, streaked in vivid grey.

"Neat! Where'd you get it?"

"It was here when I moved in. And take a look at this one." He hands her a pale cream bivalve shell, and points to a small round hole near the hinge. "Know what the hole is for?"

"So the clam can breathe?" she asks.

"Nope. So the snail can have dinner. Moon snails can drill a hole in a shell, and then they suck out the animal."

"No way! That's gross!"

He smiles at her gently. "It's how the world works. Things eat each other, and some things have to die so others can live."

She regards the shells solemnly. "I'm not going to die."

"Well, not for a long time, anyway. Would you like to keep them?"

"Sure. Thanks."

"Not so fast. There's a catch."

There's a smile in his voice, and Jennie stares into his eyes expectantly, wearing a pixie grin.

"You have to stop riding your bike on the highway and going off places without your mom's permission."

Her face turns cold, and she looks down at her hands. Then she gives the shells back to Andrew.

So much for that strategy, he thinks. "Not such a good deal?" he asks. She slips off the porch and stands quietly scuffing her toe in the sand. "You don't much care for being told what to do, do you?"

"Nope."

"Most people don't. Myself included. But your mom wouldn't give you all those rules if she didn't really care about you." He waits, but Jennie stays silent. "Me, too," he says.

She looks up. "What do you mean?"

"I wouldn't bother to worry about you riding your bike if I

didn't care about you, too."

Jennie bites her bottom lip and twists her small shoulders back and forth. She takes a deep breath. "I like the shells."

He holds them out to her.

"Are they mine, even if I keep riding on the highway?"

"Uh, huh."

She considers him carefully. "Then I won't do it any more," she says, and reaches out for the shells. She climbs back up beside him on the porch and drags the book back onto her lap. She leafs through the pages and begins to ask questions, and they relax once again into easy familiarity.

After nearly half an hour, Andrew calls a halt. "Time for you to go home," he says.

"You got anything to eat first? I'm starved!"

"And you are also a world class procrastinator."

"What's that?"

"It mean you like to stall."

She laughs delightedly. "I really am hungry, though."

"Then you're out of luck. I'm fresh out. Unless you'd like to sample a can of Old Cat's seafood supper, that is."

"Yuck!" She grins at him expectantly.

"All right. Talk about con artists. We'll go down to the canteen. But after that, straight home!"

Her face drops. "I haven't got any money."

"Never mind. At the rate I'm going, I've got more than I'll ever have a chance to spend." She brightens, not understanding the context of what he has said. He carries the book inside, finds his keys and wallet, and comes out onto the porch again.

Jennie steps forward and takes his hand, then tugs him toward the edge of the porch and down the steps. He tries to shake her off, but she hangs on to him all the way to the end of the driveway and down the road until they reach the restaurant. He opens the door, and she goes in ahead of him.

Andrew and Jennie sit across from one another at a table by the inside wall of the room, nearest to the cash register. Nadia Marshall is serving lunch to a couple in the corner booth. She finishes serving and picks up two menus from the rack on the wall. She walks over to the table and passes them out.

"Hi, Doc. This your granddaughter?"

"This rotten kid? Not likely. She's just some stray that wandered into my yard."

Jennie tilts her chin haughtily and gazes across the room toward the window, pretending to be insulted, but she can't completely hide her grin. Nadia looks from one to the other, smiling but looking puzzled.

"She's my beach buddy," Andrew says. "We've been protecting the starfish population together."

"Sounds like fun. Need some time to read the menu?"

"Not me," says Jennie, turning back from the window. "Cheeseburger and fries, please."

"Drink?"

"Coke."

"How about you, Doc?" Nadia asks.

"Just coffee." Nadia cocks her head and twists her mouth in disapproval. Jennie is listening alertly. "Oh, all right. Bring me some soup."

"That's better. It's vegetable today." She turns and heads for the kitchen.

"What was that all about?" Jennie asks.

"Nadia, that's her name, she thinks I don't eat enough."

"You are pretty skinny."

"Well, thank you!" he bristles. "I'll pay you a nice compliment someday, too."

" 'Just some stray that wandered into my yard,' you said."

He laughs. "Okay, so we're even."

"Why does she call you Doc?"

"I guess she thinks I'm one of the Seven Dwarfs."

"Come on! That's not the reason."

Andrew gives in. "I used to teach in a university. One of my degrees is a Doctor of Philosophy. She's just making fun of me."

"That's not what it sounds like," Jennie says seriously. "What's a Doctor of Philosophy do?"

"This one doesn't do much any more."

Nadia brings their order before Jennie can pursue the matter further. She attacks her burger ferociously and he samples his soup, finding it thick and rich.

Nadia stands beside the table, watching him with approval. "Pretty good, isn't it?"

"Terrible, as usual."

Nadia laughs. "You have to eat it anyway, or I'll get mad. How's Old Cat doing?"

Jennie looks up from her plate. "That's a really dumb name for a cat."

Nadia smiles at the child. "What would you call her?"

"I don't know." Jennie takes another bite, her brow creased in a frown. Then she brightens. "She's got really long fur. How about 'Hairy Potter'?"

"Literary humour from an eleven-year-old! Spare me!" he says, a broad grin on his face. Nadia laughs aloud.

Jennie's face shows delight in the adults' attention. "I told Andrew he should have gotten a kitten instead."

He puts his spoon down, surprised to see half of the soup is gone. "I'll have you know Old Cat is very special. She has medical training, in fact. Before I got her, she was the vet's assistant."

"Come on!" Jennie says.

"Absolute truth. The vet told me so. Just a week before I got her, he said that a man came into his office with a shoebox under his arm. He put it down on the counter and opened the lid, and there was a budgie lying in the bottom, all stiff and cold.

" 'Doc, you've gotta help me,' the man said. 'My bird's sick.' And the vet looked into the box and said to the man, 'Sir, your bird is dead.'

" 'No, no, doc,' the man said, 'you can save him. I know you can. Just give him some medicine or something.' " Andrew pauses to eat more soup.

Jennie and Nadia both stare at him eagerly. "So what happened?" the child asks.

He lowers the spoon again. "Well, this vet is a kind man, and he said, 'There's one more thing we can try. But first we have to be sure your bird is still alive.' Then he reached down to the floor and picked up Old Cat and put her on the counter next to the shoebox."

He returns his attention to the soup bowl, and Nadia smiles as the child bounces impatiently in her seat. "Come on, Andrew! What happened next?"

"Just what you'd expect. Old Cat stuck her nose in the box and took a sniff, then backed off, twitching her whiskers. Then she jumped off the table. 'Well, that settles it,' the vet said. 'Your bird is definitely dead.' The poor man was very sad, and he put the top back on the shoebox.

" 'Well, thanks for trying,' he said to the vet. 'How much do I owe you?'

" ' That'll be four hundred and twenty-five dollars,' the vet said.

" ' Four twenty-five?' the man shouted. 'How come so much?'

Andrew pauses, a slight grin touching his lips, delaying the punch line as he once had done so many times in his university classes.

" 'That's twenty-five dollars for the office visit,' the vet told him, 'and four hundred for the CAT scan.' "

Nadia dissolves into helpless laughter, but Jennie stares at him in confusion. "What's a cat scan?"

Andrew can't contain his own laughter. Jennie picks up her burger and tears off a bite, chewing angrily. "It's not fair! You tell a joke, and then you don't explain it."

"I'm sorry," he says, recovering. "It's a big, expensive medical machine. It's like a big x-ray, and it's called Computerized Axial Tomography. The first letters in the name spell 'cat', and so they call it a CAT scan. Get it?"

Jennie thinks it over. "That's not so funny."

"Guess you had to be there." He recites the old cliché, making Nadia laugh even harder. He suddenly realizes that his mind is clear, his memories intact. He has not only remembered the old joke, but even the name of the technology it was based on. Then he realizes he has eaten more in the last twenty-four hours than he has any other day for weeks. *Maybe eating something helps*, he thinks. *Having someone to eat with makes a difference too, even if it's just a kid.*

Nadia heads off to the kitchen, and Andrew and Jennie finish their meals quickly, and then their drinks.

"Dessert?" he asks the child.

"Can I have a cone?"

"Sure. We'll take them with us. What kind?"

"Chocolate!" They get up from the table and he leaves a generous tip. They walk over to the cash register, and Nadia comes out of the kitchen.

"Two chocolate cones," he says. Then to Jennie: "Two scoops?"

"No thanks. I'm almost full already."

Nadia pulls two cones out of the dispenser and opens the lid of the freezer. "You didn't overtip me again, did you?" she says.

"I left you *nothing!* You're a terrible waitress, and a bully, too."

She raises her eyebrows. "Somebody has to look out for you." She hands them the cones and gives Jennie a warm smile. "Come again." He pays the check, and he and Jennie walk out into the sunshine. She grabs his free hand, startling him, and he tries to pull away. She clings determinedly, and they walk back toward his cottage eating their cones.

"You've been getting on my case about lying," she says grumpily, "and then you did it."

"When did I lie?"

"Just now. The waitress asked about a tip, and you told her you didn't leave her anything."

"That wasn't a lie, exactly," he answers. "She knew I was kidding her, so it's not the same thing."

"How did she know?"

"Because I always give her a tip, and I always tell her I'll never do it again. It's kind of like a game."

"I don't get it."

He sighs. "Nadia is saving her money to go to university next year, so I gave her something extra last time to help her along, that's all. I think she worries about me a little, and so she pretends to give me a hard time about not eating enough. And I act insulted, just for fun. She's a good person."

"I think she likes you, too."

He thinks this over. "Maybe…" *Not much reason to.*

When his ice cream is gone, he opens the trunk of his car and puts her small bike inside. "Don't forget your shells," he reminds her as he climbs into the driver's seat and starts the engine.

Jennie runs over to the porch to retrieve her treasures, then scrambles into the passenger seat. Soon they are on Route 331, driving out of Petite Riviere.

Jennie sits contentedly watching Andrew manipulate the gearshift. Idly she plays with the radio dial, changing his preset classical station to a light rock selection. She examines her shells, carefully turning them this way and that.

"I just thought of something," she says finally.

"What's that?"

"You wouldn't let me go in your house in case anybody might see me, but now I'm in your car. Isn't that worse?"

"Yes, it is. So now the responsibility is yours."

"Huh?"

"From now on you have to keep yourself safe. No more going to the beach alone unless your mom says it's okay. No more bike riding on the highway. If nothing happens to you, I can't get in trouble because of it."

"Shi… Shoot!"

"That was close."

They pass Risser's Beach Provincial Park, and the turnoff for Crescent Beach comes up on the right. He twists the wheel and enters the road that skirts the perimeter of the beach and connects to the islands.

"Which house is yours?" he asks as they approach the first bend.

"Keep going." They come upon a narrow iron bridge, similar to the one in Petite Riviere, and as they cross it she says, "This is Bush Island. Slow down a little."

He eases off on the gas, and presently they approach a small shingled bungalow on the left. "Right here," she says.

The yard is neatly kept, although the grass is dry and beginning to turn brown. The stained shingled walls of the house are faded and weathered, but the trim shows evidence of a recent paint job. *Not much money in this family*, he thinks.

A weathered swing set is sheltered from the daytime sun between the western wall and a misshapen blue spruce. A double-wide dirt parking area flanks the house on the opposite side. Andrew pulls off the road into it and stops. He raises the release lever to open the trunk lid, and they get out. He lifts the bike out and she takes hold of the handlebars. She begins to wheel it toward the house.

"Thanks. See you tomorrow."

"Not so fast," he calls after her. "What time does your mom get home?"

She looks back over her shoulder. "Not for hours and hours."

"Sure. Didn't you tell me she gets back sometime before four? If I stick around I can meet her, and you can come clean about all of your crimes and adventures."

She drops the bike and hurries back to him, a worried frown on her face. "Please just go. I'll tell her myself."

"Jennie, you can't keep doing this."

"I'll tell her. Really I will. Just not right now."

"When, then?"

"Tonight. After we eat. When she comes home from work, she's all tired out, and she'll get really mad if I tell her then. Later on is better." He grimaces and shakes his head slowly, and she reaches for his hand and looks pleadingly into his eyes. "Please? I promise!"

"I'm not sure your promises are worth anything."

"I'll tell her tonight for sure, and then you can come meet her tomorrow."

"And if she says you can't go to the beach alone any more?" She looks down at the ground and scuffs the dirt, and he waits until she raises her eyes again. "Well?"

"Then I guess I have to stay home." She brightens. "But then you can come tomorrow after she gets home. Once she meets you, she'll let me go if you're going to be there."

"Don't count on it. Why don't I just stay here right now, and we'll get it settled once and for all."

"She's gonna kill me for riding my bike to Green Bay."

"All right, we'll leave that part out. But you have to tell her about sneaking out to the beach."

"Not yet. Let me do it my way."

He regards her pinched and worried face for several long minutes. Then he sighs. "This is against my better judgment." He opens the car door and slides behind the wheel. "Tonight for sure, and no excuses."

She moves up beside the window. "Are you coming to the beach tomorrow morning?"

"Even if I do, you won't be allowed to, after your mother hears what you've been doing. I'm sure of it. I'll come back in the afternoon, sometime after four, and I'll introduce myself the right way. Then we'll see what happens." She steps back. He tries to read her, but her face is blank. "Goodbye, Jennie Horton."

She waves shyly as he backs out of the driveway. "Andrew?" she calls out.

"What?"

"Thanks for the lunch."

"You're welcome. Now keep your promise." She nods but doesn't answer aloud. He puts the car in gear and drives off down the road.

* * *

Matt Burgess picks up the phone on the first ring. "Corporal Burgess, RCMP, New Minas Detachment."

"Hey, Matt, it's Jeff Comeau."

"Jeffrey, my boy, how are things on the beautiful South Shore?"

"Quiet," Comeau answers. "Haven't even had a hash boat try to land here lately."

"Tough luck. We busted another pot farm out near Canning this week. They're going high tech on us, had a hydroponic setup in an old barn behind Hillaton. If they'd had a chance to harvest it, they'd have made a couple of million for sure. What's on your mind, anyway?"

"A little followup, if you would," Comeau says. "I ran across an old guy yesterday, stopped beside the road and pretty confused. Trying to find his way home, and going the wrong way."

"Somebody from here?" Burgess asks.

"At one time, I guess. His license reads Wolfville, but he's staying in a cottage down by the shore in Green Bay. It's probably legit, but something about him bothered me, so I checked up and called his old residence."

"And?"

"I got an answering machine, woman's voice. Didn't identify herself, just the standard message, 'Leave your number and I'll call you back', so I did. But I haven't heard from her yet. The phone is still listed in the guy's name: Andrew Striker."

"So you want us to look into it?"

"Yeah, I do. It's probably nothing, but the guy didn't look right to me, as if he might be sick or something. I just want to be sure his family knows where he is."

"If they even care," Burgess says disgustedly. "I've seen too many cases like that."

"Yeah, that could be it. Anyway, see if you can track the woman down, will you? And call me back, whatever you find out."

"No problem. Give me the info."

Jeffrey Comeau reads the Wolfville address and phone number from his notebook.

"Hang on a minute," Burgess says. "Something just occurred to me." He lays down the receiver and turns to his computer screen. After a couple of false starts, he retrieves a file of missing persons and scans down the list. He picks up the phone again.

"Jeff, this guy is on our blotter. He walked out on his wife a year ago and vanished."

"So you've been looking for him?"

"Not exactly. He left a note, something about going away for the sake of his family. I can't remember all the details, but he also said something about not wanting anyone to look for him."

"But you did it anyway, right?"

"No," Burgess continued. "According to the file the wife was pretty upset, but she said we should leave it alone. Told me she was sure he'd come back on his own after a while."

"Strange. Think I should go out and talk to him again?"

"Let me try to get hold of the wife first. He didn't break any laws, right?"

"Right."

"So let's go one step at a time."

Comeau hangs up and spares another half minute in thought about Andrew Striker, then calls the Striker home and leaves another message on the answering machine.

Insights

On Tuesday after his meeting with Bob Melanson, Andrew spent the early part of the afternoon in Vaughan Memorial Library, searching through books on cognitive function, aging and senility. The more recent volumes tended to focus heavily on Alzheimer's disease, and he tried with only partial success to remain objective when reading about its symptoms.

At two-thirty he returned to his office and initiated a series of internet searches. He found pages on senility and generalized dementia as well as Alzheimer's, and was surprised at the varied forms the diseases took. He followed some links and discovered abstracts of recent journal articles. Finally he printed off a dozen web pages and sat back to compare them.

A significant finding captured his attention, one which seemed to bear on his situation. Although the theory was in dispute, several authorities considered it to be significant. According to the research, some of the types of mental declines loosely grouped under the banner of dementia tended to progress much more quickly when the victim was middle aged, as opposed to elderly. Andrew felt this could account for what he felt was his own escalating rate of memory loss.

Notwithstanding a vast array of information, the bottom line was bleak. Despite energetic research, no one was yet sure what caused the cruel and pernicious types of mental deterioration that stole both personality and intellect. In the case of the best known syndrome,

Alzheimer's, there were now some promising treatments that seemed to slow its progress. The end result was inevitable, however: a steady deterioration of mental capacity that left victims without their most precious possessions, their memories.

Andrew knew he had to face the problem head on, and to make some concrete plans for the sake of his family. To do that he needed some concrete information about his pension and investments, and some help in settling his affairs while he was still able to think clearly. At ten to four he reached for the phone.

* * *

Catherine's car was not in the garage when he arrived home. He went inside to find the kitchen empty, the house silent. Next to the refrigerator the light on the telephone answering machine blinked dimly, but he failed to notice it. He located the morning paper and sat down in the living room to do the daily crossword puzzle, never too much of a challenge. He always did it in ink, and it rarely took him more than fifteen minutes.

Nine down, four letters for "statuesque" has to be "tall". Pretty obvious. Eleven down, "Musical John"; too many letters for Elton, must be Lennon. Not too much imagination went into this one. Seventeen across, O, L, and four blanks, "Twelfth Night character" is…

Andrew frowned. He hadn't read an Elizabethan play in years, but they had been at the core of his undergraduate degree. *O, L… Shit, come back to it. Eighteen across, "Cowboys and Indians". What the hell?*

That one had to be a trick. He tried the words around it, and came up with T, blank, blank, M, S. *Teams, of course.* He went back to the missing Shakespeare clue and worked on the intersecting definitions. They yielded two more letters: O, L, blank, V, I, blank.

He sat in frustrated silence, staring across the room. The Bard's characters paraded across the opposite wall, Iago, Hamlet, Ariel, Julius Caesar… The missing name stubbornly resisted him.

Angrily he thrust the paper aside and went into the den. He

scanned the left-hand bookshelf for his volumes of drama, knowing just where he had always stored the vintage Shakespeare editions, but they weren't there. He began a methodical search, up one shelf and down the other, trying to spot the familiar leather-bound spines. Not one of the bookcases yielded results.

Now anxious and becoming upset, he started over, examining the title of each book in turn, one by one. Several seemed completely unfamiliar. He thought he knew every book in his library, had certainly read them all, harbouring nothing but disdain for collectors who never cracked a cover. Now mysterious titles jumped out at him, by authors whom he couldn't place at all.

He reached for a slim volume that seemed familiar and turned to the title page. Neatly inscribed in ink were a date, June 23, 1962, an inscription ("To Andrew Striker, with deepest admiration for a burgeoning talent") and a signature in a dramatically flowing but illegible script. He couldn't read it, and looked for the author's name below the title, but even in printed form it meant nothing to him. A signed first edition, a gift from someone he had obviously known well, and the author's face and identity had vanished from his memory, obliterated like a child's chalk drawing on a rain-soaked sidewalk.

He dropped the book on the floor and hauled out another, and then another. Some were old friends, but an alarming number were either vague and puzzling or completely foreign to him. The pile of volumes grew, haphazardly dumped at random as he searched for reassurance among them. More and more frantically he scrabbled at the shelves, until finally he collapsed among the heaps, his head buried in his hands, his eyes streaming tears of impotent rage.

* * *

Andrew lay slumped against the side of a bookcase, his eyes open but unseeing, his face a vacant mask, his hair dishevelled and the colour of his skin drained to an unhealthy waxen pallor. Nothing penetrated his consciousness until her heard the garage door open and the sound of Catherine's car going inside.

Gradually he became aware of his surroundings. He heard his

wife come through the hallway between the garage and the kitchen. He heard her call his name and tried to answer, but felt too exhausted to mouth the words. A few moments later the telephone answering machine came to life, and he heard Catherine's recorded voice telling him she would be late. Then he heard her footsteps entering the living room. She called out his name again, and again he couldn't answer.

Finally she walked into the den and gasped aloud at the carnage of their library, books scattered everywhere, treasured volumes sprawled in unruly mounds on the chairs and floor. Many lay half open, some with their pages bent back. Most of those still on the shelves lay at chaotic angles. In their midst, Andrew sat unmoving, unseeing.

Through vacant eyes he watched her pick her way cautiously among the disarray. She bent down to encircle him in her arms. At first stiff and unyielding, he suddenly collapsed within himself, and would have fallen over had she not held him close. A gasping sob rose from his throat.

Saying nothing, she coaxed him to his feet and helped him back into the living room. He was painfully aware of his cold, clammy hands, and the pins and needles that impeded his gait. She manoeuvred him onto the sofa and sat down beside him. She moved in close, stroking his hair, sharing her warmth.

Finally he stirred. "I'm sorry…" Still she said nothing, and he struggled to come to terms with what had happened to him. He breathed deeply and felt his muscle tone return. His posture stiffened. He swallowed, coughed, and reached into his back pocket for his handkerchief. He wiped his eyes and turned to look at her.

"Can you tell me what happened?" she ventured.

"Damn crossword puzzle…" Gradually the story came out, the missing name of a Shakespearian character, his search for the play, growing ever more frantic in the face of alien volumes whose titles tantalized him, almost but not quite remembered. Then a sort of madness, as if by clawing the books to him he could recapture their words, their meaning, and his memory of them.

"You moved them," she said softly.

"What?"

"The Shakespeare. Last fall you reorganized the shelves, and you moved all the things you don't use very often into Penny's old room."

"I didn't."

"Yes."

He sat in stupefied silence. *How could I forget something like that? How come I can't remember it now?*

"Come on, let's go look it up," Catherine said, starting to get to her feet.

"Never mind. It's Olivia."

"What?"

"The *Twelfth Night* character. Olivia." She sank down beside him again, and he continued. "All of a sudden I remember, and before, with only two letters missing, I just couldn't see it."

Catherine slipped her hand around his arm and laid her head on his shoulder. "It's not a big deal. This happens to everybody when they get older."

Not like this, he thought, keeping silent. *My lectures, my classes, even my students' and colleagues' names. And now my books. What next? What next?*

SIX...

Andrew rouses himself from a half doze and looks around at the dim outlines of his sparsely furnished room in the gathering dusk. He tries to remember if he has eaten an evening meal, but focusing on recent events proves too taxing. He gets up and wanders over to the door.

The evening is soft and inviting, the humidity low, and only the barest trace of a breeze disturbs the rushes that line the beach. He steps out onto the porch, intending to sit down on the steps for a while. The screen door swings shut behind him. As he stares out toward the water, the memory of the cottage fades, and he walks off, leaving the inside door standing open.

Traces of clouds paint narrow bands across the sky and the face of the rising moon. The sun is gone, but it still illuminates the heavens from behind the low inland hills, casting long, cool shadows. Across the bay, a pencil-thin frosting on the crest of the low hills shimmers with halos of delicate pastels.

He has no difficulty finding the gravel road that leads to Long Point, Green Point, and eventually Broad Cove, and he wanders aimlessly south along the shore. The bay is almost flat calm, and after about twenty minutes, with the light now waning more rapidly, he finds a spot to sit and look out over the rocks that stick up out of the miniature tidal basin within the curve of the cove. Seaweed clings to some of them, thick tendrils waving but slightly in the gentle ripples. A few herring gulls perch on their tops, the day's feeding over. Other than their muttered conversation the silence is profound, broken only by the merest hint of water lapping against the shore.

Andrew is struck by the simple beauty of the spot, the reflection of the cloud-striped moon on the bay, the solitude of the great expanse of water leading to the Atlantic. The birds seem oblivious to the immensity of their world, and he wonders, not for the first time, if any creatures besides humankind ever pause to consider the mysteries of the universe.

He finds a flat spot next to a solitary pine that clings to an outcropping and sinks down, leaning back to rest against the trunk. Gradually he lapses into lethargy, with only a few ill-defined thoughts drifting aimlessly through his mind. Then a puzzle nags at his consciousness. One of the rocks seems to have shifted, and he struggles to focus upon it. Smaller than most of the others, it lies in a shallow pool just a dozen yards from the shore. He feels sure it wasn't there a few minutes before.

Sure? I'm not sure of anything any more.

He levers himself upright and gazes at the rock for several long minutes, but his attention wavers and he slumps back against the tree once more. Images flicker before his eyes, and he seems to float above his own body, looking down upon the water, feeling it rise to meet him, cresting and ebbing impossibly in the nearly windless night.

There! It moved!

He sits up abruptly. The rock is no longer so far off shore but is now almost within reach of the land, and more of it protrudes above the surface of the bay. He regains his feet and, ignoring the pain in his arthritic knees, moves near to the water's edge.

From his closer vantage point the rock becomes a sea turtle, large and obviously very, very old, the short tail labelling her a female. Her beak is craggy, and her shell is scarred and discoloured. Andrew strains to see through the gathering gloom and notices the faint reflection of the moon in one of her dull, glazed eyes. She is making no effort to swim. Even in the buoyant water, her head seems almost too heavy for her to support. Her front legs are thin and wasted.

He remembers the poster on the wharf behind the LaHave bakery, left there by the Department of Fisheries and Oceans. He wonders if he should report this find to someone, but the thought slips away almost before it is fully formed. He squats down for a closer look, and his knee joints protest noisily. He sits.

The turtle stirs, swinging her head slowly to one side, her mouth hanging slackly open. Her back legs move weakly, and she drifts several inches closer to the shore. The effort seems to exhaust her, and her head droops down further into the water.

"Almost done, aren't you?" Andrew mutters aloud. As if in response, the turtle makes a feeble swimming gesture with one front leg, then lies still. He wonders why the beast has come to rest along the shore. Trying to remember what he once knew about marine wildlife, he seems to recall that turtles usually die in deep water. Once again, as is almost always the case this past year, he isn't sure.

He wonders about her age. He knows that turtles are survivors from impossibly ancient times. Like most sea creatures, this one was no doubt born soft and vulnerable, but somehow managed to avoid the multitude of hungry predatory mouths that sought her out in her youth. While her brothers and sisters perished by the score, she escaped them all. She survived, and must have spawned generations of her kind.

Why? he thought. *She's about to die now. What difference does it make? What difference did I make?*

Somewhere in his disturbed mind there arises an image of the turtle in broad daylight, lying nearly dead on the sand, the object of the curious stares and the rough prods of ignorant onlookers. He imagines the remains of this magnificent creature suffering the callousness of an uncaring world, subjected to indignities and maybe even amusement in her final moments of life.

The end, shared by all living things…

Not going to happen.

He gets to his feet once more and seeks out a long driftwood pole that lies beside the path. Gently and with minimal pressure, he places the pole against the turtle's shell and eases it out away from the shore, pushing it southward in the direction of the open Atlantic. Unresisting, the turtle lies barely submerged beneath the surface.

Andrew manoeuvres carefully along the stony shoreline, finally rounding the point of land where the water deepens abruptly in the lee of the tumbled rocks. With a last powerful shove he sends the turtle floating seaward and stands watching as it drifts along with the current, until finally it disappears completely beneath the surface of the bay.

After several minutes, satisfied that the creature will not reappear, he retraces his steps and finds the solitary tree once more. He sinks down beside it. He sees himself as if from a distance, his face a ruined, craggy beak not unlike the turtle's, his withered arms floating, floating…

And then behind his clouded eyes swims Catherine's face, and his son Donald's, young and vital. Last of all comes Penny, Penny at four or five, her brilliant copper hair a glowing halo and her arms waving gaily above her head as she runs to fall into his arms, only to vanish in his cold and empty embrace.

*   *   *

Enjoying her one night off a week, with her mother substituting for her at the restaurant, Nadia Marshall drives into Bridgewater and hangs out with some of her friends at the mall. They eat in the food court and cruise the clothing and music stores, and play with the puppies in the pet store. They check out the boys.

She gives two of her friends a ride home, then drives back to Green Bay and parks in the public lot. Josh Watson is cleaning the grill when she enters the canteen. She can hear her mother out back, humming a Broadway tune in her inexpert but lovely voice.

"Did we make a million tonight?" Nadia asks Josh, leaning over the counter next to the register.

"Ran out of buns," Josh says sourly. "Cones, too."

"Shit. I'm sorry." Ordering is one of Nadia's responsibilities, but she was sure there had been enough supplies on hand. There must have been more customers than expected. "The truck comes tomorrow. I'll get extra this time."

"It wasn't too bad," he concedes. "I used bread for the burgers, made like it was a special. And we didn't run out of cones until almost closing. I gave the last few kids double scoops on plates for the price of one."

"You're a genius!" she says, and reaches over playfully to pull his cap down over his eyes. Josh ducks his head, but not before she sees him blush.

"Doc been in tonight?" she asks him.

"I didn't see him. Ask your mom."

Nadia turns and goes out of the kitchen into the back hall. She spots her mother heading outside, carrying a bag of leftovers to the compost bin. She pushes open the screen door and steps out into the still, warm night, breathing deeply of the salt and pines.

"Hi, Mom!"

"Hi, yourself. Have fun tonight?"

"Bored out of my skull. This isn't exactly Montreal, you know. We have a good run for supper?"

"Full house most of the time from five thirty on. Josh is a little upset with you."

"I know. He takes it personally when I let us run out of stuff. But I buttered him up some."

Fran Marshall upends the plastic bag into the compost bin. "We'd better keep him happy. It's too late in the year to train another grill man if he quits."

"Not gonna happen. He practically drools when I'm around."

"Nadia!"

"Come on, Mom, you know it's true. He goes around with that sick puppy dog look, and if I flirt with any of the guys that come in here, he gets all quiet. I even made him blush just two minutes ago."

"It wouldn't hurt you to treat him a little better."

"I treat him okay. It's just that he wants to date me, and I'm not into that right now."

"Well, I'm not complaining about that. Too many girls your

age are already barefoot and pregnant."

"That's not gonna happen, either. I've got *plans*, you know."

Fran Marshall drops the lid of the compost bin and gives her daughter a hug. The mention of pregnancy reminds Nadia of the chapters she has read in *Amanda's Passage*.

"Was Dr. Striker here for supper tonight?"

"No, I don't think so." Fran opens the screen door and re-enters the canteen. "Did you need to see him for something?"

Nadia follows along. "No, I just wanted to know if he had anything to eat. I'm worried about him."

"Why?"

"You've seen him, he's practically a stick. Last night was the first time I've seen him eat anything much in a month. And he wouldn't have, except I tormented him into it."

"It's not your business, dear," her mother says.

"I know. But nobody's looking after him, and he seems so lonely. Besides, he's really nice, once you get him talking."

"And he's your new project, I suppose."

"Mom!"

"He's not a stray dog you can take in," her mother says. "Maybe he won't want you poking around in his business."

"I'm not poking. But suppose he's sick or something?"

Fran sighs. "And you're in your mother hen mode again. So take a walk down there and see if he's okay."

"Can I?"

"Why not? And if he hasn't had dinner, tell him we can put together something cold for him."

"Thanks, Mom!" Nadia wraps her in a warm embrace, then hurries out the front door. She turns right and heads toward the line of cottages among the trees. Thin clouds mute the moonlight, and she picks her way carefully along the deteriorating surface of the pavement. Andrew Striker's windows are glowing, and she climbs the porch and looks through the screen, finding the inner door ajar.

She knocks on the jamb. Getting no response, she calls out his name. She waits several moments, and when she hears no sound from within, she opens the screen door and steps inside.

She finds the small, empty room barren and depressing. Besides the faded sofa and armchair, the only furniture consists of a floor lamp and a narrow coffee table, plus the bookshelf on the far wall. There isn't room for much more, but the effect is nonetheless desolate and discouraging.

"Dr. Striker?" she calls. She peers around the corner into the small eat-in kitchen, sparsely furnished with typical summer cottage items. The rough boards of the drop-leaf table are heavily scarred, and the two chairs drawn up to it do not match each other. Rough pine cabinets line the wall above the sink, and a tiny refrigerator, decades old, hums asthmatically in the corner. The window is uncurtained.

An old-fashioned black telephone sits on the counter next to the refrigerator. A thin layer of dust covers the handset, lacking even a single fingerprint to indicate it has been used. There is no pencil, no notepad to take down a message or to copy down a number for future reference. Expecting the line to be dead, she picks up the receiver, and is surprised to hear the buzzing of the dial tone.

Nadia replaces the phone and backs out of the kitchen. She finds the hall leading to the single bedroom. She looks into the open, vacant bathroom on the way, then reaches the end of the hall and surprises Old Cat, who has been washing herself on the foot of the bed. The animal spreads her toes and lays her ears back at the sight of the intruder.

"Hey, it's only me. Remember?" Nadia offers her hand slowly and deliberately, and Old Cat stretches cautiously to sniff it. Nadia ruffles the fur beneath her chin. "Where's your playmate?"

The cat collapses sideways on the bed, exposing her belly to be petted, and Nadia laughs and strokes her soft coat. "He must be close, huh, old girl? He wouldn't go out and leave you all alone with the door unlocked." She turns from the bed and retraces her steps to the living room. The silence seems even more intense than before, as if the cottage has been abandoned.

She spots a wallet and keys lying on the end table. Even in the relatively safe rural environment of Green Bay, leaving them in plain sight with the door unlocked would seem unwise, and atypical of a retired college professor. Concern prods her to go outside, and she stands on the porch and stares at the surrounding woods, trying to penetrate the darkness.

The previous evening, she remembers, when she was sitting on the porch waiting for him, he came from the direction of the old coast road. She turns and pulls the inside door of the cottage shut, then steps down off the porch and heads for the trail that winds through the pines.

When she clears the last of the trees and approaches the gravel path through the dunes, she discovers that the clouds have moved off to the east, leaving the moon to shine brightly on the surface of the bay. It dances and sparkles on the gentle ripples that lap the shore. The grasses stand out in sharp relief, black against the lighter background of the sky, painting a scene both lovely and serene.

Nadia continues onward, rounding the glacial rocks at Long Point and coming upon a narrow stream that bisects the path. She crosses it easily, then stops to listen. With almost no wind and only the gentlest of waves foaming slightly on the gravel beach, the near silence is peaceful and comforting. Her eyes are now fully adjusted to the approaching night. She scans the horizon, the woods behind her and the path and beach ahead, hoping to see the silhouette of her elderly friend. Her ears strain to catch the sound of his footsteps.

She decides to go as far as Green Point. The path slopes upward, and she climbs with youthful agility to a raised, dam-like crescent where large stones in the pathway make the footing less secure. She pauses before stepping across a thin stream that meanders from the forest to the shore. She debates going back and strains to see as far as the ancient, gnarled pine that stands with lonely courage above the water at the very edge of a squat, eroding cliff.

The trunk of the tree seems to move. Intrigued, she takes another dozen steps forward, and the shadows at its base begin to separate into distinct, disparate forms. She hurries on and comes up to the tree on the landward side. The moon resolves the shadows into a shoulder and an arm, just visible behind the trunk.

Andrew Striker sits propped against the tree, his legs splayed awkwardly over the sloping edge of the cliff. Nadia circles around until she can see him in profile.

"Hi, Doc."

No answer. He doesn't move, doesn't acknowledge her presence in any way. She leans down to look more closely at his face and into his eyes, which are open but glassy as he stares out over the water. His jaw hangs agape. His right hand lies loosely in his lap, palm upward.

She touches his shoulder. "Dr. Striker?"

He turns his head slowly toward her. "Catherine?"

"It's Nadia. Are you okay?"

"I'm waiting for Penny," he mumbles.

She wonders who he means. She thinks of the child he was with at lunch. She can't remember the girl's name, but Penny sounds wrong. "Is somebody out here with you?"

"Penny should be home by now," he mumbles. "She's too little to be out after dark."

Confused by his slurred speech and lassitude, she squats beside him, waiting for him to go on. His attention returns to the water. His entire body lies slack and awkward against the trunk of the tree, devoid of animation.

Nadia wonders what has happened. *A stroke, maybe?* Despite her medical ambitions, her experience with illness is limited. She debates going back for help, but is reluctant to leave him there alone. Finally she makes up her mind. She grips his arm above the elbow, encouraging him to rise.

"Let's go back now, okay?"

He stirs slightly. "I have to wait for Penny."

She tugs on his arm, but he is dead weight. "Penny is back at your cottage," she improvises. He turns his head again and looks at her without recognition, confused.

"Please, Dr. Striker, we have to go back now."

Andrew draws a deep breath and struggles to his feet. His right knee buckles, and Nadia catches him and helps him to regain his balance. She leads him back from the edge of the cliff and onto the path, moving slowly so that he won't trip on the irregular rocks that stud the gravel surface. He shuffles along, compliant but otherwise unresponsive.

Nadia begins to talk. She chats aimlessly about her day, the beach, anything that comes to mind. He doesn't answer her, but his pace begins to increase, and by the time they reach the edge of the woods and the first stretch of roughly paved roadway, his step is somewhat more secure. She no longer has to urge him forward.

They come to the cottage, and Andrew continues walking past the driveway. Nadia takes his hand and turns him toward the path to his porch. They mount the steps, and she opens the door and leads him inside. He looks around in distracted confusion as she helps him over to his chair.

"Penny?"

She stands before him, not knowing what to do next. Andrew stares through her, his chin down, his eyes clouded. She shakes her head sadly and turns to go into the kitchen.

She picks up the phone and calls the canteen. Fran Marshall picks up on the second ring.

"Mom? I need help."

Her mother is instantly alert. "What happened? Are you all right?"

"It's not me, it's Dr. Striker. He's sick."

"What's wrong with him?"

"I don't know. I found him down by the water, almost all the way out to Green Point. He doesn't even know me. He thinks I'm somebody named Catherine, and he keeps asking about Penny."

"Oh, Lord, that doesn't sound good. Where are you?"

"I brought him back to his cottage," Nadia answers.

"I haven't got the car. Your dad is off bowling. Maybe we better call nine-one-one."

"Can you just come and take a look at him, please?"

"Did he walk back by himself?"

"I had to lead him, but he walks okay. He's just so vague. Nothing I say gets through to him."

"All right. I'll be right there, and then we'll decide what to do."

"Thanks, Mom."

She hangs up and hurries back into the living room. Andrew

is still seated in the armchair, and she walks around in front of him. He looks up at her approach and focuses on her face.

"Hello, Nadia. When did you get here?"

Relief floods through her, followed by an immediate return of anxiety. "Don't you remember? You were down at the Point, and you walked back with me."

"I did?" His eyes look clear to her, not clouded and vacant as before. "I can't seem to remember."

Hurried footsteps climb the porch, and Fran Marshall pushes through the screen door. She scans the room quickly, and Andrew meets her eyes.

"Good evening, Mrs. Marshall. To what do I owe the pleasure?"

Fran looks at her daughter in confusion, and Nadia shrugs helplessly.

"Nadia called me," she says. "She thought you might be feeling ill."

"No, I'm fine. I seem to have had a bit of a memory loss, that's all." He turns to Nadia. "I'm sorry if I upset you."

"That's okay." She and her mother exchange concerned glances. "I just came by to see if you wanted some supper at the restaurant."

"Is it that late already?" He looks toward the door and frowns at the darkness outside.

"It's pretty late," Nadia says. "How long were you out at the Point?" He looks at her in confusion. "Never mind. How about a sandwich? I can even make you some soup if you want."

Andrew grimaces. His face becomes more alert, and his speech changes from languid to precise. "No, thanks. I'm okay."

"Dr. Striker, who is Penny?"

He smiles at her, and she sees some of his old mischief creep back into his eyes. "Why so formal? What happened to 'Doc'?"

She returns his smile. "That's just for when you tease me too much. Who's Penny?"

"She's my daughter."

"Is she here visiting with you?"

"No, she lives in Ottawa."

"You were asking for her," Nadia says.

"I was? I must have been dreaming a little." He shifts position and sits more upright in the chair. "I've been known to sleepwalk, you know."

Nadia frowns at him, not knowing whether to believe him. "Who is Catherine?"

"My wife…" he says vaguely. His gaze wanders again to the door.

"Penny is such a pretty name," Fran says. "Short for Penelope?"

His attention sharpens again. "No, her name is Rebecca. Please, won't you sit down?"

Fran and Nadia move to the sofa, and the girl says, "Come on, Doc, you're kidding us. How do you get Penny out of Rebecca?"

He is becoming more animated. "You should have seen her when she was little. She was born almost bald, just a little light fuzz. When her hair started to come in, it was a bright reddish gold colour." He laughs. "It was really quite striking. You wouldn't know it to look at us now, but both Catherine and I have redheads in our families. We figured the recessive genes from both of us must have ganged up on the baby. Anyway, one day her three-year-old brother said, 'Her head looks like a penny,' and that was it. She was Penny from that day on."

"Is she still a redhead?" Nadia asks.

"No. It darkened to auburn by the time she was in high school." He smiles, remembering. "One of her children has the same colouring, though, the youngest one." He pauses. "I haven't seen them in a while…"

Suddenly he pushes himself fully upright. "I'm being rude. May I offer you some coffee? I'm afraid I don't have anything else in the house."

"We came down to invite you for the same thing," Nadia lies. "Why don't you come on back to our place?"

"I'm sorry, I can't. It would be too much to impose like that. But it's nice of you to ask."

Fran and Nadia search each other's faces. "Are you sure?"

Fran asks. "It wouldn't be any trouble at all."

"No. It must be very late." He turns formally to Nadia. "I apologize again if I worried you."

The women stand up to leave, reluctant but not knowing what else to do. Andrew walks with them to the door.

"We open at seven," Nadia says. She steps out onto the porch and turns back to face him. "How about some blueberry pancakes in the morning? On the house."

"You won't get to medical school by giving away the profits," he laughs. He swings the door open, leaving them no choice but to go outside.

"The way you've been tipping me lately, I can stay in university for the rest of my life," Nadia says.

"My pleasure." He steps back and the screen door swings shut. "Good night." He turns and vanishes into the gloom of the cottage, and the inner door closes to shut them out. Nadia and Fran stand on the bottom step, looking at each other.

"Do you think it's okay to leave him?" the girl asks.

"I have no idea. You say he didn't even know you when you found him?"

"He was completely out of it, right up until I called you. Then when I went back into the living room, it was like he had just waked up. Maybe he wasn't kidding when he said he's a sleepwalker." Reluctantly, they start down the path toward their home. "I'm really worried, Mom. Maybe there's somebody we can call."

"Is his wife still alive?"

"I don't know. He's never said anything about her to me before." They pass the canteen and start up their own driveway.

"The best we can do is keep an eye on him," Fran says. "If he comes to breakfast, why don't you see if you can find out where his wife lives, or his daughter. She probably goes by her married name, but if you can find out what it is, we could try to get hold of her."

Nadia stops at their door and looks back up the road. "He shouldn't be all alone."

Fran squeezes her daughter's shoulder. "There's only just so much we can do. He seemed pretty good when we left."

"Even so…"

"Come on inside, Mother Hen. We'll see what can be done in the morning."

Investment Counselling

It took Andrew and Catherine almost an hour to return their books to the shelves. Aside from a couple of cracked spines and some wrinkled pages, there was little damage. Andrew worked in silence. When they were finished, he went to Penny's room and stood before the bookcases he had lined up against the wall next to the closet half a year before. He remembered moving the furniture into the room, but not the act of filling it with the treasured volumes.

He ran his hand down the rich, gold-embossed leather binding of "Twelfth Night", one of a complete set of Shakespeare's plays printed in England over a century earlier. Catherine had found them on the occasion of their third anniversary, the year of his dissertation. Buying them had been an incredible extravagance.

With a new baby (Donald was barely six months old) and the graduate school bills mounting alarmingly, they struggled from payday to payday, never seeming to get ahead. But she had convinced the owner of the town's used bookstore to put the volumes aside for her, and for nearly a year she squirreled away every spare cent. The night she presented them, he insisted that it was too much, that she should return them. She was just as adamant that he should keep them.

As he stood now examining them, Catherine came up behind him and put her arms around his waist. "Feeling better?"

"Much. Thanks for helping."

"Now will you please, *please* do as Bob says? Take the rest of those tests, and let him help you figure out what's bothering you."

He turned around and embraced her. "It's going to be okay. I know what's wrong now."

She leaned back and searched his face. "What? Tell me."

"I love you, you know that?"

"Of course I do."

"So you just have to believe me when I say that everything

will be all right."

"Andrew…"

He placed his index finger across her lips. "Shh. Trust me."

She kissed his finger, then moved it aside. "Only if you promise me something."

"What?"

"If anything else happens again like tonight, if you get upset or anything, you'll tell me, or you'll call Bob. Promise me you won't try to face it alone."

"You worry too much."

"Promise me!"

"All right, I promise," he said. *But there won't be any more times like tonight. Tomorrow I'll make sure of that.*

* * *

The following morning Andrew arrived at his office an hour earlier than usual. He sat at his desk and reviewed the notes he had taken concerning his pension options. Then he made a checklist of things to be accomplished within the next few days.

At nine he called the local investment firm, and asked Russell Baxter's secretary to make an appointment for the noon hour. Then he called the Bank of Montreal and arranged to see the manager at one thirty. After teaching his morning class and meeting his other appointments, he walked downtown and arrived at Baxter's office five minutes early, finding his advisor ready and waiting for him.

"Come on in, Andrew. Decided to visit your money? You haven't been in here for a long time." He motioned Andrew to a chair and sat down behind his desk.

"Here to give it some exercise, I think. To be as direct as possible, how much am I worth?"

Baxter opened a file folder and extracted a thin sheaf of documents. "Want to cut right to the chase, do you?" He points to a page of rising jagged lines. "These graphs show the increase in your portfolio since the last time you were in. What I did was…"

"I'm an English prof, Russ, not a CPA. Just the bottom line, okay?"

"You don't want me to have any fun. Okay, given the fact that you've been in pretty conservative stuff all along, nothing volatile, you didn't get in on any of the skyrockets. On the other hand, you didn't take a bath when the high tech stuff tanked, or after the nine-eleven mess. Bottom line, between the two accounts you've averaged thirteen-point-four percent over twenty-one years, compounded, of course, and most of it tax sheltered. Not too shabby."

"So what am I worth?"

Baxter drew out the bottom sheet and pointed to the last entry in a column of figures. Andrew squinted at the small print. "Whoa! Looks like you've been giving my money *plenty* of exercise."

"Blue chips, buying bonds at the right time, riding out the bad times and buying in when the others are bailing out. It all adds up, my friend."

"Thanks to you. I wouldn't have known where to put it."

"That's what I'm here for. And when you make out, I make out."

"So with this, my insurance and my pension, would you say I'm pretty well fixed?"

"Unless you're contemplating a six-month fling in Las Vegas or an expensive mistress, you won't ever have to touch the capital. Your grandkids will bless your name some day."

"Provided I can keep the government at bay," Andrew says. "Is there anything we can do about that?"

"Sure. That's what estate planning is all about."

Andrew leaned forward seriously. "Russ, I'm going to outline what I want to do. Then I'm going to trust you to set it up for me. And to keep your mouth shut about it."

* * *

Andrew left Baxter's office and headed west up Main Street. He turned in at the Bank of Montreal and walked to the back counter. Trevor Nelson, the branch manager and Andrew's personal friend for over half his tenure at Acadia, came out to meet him.

"Come back to my office," he said. "How are Catherine and the kids?"

"Everybody's fine," Andrew said, entering the cubicle and taking a seat in front of the desk. "And yours?"

"Third grandchild expected any day. You've got just the two, haven't you?"

"Penny's kids, both boys. But Donald's been making noises about getting married and starting a family, too."

"That's great," the banker said. "Now what can I do for you?"

"I need to know that anything we say is confidential. Even from Catherine, at least until I'm ready to tell her."

Nelson turned serious. "Of course, if that's the way you want it. What's going on?"

"It isn't absolutely definite, but I think I'm going to retire in July."

The banker sat back and stared at his friend. "That's the last thing I expected to hear you say. I thought teaching was your greatest love. After your family, that is."

"It is," Andrew said sadly. "But nothing lasts forever. Anyway, in case I decide to follow through, I need to put some things in motion now." Nelson took out a legal pad and picked up his pen. "First of all," Andrew continued, "I'm going to update my will, and I want the Bank to serve as executor." Nelson made notes.

"Next, Russ Baxter is setting up a couple of trusts for me. He'll send you the details. And I'm going to have my pension sent directly here, to go into our joint account so Catherine will always have access to it."

Trevor Nelson stopped writing and looked up with concern. "How about levelling with me. Are you ill? Is that why you're keeping all this from Catherine?"

Andrew sighed. "Not exactly. I'm just taking precautions, that's all, in case I'm not able to make the right decisions later on. The way Russ and I have it worked out, Catherine won't ever have to worry about any of the details, or the kids either."

"So what's the rush? You know that I'd look out for them if it ever became necessary. You and Catherine are like family."

"And you know how much I appreciate it. But there's a little more to it than that. Do you have a branch on the South Shore?"

"Several of them. What area?"

"I'm not sure yet," Andrew said. "Maybe Lunenburg or Bridgewater. In any case I'm going to want a separate account there, something in my name only. And it has to be confidential."

"Damn it, Andrew, what's going on? Are you laundering drug money or something?"

"I'm sorry, Trevor. I can't talk about it just yet, but it's nothing illegal. When the time comes, I'll explain as much as I can to you."

Nelson grimaced and stared at his friend for several long moments. Then he raised his pen again. "All right. I just hope you know what you're doing."

"When you see how I want it set up, I think you'll agree that it protects Catherine in every way possible. And Russ is working on an estate plan for me."

"Damn it, you *are* sick, aren't you?"

"Please, Trevor. Just listen to me, and help me get everything in place." For the next half hour, the two men arranged Andrew's affairs and opened the required accounts.

*   *   *

Andrew arrived back at the arts building just after two thirty and found his class already assembled in the lecture hall. He stopped in briefly, asked them to wait while he retrieved his notes from his office, and went upstairs. He picked up the phone and called his lawyer's office. When the receptionist answered, he stated his intention to make some changes in his will and made an appointment for the following morning.

Later that afternoon, just before starting for home, he consulted his checklist once more and marked off what he had accomplished. Satisfied that he hadn't forgotten anything, he packed up his briefcase, put on his coat, and headed out the door. He decided to take Catherine out to dinner.

Most important, he resolved to maintain a tight rein on his

emotions from that day forward, until everything was finally in place. He had already given his wife too much cause for concern, and he had to convince her that he was perfectly normal again. And he had to keep Bob Melanson at bay.

No more red flags. No more upsets.

SEVEN...

Andrew awakes as the first faint light of morning touches the windowpanes of his bedroom. An uncomfortable weight rests on his midsection, and he opens his eyes to see Old Cat perched on his stomach, licking her paw and passing it behind her ears.

"So now I'm your bathtub, am I? You're just a little too presumptuous." He pushes her off gently, and she stalks to the edge of the bed and jumps down. She leaves the room and heads for the kitchen, and a minute later Andrew hears her plaintive "I'm hungry!" cry.

He gets up and shrugs into his robe. The previous evening's visit from the Marshalls comes back to him, and he frowns in irritation. *Must have been the lights and the open door that made her come looking for me. Can't let that happen again. If they start worrying about me, they might stick their noses where they don't belong.*

He finds his way to the kitchen and starts the coffee. Old Cat makes a pest of herself, and he attends to her food and water dishes. Then he sits at the table, waiting for the coffee to finish brewing. He can't remember leaving the cottage the previous evening, and only vaguely recalls sitting out beside the shore.

Something about a turtle...?

The earlier part of the day stands out clearly in his mind,

however: Jennie's bike ride to the cottage, their lunch, and him depositing her back home and extracting her promise to stop lying to her mother.

I came out here to get away, not to get embroiled in someone else's problems. If people can't look after their own kids, it's not my business.

He hears Penny's voice behind him, so real as to make him start. The words mean nothing, just vague echoes and the silvery laughter of the little girl he sired and feared for and finally turned loose into the world, competent and self-reliant. The guidance of two parents was there when she needed it.

There are a lot of fatherless kids in the world. The strong ones will make it on their own. The others don't deserve to.

Inertia keeps him rooted to the chair. Warring factions draw their battle lines in the sands of his mind, his reclusive depression aligned against fading memories of a lifetime spent in the guidance and education of youth. He tries to ignore them.

He drains his tepid coffee and sits staring out at the brightening day. Briefly he misses the morning paper, and regrets cancelling the subscription. It had become a great source of frustration to him, however, a constant reminder of his deteriorating faculties. Except on rare good days, he had trouble putting the developing world events in their proper context, and the daily crossword puzzle, once a minor mental exercise, now angered him with the inaccessibility of its ingenious definitions.

Finally he overcomes his lethargy and returns to the bedroom to get dressed. Old Cat follows him and begs for attention, and Andrew spends ten minutes giving her long hair a thorough combing. She is, he suspects, the result of an unplanned congress between a Persian and a Siamese, the former giving her a beautiful coat, and the latter her slightly crossed eyes and obnoxious, penetrating howl.

I didn't need you in my life, either.

*   *   *

His mind wanders back to the day he got her, fresh from the

disaster of trying to heal the bedraggled stray that had wandered into his yard. When he arrived at the clinic, Emily McKinley welcomed him brightly. "Here to look at our old cat?"

"I suppose so," he grumbled, annoyed at himself, and at her for trying to capitalize on his weakness.

"She's back here." Emily beckoned him through the left hand door in the wall behind the reception counter. He stepped through into a crowded room lined with floor-to-ceiling cages, more than half of them occupied. He wrinkled his nose, expecting the dense odour of an ill-kept pet shop, and was surprised to find the air sweet. A chorus of barks and meows greeted them.

He hesitated just inside the door, unaccountably anxious and uncertain. "This isn't a good idea," he said.

"Why not?" the young woman said. "What's the harm in looking? Here she is, over here." She stopped before the right hand bank of stacked cages and motioned toward the third one from the top.

Andrew stepped forward reluctantly. At the back of the cage, a solid grey long-haired cat sat in aloof boredom. Emily tried to coax her toward the front but was ignored. He looked closer. Although obviously far beyond kittenhood, the cat was small and compact. Her washed-out yellow eyes, pale but penetrating, conveyed an "I've seen it all" nonchalance.

Emily opened the cage door and brought the cat out into the light. She ruffled her coat. "Look how beautiful her fur is. It's actually two colours. She's got a light grey undercoat, almost white."

She picked the animal up and carried her to an examining table in the centre of the floor, chatting cheerfully. "You wouldn't know it to look at her, but she weighs a ton. Dense bones, I guess." The cat resisted passively, her posture stiff and her small rounded ears drawn back half way and twitching.

Andrew watched in quiet distraction. *What am I doing here? I don't need anything around to look after. I don't even know how.* He reached out tentatively and stroked the cat's disturbed fur back into place. The cat turned her head at the unfamiliar touch. She fixed her baleful yellow eyes on his face and hunched down on the table.

"I'm sorry," he said. "I guess I shouldn't have come. It just wouldn't work out." Emily's face fell, and he turned from her and from the cat and started out of the room.

A piercing yowl brought him up short. The cat had a voice like nothing he had ever heard, something akin to a fire siren. Startled, he looked around to see the beast standing at the very edge of the table, her chin stretched out belligerently. He smiled in spite of himself.

"She ignores me completely, except when it's time to eat," Emily said hopefully. "I guess she likes you, though."

"Not likely." He returned to the table and extended his hand. The cat turned her head sideways and leaned out alarmingly, almost losing her balance. She scrabbled at the slippery stainless steel, and he steadied her. Then he rubbed the fur on her cheek, and she rumbled her approval.

"I'll be darned," Emily said. "I've never heard her purr before. I didn't think she could."

"Who are you kidding!" he said, gruffly but good-naturedly. "This whole dog and pony show is just a setup for my benefit."

Emily ignored his protest. "Ever since we got her, she hasn't trusted anyone. Abandoned animals are like that sometimes. Some of them beg for affection, and others turn away from everybody. This is the first time she's responded positively to anyone."

"You really expect me to swallow that?" he said.

She pretended to look hurt at being disbelieved. She started to pick the cat up to put it back in the cage, and the animal stiffened and uttered its strange cry again.

"What's wrong with her voice?" Andrew asked.

"Nothing. Cats don't all sound alike. This one is probably part Siamese. Most of them can wake the dead."

He laughed. "Put her down again. Let's see how much of a con artist she is." Emily did so, and the cat took a few quick licks down her flank to smooth her rumpled coat. Then she looked directly into Andrew's eyes and wailed at him again. She crossed to the edge of the table and stretched her head out to be stroked.

Emily kept silent, letting the cat do her own persuading. She butted her head against his hand, then turned to present her rump to him. "What does she want?" he asked.

"Try rubbing the fur on her back just forward of her tail," Emily said. "Both ways, sort of brisk." He did so, and the cat arched her back and began to purr again. "A lot of them like that."

"If I take her, how much are you going to gouge me?"

Emily smiled. "No charge. I told you, she was abandoned. Grandfather says she's in perfect health, so all you have to do is feed her and change her litter. Bring her in every six months for a checkup and to have her teeth cleaned. That's all."

"There's got to be a catch to it."

"Nope. I'll even let you keep the litter pan we let you borrow. And I'll throw in a comb and brush. You'll have to groom her, or she'll get knots in her coat."

"Wow, a bonus!" he said sarcastically. "What does she eat?"

"The same stuff you already have. It's a balanced diet for older cats. You can get her some cans from the super market, too, but save that kind for a special treat. It's not as nutritious, but most cats like variety."

"How old did you say she is?"

"We think about fifteen."

"How long do cats live?"

"It varies. If they don't go outdoors and tangle with cars or other animals, cats do pretty well. She's probably got a few good years left. I had one that lived to nineteen, and some make it well past twenty."

Damn thing will probably outlive me. "All right, I guess I've got a cat. Tell her to pack her suitcase."

Emily smiled with pleasure. "It's great having something alive around the house. You won't be sorry."

"I expect I will. Probably the first time she yowls like that in the middle of the night, in fact. How do I get her home?"

"We can sell you a cat carrier." He looked at her askance, and she laughed. "Okay, just try putting her on the front seat. She'll probably settle down as soon as you start to drive."

He bought extra food and another bag of litter and loaded it into the back, along with the free comb and brush. Emily followed him, carrying the cat, and he took it from her and placed it on the front passenger seat. The cat promptly turned around twice and settled down to wash, thoroughly at home.

"You should be selling real estate," he said to Emily as he got behind the wheel.

"I didn't sell her. She sold herself. If you have any problems, call us. And thanks. She's a good old girl, and deserves a home." She gave the cat a farewell pat through the open window. "What are you going to call her?"

He put the car in gear and pressed the button to raise the window. "Old Cat. What else?"

* * *

Shit! Responsibility wins the battle, the legacy of his profession. He decides to make another trip to Crescent Beach. He has no doubt that the child's mother will have taken steps to keep her at home, but he wants to make sure. He *has* to make sure.

The morning is becoming uncomfortably warm, and he decides to take a cooling shower before getting dressed. Then he shaves off three days' growth of beard, and selects a golf shirt and his lightest cotton pants from the closet. It is past seven thirty when he finally leaves the cottage and walks out to his car.

A square of paper flutters beneath the windshield wiper. He plucks it out and finds Nadia Marshall's neat script: "The pancakes are ready whenever you are." She has signed it with a happy face.

Andrew considers stopping at the restaurant, but he feels no hunger. He resolves to begin fending the girl off, afraid that she is already too much aware of his worsening condition. *Better to keep her at a distance from now on.* He gets into the car and starts the engine. He backs out of the driveway and drives slowly away from Green Bay.

He glances briefly at the canteen as he passes, and sees Nadia Marshall looking out the window. He stares straight ahead through the windshield, ignoring her wave. He continues up the road toward Petite Riviere.

He arrives at Crescent Beach a few minutes later and drives down onto the sand. Only a few other cars are there ahead of him. He parks and gets out, and squints eastward along the beach. He is looking for Jennie's small figure at her usual spot, halfway to the distant rocks and islands. He doesn't see her.

He begins to walk along the water's edge. The moderate wind that crosses the beach is hot and dry, and several of the early arrivals are seeking relief in the water. Several hundred yards further along, a small sedan is drawn up next to the log fence, and a young mother sits on a blanket, watching two children paddling in the surf. Another small head breaks the water some twenty-five yards distant and a dozen yards off shore. He wonders why the woman is letting one of her charges play so far away.

Some people have kids to spare, I guess.

The beach is surprisingly clean. Whatever conditions of wind and tide had prevailed overnight, they must have prevented fresh seaweed from washing ashore.

Not too many starfish to be found today.

He passes the children at play in the shallows and skirts the splashing surf. He looks up and sees the most distant child swimming toward him, her arms cutting strongly through the water. She gains her footing in the shallows and splashes up onto the sand.

"Hi." Jennie is wearing a faded yellow and blue swimsuit, well worn and a size too small. Her hair is pinned back close to her head. "Hot today."

"It is that," Andrew says. "You're quite a swimmer."

She shakes the water out of her hair and grins up at him. "Thanks. That's about the only thing Dad ever taught me that did me any good."

"So your mom decided you could keep coming out here, did she?" he asks. Jennie looks down at her feet. "Well, did she?"

"I didn't tell her," she admits in a soft voice.

"Damn it, Jennie…"

"She didn't get home until late," the child says hurriedly. "She had to take my sister to the doctor after day care. She's got an ear infection or something. So supper was late, and Mom was tired, and I just didn't get around to it."

"You promised."

"I know." Suddenly she brightens. "How about if I take you to meet my grandma instead? You'll like her. We can tell *her* that I've been coming out here, okay? And even about me riding my bike out to see you, if you want. Okay?"

Andrew regards her carefully, expecting another con. "That's not the same as telling your mother."

"So we can do that later. What's the difference, as long as Gram knows where I am."

"Why do I get the feeling you're pulling another fast one on me?"

She grins delightedly. "Want to see me do the butterfly? I figured out how by watching the Olympics on TV."

"Why not?" He sinks to the sand as she trots back into the water. When it reaches her waist she throws herself forward, her arms windmilling in inefficient circles. Her head bobs in and out of the water. She expends great amounts of energy but makes little progress. About a dozen yards farther out she regains her feet and waves at him. The water now comes up to her neck. He applauds her politely, more for her effort than for her technique.

She plunges back into the surf and splashes to shore, this time with a less awkward overhand crawl. She runs up to him and sprawls by his side. "Can you swim?"

"I used to. Haven't in a long time."

She bounces up again and grabs his hand, trying to pull him to his feet. "Come on! Come in with me!"

Laughing, he resists her. "I'm not dressed for it."

"Coward!" She drops his hand and runs back into the water. He watches her for another ten minutes as she splashes back and forth parallel to the shore.

He wonders what to do about her. *She shouldn't be swimming alone, shouldn't even be out here without someone to watch over her. And I shouldn't be getting mixed up in this, either.*

Jumbled images crowd his mind: the child's head disappearing under the water, not coming back up; her broken body lying by the side of the highway, tangled in the smashed remains of her bicycle; a dark and shadowy figure leading her from the beach to his car. He despairs of getting her to stop deceiving her mother and resolves to bring matters to a head himself, that very afternoon.

Jennie flounders out of the water and drops down beside him again. She draws up her knees and hugs them, and turns her small face toward his. "So what's your kind of doctor do?" she asks.

"What are you talking about?"

She tilts her head coyly and rests it on her knees, looking at him sideways and grinning. "You told me yesterday you're some sort of a doctor. What kind? What do you do?"

"I have a university degree called Doctor of Philosophy," he says. "I'm not like a regular doctor who helps sick people."

"I don't get it."

"It just means I went to school for a lot of years, that's all. I studied English and literature, so I'd know enough to be able to teach." He changes the subject. "Does your grandmother live with you?"

"Nope. Do you teach at a school like mine?"

"I don't teach at all any more. I used to work at Acadia University." He frowns, trying to sort out his memories. "Didn't I tell you that yesterday?"

"How come you stopped?"

He looks away from her. "Just got old, that's all."

"You're not so old. What did you teach?"

He sighs, knowing she is stalling again. "I taught courses about famous authors, and creative writing."

"What's that?"

"How to write short stories, feature articles for newspapers, even novels. Where does your grandmother live?"

"Almost to Pleasantville. Did *you* ever write anything?"

Pleasantville? He tries to recall a town by that name. *Isn't that a movie?*

"What road is that on?" he asks.

"This one, about halfway to Bridgewater. So did you ever write a book?"

"Yes, you little procrastinator, and don't tell me you don't know what that means."

"Have I ever read it? What's it called?"

"I'm sure you haven't. And I'm not answering any more questions until we settle the issue of visiting your grandma."

"Can I see it some time?" she persists. Andrew keeps silent, and she tries again. "Let's go to your place, and you can show me."

He turns and looks directly at her, raising one eyebrow dramatically. She bursts out laughing. "Okay, fine. But after we see Gram, will you show me your book?"

"Do you ever do anything without trying to get something in return?"

"Not if I can help it." Her irrepressible energy keeps her bouncing and fidgeting by his side. "Want to see me do the back stroke?"

"No! I want to meet your grandmother." *Except I don't! I want to be free of this kid, free of feeling responsible for her safety.*

"Oh, all *right!*" She stands up and brushes the sand off her bottom. "You'll have to drive me there."

"Let's go, then."

"I have to go home first. Mom's gonna call me, so I have to be there, and then I have to change clothes."

Andrew climbs wearily to his feet. "Go ahead. I'll pick you up at your house."

"Can't I ride with you?"

"You'll get my car seat all wet."

"Please? I can sit on my knees."

He starts off toward the west end of the beach. "Come on, then." She hurries to catch up, and reaches for his hand. He lets her hang on, and they walk the rest of the way to the car, he in silence and Jennie humming happily to herself.

* * *

Andrew steers the car into the Horton driveway and Jennie gets out. She hears the telephone ringing inside the house.

"Oh my gosh!" She sprints for the door, fumbles her key into the lock, and disappears inside.

He gets out and walks toward the far end of the driveway and then into the small back yard, sandwiched between the house and a line of scrub pines. The sides of the yard are similarly screened, hiding the property from the view of any other homes along the road. There is a small sandbox at the far corner of the lot, with a handful of plastic toys scattered about. He wonders how old Jennie's little sister is.

He turns and surveys the building. Like most of the homes he has seen so far on the islands, it appears to be many decades old. The spruce shingles that make up the siding are cupped and split, and the trim at the corners and around the windows shows signs of many coats of paint. He ponders the problems of a single mother with two children, apparently abandoned by an unpredictable husband and newly hired at a fast food restaurant, no doubt at minimum wage.

How long before she gives up trying? Maybe I can help somehow...

There is nowhere to sit in the back yard, and his right knee begins to throb. He retraces his steps and opens the car door to get in, but the air inside has warmed to an uncomfortable level. He goes toward the front door of the house and sits on the steps instead, sheltered from the direct rays of the sun.

A few minutes later Jennie reappears, this time in shorts and a threadbare tee shirt. "Let's go."

He stands up. They start walking to the car. "Did you talk to your mom?"

"Yeah. Missed her the first time. When I picked up the phone, she had already hung up, but I called her right back." She opens the door to get in. "Wow! Hot!"

"Leave the window up," he says. "The air conditioner will cool it down fast." He gets in and starts the engine.

She settles in and buckles the seat belt. "Anyway, I said I was out in the yard when she called. I think she believed me."

He stares at her in frustration, then shrugs off her deceit. He backs out and heads for the bridge at the end of Bush Island, skirts Crescent Beach, and turns right onto Route 331.

Closing Some Doors

The President's secretary ushered Andrew into the anteroom. "Dr. Reynolds will be with you in just a moment. Would you like some coffee? Or perhaps water?"

"Thank you, no."

She retreated, leaving the door open. He took the closest chair, and presently he heard the muted clicking of her computer keyboard.

He glanced around the pleasantly furnished room, more like a residence than an institutional office. In place of purely functional seating, a pair of comfortable sofas and several upholstered chairs were tastefully arranged around a low coffee table. Brass lamps graced the end tables, and the room was pleasingly lit by immense windows in the two outside walls. Four paintings by Alex Colville hung opposite them, reminiscent of that famous artist's service as the university's Chancellor some years before.

The door to the President's inner office opened, and Dr. James M. Reynolds entered. Andrew stood up as the man crossed to him, his hand extended in greeting.

"Andrew, so good to see you. It's been a while."

"It's good of you to make time for me, Jim."

"On the contrary, it's good of you to take me away from all that work on my desk. What can I do for you?" He waved Andrew back to his chair and pulled another up closer and sat down.

"I've reached a crossroad, I guess," Andrew began. "I'd like to take early retirement this July."

James Reynolds stared at him seriously. "What brought this on?"

"A number of things. It just seems like the right time to go."

"You're not running off to some other institution, are you? Or are you and Catherine planning to do some travelling?"

"No to both, at least for now. I'm not sure exactly what I'm going to do."

The President sat back thoughtfully. "Of all the faculty members I've dealt with over the years, I can think of no one who loves being in the classroom more than you. Are you sure this is what you want to do?"

"What I'm the most sure of is, I may not be as effective as I once was."

"How so?"

Andrew considered his answer carefully before speaking. He had already inadvertently revealed more than he intended. "I think I'm just tired," he said.

Reynolds regarded him critically. "When a faculty member comes to me to resign or retire, I normally don't try to change his or her mind. That isn't my place. But you and I have been friends for quite some time, and this just isn't like you."

"I appreciate your concern, Jim, and especially your friendship. But I really need a rest."

"Take a leave, then. Six months, even a year. How long have you got to go before sixty-five? We can do without you for a term or two."

"It's not just that. It's time you hired somebody younger, that's all."

"Nonsense!" Reynolds exploded. "The Dean has the highest respect for you, and I do too. And no one in this whole place gets better student evaluations than you do."

Andrew was surprised that the President was aware of the details of his reputation, and his face showed it. "I keep track," Reynolds said. "Your classes are always oversubscribed, and your list of publications is the envy of the entire Arts Faculty."

He looked at Andrew critically. "What the hell is going on?" he asked frankly. "A crisis of confidence, maybe?"

Andrew sighed. "Not really," he lied.

The silence between them grew. Finally Reynolds shifted his position, waiting, but Andrew was reluctant to provide any more information.

"At least take some time to think it over," the President said. "The end of the term isn't far off. Take the summer break to get your feet under you again. You may feel differently in the fall."

"I'm sorry, Jim. I've made up my mind. It's time for me to go."

"I really don't understand," Reynolds said sadly.

"Maybe I don't either," Andrew admitted honestly. "But this is something I have to do."

* * *

Shortly before noon on a Saturday in the last week of June, Andrew stood in the doorway of his office and looked around for one last time. Just two small cardboard boxes stood by the door, waiting to be taken down to his car. The rest of his books and possessions were already gone, packed away perhaps for good.

He felt very much alone, but he knew it had to be that way. The previous afternoon, at the President's annual spring get-together for faculty and staff, he and other retiring colleagues had been the centre of attention. James Reynolds presented him with a plaque engraved with the dates of his service and bearing the thanks of the Board of Governors. It was a kindness he deeply appreciated, but it drew a type of attention to him that he would have preferred to avoid. He really just wanted to fade quietly away.

Shortly after the Board accepted his application for retirement, the President and the Dean of Arts had proposed a dinner to honour him, but he declined. Nevertheless, his colleagues refused to allow his departure to go unnoticed, and with Catherine's collusion they had organized a surprise gathering of faculty and students during the second week of examinations in April. Lured on a flimsy pretext to the Michener Lounge of the Student Union Building, he could not escape the party with good grace. He endured with feelings of unworthiness the praise and plaudits of the many who had benefited from his work and friendship over so many years.

Now he saw his years at Acadia reduced, at least in his own mind, to the sad sterility of a vacated office. The next month, or the next, a fresh and eager young intellect would fill it with energy and promise. In a surprisingly short time Andrew would fade from everyone's memory, just as the details of his career was fading from his own.

Want to see how much you'll be missed when you're gone?

Stick your hand in a bucket of water, pull it out, and see how much of a hole is left.

He turned and shut the door, leaving it unlocked. He picked up the two cartons and carried them down to his car. It surprised and saddened him to see the small amount of space they occupied in the trunk. Then he got in and drove up Highland Avenue to the Student Union Building and parked in the lower lot. He climbed the back stairs to the Security Office.

He encountered an unfamiliar face behind the reception desk, a youthful commissionaire in uniform who sat typing at a computer console. "I've come to turn in my keys," he said, loudly enough to get the man's attention.

The commissionaire turned toward him. "Name?"

"Andrew Striker."

With one keystroke the man cleared the screen, then called up another file and scrolled through until he reached the "S" column. "Which ones are you returning?"

"Everything," Andrew replied.

The youngster looked at him with mild interest, taking in the grey hair and weathered face. "Retiring?"

"That's right."

"Lucky man." He highlighted the entry on the screen, and somewhere under the desk a printer whirred and clicked. He reached down and plucked a sheet from the tray. "Keys?"

Andrew placed his ring on the counter. Methodically the commissionaire compared the numbers on the keys with those on the printout, checking off each one as he located it.

"All here," he announced. "Sign at the bottom, please."

Andrew took his pen from his shirt pocket and clicked the point out. He hesitated over the signature line.

So easy. A few pen strokes and it's as if I had never been here. He sighed and wrote his name, and slid the paper across the counter.

"Anything else I should do?" Andrew asked.

"Nope, that's it." The young man took the form and the keys and turned toward a wall cabinet at the back of the office. He opened the door and began replacing the keys in the various drawers.

Andrew stood watching him for a few moments. He started to say goodbye, then thought better of it. He walked away from the counter and headed down the stairs and out to his car.

* * *

Catherine met him in the garage as he eased his car in between the lawn mower and the rack of garden tools. "Need any help carrying things?" she asked.

He tugged on the trunk latch and eased himself out of the driver's seat. "There isn't much. Just the stuff from my desk." He lifted the boxes out, and Catherine took one of them from him. They went in through the kitchen door and carried the boxes down the hall to the den.

"I've got some soup on the stove," she told him. He tried unsuccessfully to hide his dejected mood, and she stepped up to him and put her arms around him. "I'm so glad you did this. I need you all to myself for a while. More than you know."

He forced himself to smile at her. "Soup sounds good. Lead me to it."

For the previous few months, despite the progressive decline in his mental powers, he had managed to conceal from her most of the despair he felt. Not knowing what to expect when he told her of his decision to retire, he was surprised at the level of her enthusiasm. Immediately she began to plan visits with their children, which had happened too rarely while he was working full time.

"Penny called this morning," she said as she stood at the stove, ladling out the soup. "Any time after the fifteenth is fine. Paul's vacation is in August this year, so they'll be home until then."

"How long do you want to stay?" he asked her.

"As long as they'll have us. We haven't seen the babies in a year."

"Has it been that long?"

"You know it has. And they change so quickly when they're small." She placed the bowls on the table, and they sat down to eat.

"I'm not sure I'm up to a trip right now."

Concern and disappointment crossed her face. "What is there to keep you home? I thought that was the whole point of retiring, so you could be free to do what you want. And what's more important than seeing our family?"

Irritation bubbled up inside him, but he forced it back down and kept his face bland. "I just feel like I'm imposing on them."

"That's ridiculous. Penny's always asking why we don't come more often."

"I know…"

"And we have to be prepared for a trip to Calgary sometime soon, anyway. My guess is that Donald will propose to Susan by Christmas at the latest."

"Maybe they'll elope."

"I'll kill him!" she said vehemently, then laughed. "I've already told him I'll never forgive him if I'm not there when he gets married."

"You know what he's like," Andrew said. "He hates any kind of fuss made over him."

"I'm not trying to talk him into a big wedding. If he wants to keep it simple, fine, but at least his own mother and father should be there." She stood up and took her empty bowl and spoon to the dishwasher and placed them inside.

Andrew finished his own soup and handed her the bowl. "How about a compromise, then. I'll go with you to Ottawa for three or four days, and then fly back early. That way you can stay as long as you like. I'll get to see the kids that way, but I won't feel like I'm imposing."

"So you're saying I'll be imposing."

"Please, Catherine, don't put words in my mouth." This time he couldn't conceal his annoyance. "You fit in there much better than I do. You and Penny get along like sisters. After a few days I'd just be sitting around looking for things to do."

"What's so important for you to do back here?"

"That isn't the point. I'm just more comfortable here."

He saw Catherine's face shut down. She turned to the sink and washed her hands, then turned and walked out of the room. It was a tactic against which he had little defence. Reluctantly he followed her.

"Okay, a week then," he said as she entered the living room and walked over to stare out the window. "Damn it, you know how I get when I'm away from home too long. I'm like a bear in a cage, and I make everyone else miserable."

She turned to him and stepped into his embrace. "You never do that. All right, a week."

"Good. You can stay as long as you like after that."

"I won't intrude on their vacation. They'll probably want to take another camping trip this year. Penny mentioned the Rockies in her last e-mail. Suppose I come back toward the end of the first week in August?"

"I'll leave it to you to make the reservations."

She squeezed him tightly. "I'm so looking forward to this. And I'm so glad you decided to retire. I know you did it partly for me, and I love you for it."

He smiled down at her sadly, aware that what he really had to do for her would hurt her more than he could bear.

* * *

Andrew stopped the car by the curb on the upper level at Halifax International Airport. He opened the trunk and placed their suitcases on the sidewalk, one for himself and two for Catherine's longer stay in Ottawa.

"I'll find a baggage cart while you park the car," she said to him.

"Won't take me long." He closed the trunk lid and got back behind the wheel. Carefully avoiding the line of taxis and limos strung out along the curb, he drove to the far end and took the ramp down to the parking lot. He took a ticket from the automated dispenser and drove to a far corner of the lot, then locked up and headed for the terminal. Catherine was already waiting in the Air Canada lineup when he reached the upper concourse.

"Is anyone meeting us at the airport?" Andrew asked.

"Penny is. Paul couldn't get time off without taking it from his vacation."

"We could have taken the shuttle," he said. "There's no sense in her having to take the babies all the way out to the airport."

"I offered, but she wouldn't let me. Besides, this way we get to see them all that much sooner."

Andrew lapsed into silence. He fully expected that the week ahead would be his last with his daughter's family, and wondered if he'd ever see his son again.

The line moved and their turn at the counter came. After a careful passport check and the assignment of seats (an aisle for Andrew, so he could stretch out his arthritic knee), they headed for the security gate. He carried no hand baggage in anticipation of an exhaustive search, and was surprised that Catherine's bag was not examined more carefully, given the official paranoia that followed the World Trade Centre disaster.

Guess we don't fit the profile of terrorists, he thought. *And if I'm smart enough to figure that out, the real terrorists are, too. Next we'll have bomb-toting grannies on these planes.*

After a twenty minute wait in the departure lounge they boarded the plane and settled in for the short flight to Ottawa. Andrew regarded Catherine's happy smile with sadness and regret. He knew she hoped that his retirement meant a new kind of liberation for her, and that this would be only the first of many such visits. It was a chance to exercise her grandmotherhood to its fullest extent, but he hid the fact that she would be making future trips alone.

EIGHT...

"That's it! The one with the stone wall out front."

Andrew follows Jennie's finger, and sees a heavily gingerbread-laden three-story Victorian home set back from the narrow side road. The spacious grounds slope down toward the LaHave River behind it. The lawn is well watered and carefully manicured, and bright perennials line the foundation. Baskets of colourful annuals hang at intervals along the veranda.

He turns in between two stone pillars and notes the modest sign mounted beside the open gate: Willowbrook Home For Special Care.

"Your grandmother lives here?" he asks her.

"Uh, huh. You can park around the back."

He aims the car where she points and follows the curving driveway past the end of the building where a broad paved area spreads beneath the thickness of venerable red and sugar maples. He stops, and she jumps out eagerly.

A more modern addition sprouts from the back of the house, two stories high and austere in its angular regularity, like a dormitory. Broad cement steps lead to a double-wide rear entry, and Jennie takes his hand and tries to hurry him along. He follows her inside. A kindly, white-clothed woman of indeterminate middle age sits behind a modern desk. The sign beside her lists visiting hours: ten to twelve in the morning, two to four in the afternoon, evenings by arrangement.

Jennie steps up to the desk. "May I see my Gram, please?"

"Name?"

"Norma Creighton."

"Oh, you're Jennie, aren't you?" the woman says. "You've grown so much I didn't recognize you. Where's your mother?"

"She started a new job this week, in Bridgewater. This is my friend Andrew."

Andrew steps forward and takes the woman's offered hand. "Andrew Striker. I'm pleased to meet you."

"The pleasure is mine. Call me Hannah. Just a minute, please." She turns to pick up the telephone and punches in an extension. She speaks briefly, too softly for Andrew to hear. She replaces the handset and turns back to Jennie with a smile.

"She's just had her bath, and she'll be going back to her room in a few minutes. They'll let me know when. You can wait out front."

"Thank you," Jennie says politely. She takes Andrew's hand again and leads him off down a hall to the left. He can tell she's sure of where to go. They come out into a pleasant old-fashioned parlour, brightly lighted by tall windows and furnished with modern reproductions of antiques. She tugs him toward an ornate carved Victorian love seat, and they sit side by side.

"Nice place," he comments. The building is gently air-conditioned against the heat of the day. "How long has your grandmother lived here?"

"A couple of years…" She trails off. He waits for her to say more, but she stays quiet. He looks around the room, noting the excellent maintenance and the quality of the furniture.

A young woman, dressed similarly to the receptionist, walks through the room on her way to the back hall. "Hi, Jennie." The child waves back.

"Who's that?" he asks.

"I don't know her name. Lots of people work here. Most of them are really nice."

Andrew puzzles over the inconsistency of Jennie's grandmother living in such comfortable surroundings, as compared with the child's own modest home, close to the poverty line. He is about to probe the issue when the receptionist calls to them. "You can see Mrs. Creighton now."

"Thank you!" the child calls out. "Come on, Andrew." She bounces up and heads for the staircase. They climb and come out in a wide upper hallway lined with extra-wide doors. A compact nurses' station sits in an alcove at the far end, unoccupied.

"Gram's room is down here," Jennie says, making her way to the third door on the right. They go inside, to cheerful flowered wallpaper and clean white woodwork. A motorized hospital bed sits to the right, and next to the window, just out of the direct sunlight, an elderly woman sits in a wheelchair. Her hands lie placidly in her lap, and a thick soft collar around her neck supports her head.

Jennie goes to her and drops to her knees in front of the wheelchair, manoeuvring herself into the old woman's line of sight.

"Hi, Gram." There is no response. "I brought my friend Andrew to see you."

She waves to him, and he steps forward. Jennie's grandmother is staring vacantly toward the child, her eyes unfocused. Her chin rests heavily on the padded collar. Her chest rises and falls in slow, shallow breaths.

"Hello, Mrs. Creighton," he ventures.

"I met Andrew on the beach, Gram," Jennie says. "He looks out for me. He said I had to tell you, so you'd know it's okay for me to go there." The old woman stares serenely ahead. The child gets to her feet and leans forward to kiss the seamed and weathered cheek.

Norma Creighton stirs. To Andrew's surprise, awareness creeps into her eyes, and she tilts her head to one side. She smiles. "Elizabeth?"

"No, Gram, it's me. Jennie."

"Are we going home today, Elizabeth?"

Jennie turns to Andrew and speaks softly. "Sometimes she gets a little confused." She turns back and speaks loudly again. "You are home, Gram. This is your room, just like always." She grins broadly, but Andrew sees a tear in the corner of her eye. She wipes it away brusquely.

Norma Creighton's forehead wrinkles in a frown, and her body tenses. She looks into the child's eyes, bewildered but, Andrew thinks, somewhat more aware.

"Want me to read to you?" Jennie turns to Andrew again. "Do you mind? Can we stay for a while?"

Andrew nods silently. He makes his way across the room to sit in a straight wooden chair. Jennie goes to the nightstand beside the bed and finds a small stack of children's books on the lowest shelf. "It doesn't matter what I read," she says to him. "She just likes to hear me talk."

She selects one and goes back to her grandmother's side. She finds a low footstool along the wall and drags it over beside the wheelchair. She sits down and opens the book.

Her clear, youthful voice fills the room, and Andrew glances again at the old woman's face. At the sound of Jennie's sweet cadence, Norma Creighton's features smooth out and her eyes return to their calm gaze at nothing at all. Her withered mouth purses twice, then relaxes into a gentle half smile.

Andrew compares their faces, the very young and the very old, two sides of the puzzle of life. Their eyes are the same, he notes, an intense dark brown amid fair skin, vibrantly pink and fresh on the child, translucent and blue-veined on the grandmother. But where the younger one's eyes are animated and vivacious, the elder's are empty and vacant.

Their faces are also similar, slightly heart-shaped with a softly rounded chin and high, strong cheekbones. Worn and sadly shrunken, Norma Creighton is still a beautiful woman, as only the very old can appear to one who soon will join their ranks.

He can stay no longer. He rises and crosses the room. He touches Jennie's shoulder, and she looks up from her book. He raises his hand, palm forward in front of her face, and waggles it back and forth as if to say, "It's okay, stay here." Then he makes his way out of the room and goes down the stairs.

He steps outside into the sun's intensity and turns toward the riverbank beyond the parking lot. A miniature cove dents the shore, and the breeze, no longer brisk, barely disturbs the surface of the water. A wrought iron bench welcomes him, and he sits down gratefully.

I've seen the future…

*   *   *

Time passes. The sun is nearly overhead when Jennie emerges from the back door and spots him down by the river. She hurries to his side and boosts herself up on the bench.

"Did you like my Gram?"

"Of course I did. And you conned me again, didn't you?"

"I didn't mean to."

"You little monster! You talked me into bringing you here because I thought she could give you permission to go to the beach in the morning."

Jennie hunches her shoulders and shrugs. She stares sadly out over the water.

He relents a bit. "She has Alzheimer's, doesn't she?"

Her eyes are wet when she turns back to him. She nods miserably. He takes out his handkerchief and blots her cheeks gently.

"How old is she?"

"I don't know exactly. Pretty old. She was forty-something when she had Mom, and Mom was past thirty when I was born." She takes a deep breath and straightens up.

"I'm sorry I fooled you," she says.

"You love your grandma, don't you?"

"Uh, huh. She used to live with us until Mom couldn't take care of her any more. We started to run out of money after Dad left, and Mom had to go to work and couldn't stay home with her."

"Where did she work before McDonald's?" he asks.

"At a software place in Bridgewater. She's real good with computers. But they went out of business last month, and she couldn't find anything else." She brightens. "She's been looking for a job in Halifax, though. Maybe we can move there some day."

"I hope so," Andrew says. "Do you know who pays for your

grandmother to stay here?"

"I don't know how it works. Gramps had some kind of insurance. I think Mom said it was just for a nursing home. And there's something else, some kind of a fund…"

"A trust fund, maybe?"

"That's it!" she says. "Gramps was a shipbuilder down in Lunenburg. He had lots of money, Mom says, and he left some of it to us. But I think Dad must have spent it all. He used to work sometimes, but then he'd get drunk and get fired."

"Is your Gramps dead now?"

"Uh, huh. I don't remember him very well, except that he was real nice. And he smelled good. Mom called it bay rum, but I never could figure out what that was."

It seems clear to Andrew that Jennie's maternal grandfather had sized up the child's father pretty well, and had taken steps to protect his own wife. *Too bad he couldn't have done the same for his daughter and granddaughter.*

"So we're right back where we started, aren't we?"

"How come?"

"Well," he says, "you're still going to the beach alone without permission, and riding around with strange men…"

"You're not strange!"

"To your mother, I am. How about if we drive on into Bridgewater and talk to her right now?"

"I'm not allowed."

"Oh, so all of a sudden you're concerned with obeying the rules? That's a switch!"

Jennie slides down off the bench and starts back toward the parking lot, her back rigid and her steps aggressive with barely restrained anger. He watches her go, and when she reaches his car she keeps on walking without looking back. He starts to follow her, and she is halfway to the road before he catches up with her.

"And you're going where?" he asks.

She turns to face him. "Home. I'm going to hitch hike."

He stares at her in exasperation. "You're eleven years old, and you're going to beg a ride from someone you've never met? That's really smart."

"I don't care! I don't want to be with you any more!" She whirls around and stamps off toward the road. She reaches the pavement and starts down the lane to the highway.

How did I get myself into this? He starts after her: "Hang on a minute and let's talk this over."

She keeps on walking, resolute. "You're not very nice, saying I'm stupid!"

"That isn't what I said. I just meant that hitch hiking isn't safe, that's all. Look, slow down a minute. This is really hard on my arthritis."

She skids to a stop. "I didn't know you had arthritis."

"Well, I do." He leans against the split rail fence that lines the road, flexing his knee joint.

She stands looking at him, then moves over beside him. "I'm sorry your leg hurts."

"It's not so bad. Suppose I take you home again, and we do what I suggested yesterday. Later this afternoon I'll come back when your mother gets there."

She stares morosely at the ground. "I'm in a whole lot of trouble, aren't I?"

"Not as bad as it could be."

She looks up at him. "I didn't mean it."

"What?"

"When I said you aren't very nice. I really like you a lot."

"And I really like you a lot, too, Jennie Horton. But if we don't make things right with your mom, we're *both* going to be in a whole lot of trouble with her. So let's do it right this time, okay?"

"All right," she says quietly.

"Come on, I'll race you to the car."

"How about your arthritis?"

"I said I'd race you." He grins. "I didn't say I'd win."

* * *

Andrew pulls into his driveway at quarter after one and gets out of the car. He is reluctant to leave its air-conditioned comfort, but the breeze has returned, this time directly off the bay, and the air is agreeable. He goes inside and checks on Old Cat, finding her asleep in her accustomed place on the windowsill. He goes out to the kitchen and looks in the refrigerator, then in the cupboard. He hasn't been to a store in many days, and there is nothing to eat.

He searches through the drawer beneath the telephone for some stationery, an envelope and a pen. He sits down at the table and begins a brief letter to Russell Baxter, explaining his intention to set up another trust fund and to link it to his will. He names the beneficiary: the juvenile named Jennie Horton, daughter of Elizabeth Horton, resident of Bush Island, Lunenburg County. Then he copies the essence of the letter on another sheet of paper, this time addressed to his lawyer. He signs them both and addresses and stamps the envelopes.

Another thought occurs to him, and he draws out two more sheets of paper. He writes a second letter, brief and to the point, establishing an education fund in support of Miss Nadia Marshall of Green Bay. He makes a second copy for the lawyer, places them in the envelopes, and seals them.

Catherine and the children will still have more than they need. She'll understand. I hope.

He goes outside again and heads for the canteen. As he passes the takeout window he sees Josh Watson waiting on a customer. He waits for the young man to finish, but a line is beginning to form. He steps up close to the side of the window.

"Josh, can you do me a favour?" he interrupts, waving the envelopes. "I need these to go out in the mail today."

"Just leave them on the counter inside. I'll run them up on my way home."

"Thanks. I really appreciate it."

"No problem."

Andrew steps inside and places the letters next to the cash register. He looks around the empty dining room and is reminded once more of Nadia. Another thought crosses his mind, and he resolves to do something about it right away, in case he forgets later. He leaves the canteen and returns to his cottage.

Once inside, he enters the kitchen and locates two more sheets of paper. On the first he writes a simple sentence: "All of the books on this shelf are to be given to Miss Nadia Marshall, waitress at the Green Bay Canteen." He signs his name at the bottom.

He takes the second sheet and writes, "This book is to be given to Miss Jennie Horton, Bush Island." He signs that one too, then carries both pages into the living room and walks over to the bookcase. He slips the first sheet under the row of his novels on the top shelf, hanging out part way over the edge in plain sight. Then he finds the book about marine life and puts the second sheet between its pages, sticking up well above the top.

Satisfied, he goes outside again and crosses the road. The fine white sand and clear, clean water across the road from his cottage have attracted many residents and casual visitors on this hot August day, and the beach is more crowded than usual. He has no desire to be among strangers.

He trudges along the shoreline, leaving the sand behind for the less hospitable gravel bed that stretches south along the unpopulated part of Green Bay. He circles a rock outcropping, seeking solitude, and hears instead a voice calling out his name. He turns and sees Nadia Marshall running to catch up.

Penny reaches his side. Her soft, red-gold hair bounces on her shoulders, and he reaches out to brush it from her face. She smiles up at him.

"Hi, Dad!"

"Hi, sweetheart."

"What did you call me?" Nadia says, surprised.

Andrew recoils abruptly. Penny's face evaporates, becoming first a stranger's, then reforming itself into Nadia's again. Dark-haired Nadia, not Penny. He recovers. "I'm sorry. I thought you were someone else."

"That's okay. Where've you been?"

"Just out driving." He notices her swimsuit. "How come you're not working today?"

"We don't get much business after about one thirty. Josh and I trade off every other day, and today's his turn. Did you have lunch?"

He puzzles over the question. "I think so."

"Bet you didn't. Come on, let's get a burger."

"I'm sorry, Penny. I'm just not hungry."

She regards him with concern. "I'm not Penny, Dr. Striker."

"Of course you're not!" he says impatiently. He turns in embarrassment and heads off down the beach again.

"Hey, wait up!" She reaches his side once more. "Want some company?"

"Not really."

She stops walking, and he continues on. After a dozen steps he turns and sees her standing there, staring sadly after him. "I'm sorry, Nadia. I didn't mean to be rude. I'm just not likely to be a very good companion today, that's all. You should be off with your friends, people your own age."

She starts forward slowly. "My choice," she says.

He grimaces, wanting to brush her off but reluctant to hurt her feelings any further. Vague tendrils of fog begin to tease the edges of his consciousness.

"It's nice out here, isn't it?" she says. "Mom thinks it's the best spot in the whole world. Dad says we're never going to sell our place. Then I'll always have it to come back to, even after I graduate."

He walks on in silence, but she refuses to be put off. "Mom says God must love Nova Scotia to make it so beautiful here." He turns his head and gives her a sceptical glance, then shrugs and continues on.

"Not a believer, huh?" she says.

"Two things I try never to discuss are politics and religion. They always lead to arguments."

"So you must think the whole world is just some kind of accident, right? That's what my science teacher says."

"See what I mean? You're trying to start an argument."

"No I'm not. I haven't really figured out what I believe yet, and I like to ask questions."

"Good for you," he says. "When it comes to religion, the questions are a lot more important than the answers, although many people will try to tell you otherwise."

"So I suppose you don't think the world was made by God.

That it all just came together on its own."

"There's no evidence of anything else."

"Sure there is. The Bible, for example."

They reach Long Point, well out of sight of the Green Bay beach and canteen. Andrew's knee begins to pain him. He finds a path that winds between a saw grass-covered dune and a low escarpment, and heads down toward the water. Nadia follows along. The rocks lie in a gentle crescent, forming a natural sheltered cove, edged by fine white sand and out of the wind: a miniature natural cathedral.

"Haven't you ever read the Bible?" she persists.

"Of course I have, and it's wonderful literature," he agrees. "But so is the Talmud, and the Koran, and... Look, the basic premise behind all holy books is that they're either the work of some god, or that the writers were divinely inspired. To accept that, you have to believe in an overall intelligence, a supernatural personality of some kind that affects human affairs."

"So what's wrong with that?"

He sinks down on a flat boulder and stretches his right leg out to knead his knee. She folds her legs in a modified yoga squat and sits on the sand in front of him.

"There's nothing wrong with it, if that's the way you want to believe the universe operates. But there's no way to prove it, either. No independent evidence. And it doesn't fit in with what I think I've learned and observed."

"Which is what?" she persists.

"Years ago, before humans began to understand how the natural world works, it was easy to ascribe everything, good and bad, to the gods. Storms and floods and diseases were divine vengeance. Remember the Ark story?"

"Our minister says there's lots of evidence for a world-wide flood."

"The known world then, maybe. All the evidence points to the Mediterranean Sea overflowing into the Black Sea at the Bosporus a long time ago."

"Where's that?" Nadia asks.

"Turkey, at Istanbul. Anyway, when the Bible was written,

people didn't have any way to travel very far. Most of them thought that where they lived was the whole world, so a flood like that would seem to be world-wide."

Nadia leaned forward eagerly, her eyes shining with interest and curiosity. "So the Noah story is true!"

"Whoa! That's a big leap. Just because there was a flood of some kind, that doesn't prove some man built a boat to save all the animals. Think about how many different species there are on earth. That would have to have been some big boat."

"Lots of people believe in it."

"Besides," Andrew continued, "the flood legend didn't start with Noah. Ever hear of Gilgamesh?"

"Who's that?"

"Supposed to have been a king of Sumeria, and there's a flood story about him too, even older than the Bible."

"There!" She sat straight up abruptly. "It must have happened, then. My teacher says any time you find corroborating evidence from another source, something is more likely to be true."

Andrew smiled at her attempt at logic. "It supports the theory that there was a flood. But not that there was an Ark. See the difference?"

Nadia cocks her head to one side. "Not exactly."

Andrew takes a deep breath. The first faint pulses of headache throb at his temples. He adjusts his position, leaning over onto his left hip and taking the weight off his other leg.

"Look at it this way. There are always events in the world that are hard to explain, good things and bad. Like an epidemic, or a bunch of people killed in an earthquake. Or good things, like a big crop of wheat or a victory in war. These were facts, things that actually happened, and once ancient people developed written language, they wrote them down. That's history."

"What's that got to do with…"

"Hang on, I'm getting to it. When something happens that's out of our control, people tend to look for a reason why it happened. And if they can't find a logical explanation, they invent one. That's often called folklore."

"Myths and stuff."

"Right. And practically every civilization has stories about some sort of gods, very powerful beings who look like us and who rule the world and make things happen, good and bad."

"What's that got to do with history?"

"Suppose we know from a variety of sources that a war happened someplace, and it was a great victory for one of the sides. That's verifiable history. But if one of the winning generals records that he prayed to his god before the battle, and that's why they won, that's folklore. There's no way to prove cause and effect between the prayers and the victory."

"But doesn't every culture have some sort of religion?"

"Just about," he concedes.

"And like Noah and Gilga-whoever, don't they sometimes have the same stories?"

"Sometimes."

"So if two different civilizations have the same stories," Nadia says reasonably, "doesn't that mean they could be true? Corroborating evidence again."

"But if one person *makes up* a story, and a thousand other people believe it and repeat it, that doesn't make it true. Later on it just seems like it's coming from all those different sources, that's all."

She considered this a moment. "So you think the Bible is all myth?"

"No. There's plenty of evidence from many other reliable sources that a lot of the events in holy books like the Bible actually happened. But that's not the same as saying that some kind of god made them happen."

"Okay, now I see. But that doesn't prove that our god doesn't exist, either."

"You're right. There's no reliable evidence either way, so we're free to believe whatever we want to."

"So I suppose you don't believe in prayer, either."

"On the contrary, I think it's a very powerful force in the world. But not for the obvious reason." His head has begun to ache in earnest, and he has to focus his attention carefully, examining each thought before he speaks.

"What's the obvious reason?"

"Okay, let's take a really foolish example, one that makes me laugh every time I hear about it. Apparently it's the custom for some supposedly Christian athletes, and even some whole teams, to pray for success before every game."

"So what's wrong with that?"

"Think about it. The universe is so vast we haven't even begun to see the end of it, even with our most powerful telescopes, and our whole planet is the tiniest possible speck lost somewhere in the middle. If all of this was deliberately made by some god, some supernatural person or thing, that being would have to be unimaginably immense and powerful. And should we expect this fantastic superbeing to take sides in a football game?"

She laughs. "Good point. But what's that got to do with whether prayer works?"

"It works because that football player *thinks* it does. He convinces himself that God is on his side, and it pumps him up. He works like hell at being the best player he can be, and that makes him more successful. So when he wins, it has to be because God has answered his prayer. It's self fulfilling."

"What if he loses?" she suggests.

"Well, perhaps he thinks it's because he's unworthy of God's help. So he tries all the harder to be worthy. Faith is a funny thing. If you really believe, you have a vested interest in doing everything possible to prove your belief is justified."

Nadia is intrigued. "Why can't it be the other way around? Why can't he win the game because God *does* think he's worthy, and helps him?"

Andrew sighs, frustrated at the encroaching tendrils of fog that cloud his mind and keep him from formulating a convincing scenario. "Could be. I'm not saying I'm right. I just don't see any evidence that there's a god of some kind that picks winners and losers among the human race."

They fall silent for a few moments and he gazes out to sea. He feels her eyes on him and turns to see expectation in her eyes. He tries again.

"Look at it this way. The Judeo-Christian Bible says God is perfect, right?"

"I guess."

His head throbs, and he struggles to form an argument that won't seem banal. "So if he's perfect, he's above all the things that make us humans so miserable: hate, envy, spite, even competition, like the need to win. If he's the *only* god, he's *already* won. What possible pleasure or reward could such a magnificent being derive from choosing to favour one person, or one football team, over another? How could he be so petty?"

"Okay, so the football analogy is silly. But how about praying for more important things?"

He searches for something more meaningful. "September Eleventh is a better example. As far as we know, the terrorists believed that their god wanted them to attack the United States. Because they believed that, they decided that what they did was justified. In their minds, that made it good, not evil."

"They were fanatics, that's all. Crazy."

"Sure. But they succeeded, didn't they? Thousands of people died. And when it was over, people here began to pray to our god to protect them from any future attacks. Apparently it didn't occur to them that a lot of the people on those planes, the ones that hit the World Trade Towers and the Pentagon, must have been praying, too. And it didn't do *them* any good."

"Still…"

"Look, Nadia, right after the attacks, when the United States started to mobilize its attack against the terrorists, what was the slogan that popped up all over, on TV and in magazine ads, everywhere?"

"I can't remember."

"It was 'God Bless America.' And that's just another way of saying, 'God is on our side.' How was that different from the terrorists thinking that their god was on *their* side?"

"But they were fanatics…"

He shrugs. "Right. Which means they believed strongly that they were right, and that they must be doing what their god wanted them to do."

"And you're saying the Americans believe the same thing? They're fanatics, too?"

"Some of them, maybe. It doesn't seem so very different to me. Don't get me wrong, I believe we have to fight terrorism. What happened on September Eleventh was very wrong, a terrible evil. But if God is real, and he actually takes sides in such matters, would he have let it happen in the first place? Or maybe he was on the terrorists' side after all, but that's too frightening even to contemplate. In our western civilization, God has to be good, not evil. But that's what we *believe*, not what we can prove."

Nadia sighs. "This is all too complicated for me." She brightens. "God must look after some people, though. Remember the end of last winter, that awful car crash on Highway 101 in the Annapolis Valley? The trailer truck that smashed into a van outside Coldbrook?"

"I remember."

"So the whole van was smashed flat, and the whole family was killed, the mom and dad and three kids, thrown all over the highway. Except one little baby in a car seat was tossed out, and landed in the ditch under a culvert. They didn't even find him until the next day."

Andrew shifts uncomfortably. "What's the point?"

"So he wasn't hurt, but it was freezing cold. Nobody could figure out why he didn't die, so they said God took care of him. It was in all the papers, and it makes sense to me. God looked out for him."

His eye is on the sparrow, Andrew thinks.

"I remember," he says. "But God didn't save his mother or father, did he? Or his brothers and sisters. Why him and not them?"

"I don't know."

"And that same day, in a South American country, I think, a bus crashed into a truck and twelve children died. In Italy an earthquake struck a town, and the only building that collapsed was a school, killing all the children. So should we believe in a God who chooses whom to save and whom to let die? Is that how the creator of this amazingly complex universe would be likely to operate? By choosing favourites?"

Nadia sits still for several minutes. "I'm going to have to think about this. A lot!"

"Good. And remember, I may be way off base. You have to reach your own conclusions, and I'm not trying to convince you of anything. But I just don't believe these questions have been answered yet, despite what fanatics, and even moderate believers, have to say. Anyone who says God is on their side is claiming to know the mind of God, whatever that is, and I don't think the evidence is all in yet."

Nadia stands up and looks at her watch. "Guess we won't solve all the world's problems this afternoon. And I've got to go back to work soon."

Andrew flexes his knee and gets to his feet. Nausea strikes him, but he tries to hide it from her. His mind feels fuzzy and unclear. "I'll go back with you. Old Cat will be getting hungry too."

They leave the cove and start off in the direction of the canteen. He limps painfully, and she waits for him to catch up. They make their way slowly toward Green Bay.

"I don't suppose you believe in life after death, either," she says quietly.

"Again, there's no evidence for it."

"Not even spirits? Practically every culture has had legends about them, like that folklore you were talking about. If everybody believes it…"

"Ever seen a ghost yourself?" he interrupts.

"That's not the point. Aren't legends the way history used to get passed down? Real events, I mean."

"Sure. But fiction survives that way, too. The only way to be sure which is which is to have that independent corroboration you mentioned, and some way to be sure someone didn't just make it up. To the best of my knowledge, there's never been any supernatural occurrence that couldn't be explained in some other way."

"How about when the Holy Spirit visited the Virgin Mary so that Jesus could be born? If that isn't true, how come the story has lasted for so many years?"

"It's a powerful story," he agrees, "and many, many people believe it. But faith isn't evidence. Faith is most often what people *want* to believe, not what really is."

Andrew is reluctant to pursue the topic further. He pauses by the shore and studies a flock of gulls on a solitary rock fifty yards offshore from the beach.

Nadia steps up close to his side. "People have to believe in something, don't they?" she says quietly.

"Do they?" He bends and picks up a flat rock and skips it over the water. One, two, three bounces, then out of sight forever.

Forever...

He tries again. "Look, the story of the virgin birth is a great miracle, right?"

"I think so."

"And have you ever read the mythology of Greece and Rome? All the old gods were forever coming down to earth and copulating with mortals to produce offspring. It was a staple in many of the legends."

"That's sick! And those stories were just made up!"

"I think so, too. So how is that different from the story of the Holy Spirit impregnating Mary?"

Nadia bristles. "That's not how it was!"

"So myths are always fiction, but the Bible stories are true, right?"

"Yes! Maybe not always, but in this case, yes."

"And we know this because the Bible says it's the word of God, right?"

"Right!"

"Just like all holy books say they're the word of their god..."

"Now wait a minute..."

"And the corroborating evidence is...?"

She grimaces and turns halfway away from him, her shoulders rigid with frustration.

"You see what I mean?" he says to her back. "That's why I try never to discuss religion with anyone, and I shouldn't have done it with you. Look, I'm probably wrong, okay? Let's just forget it."

She turns back to face him, her expression bleak. "So you don't believe in anything?"

He shrugs and turns away again. Her quiet voice penetrates

the still air.

"It's no wonder you're so sad."

His head is pounding. He tosses another stone, then backs away from the water and starts walking again. She waits a moment, then hurries to catch up with him. They trudge on in silence. Finally, trying to lighten the mood, he asks, "What time do you start serving dinner again?"

"I have to be back by four. We don't get many in before five, but I have to start making the chowder and stuff, and get everything set up."

"It's almost that time now. Maybe I'll come by a little later and see what's on the menu."

"That'll be great! Mom bought some haddock down at the pier this morning, and she's going to bread it. She's got a real good recipe that my aunt used to make."

He doesn't respond, and she stares at him intently, wondering if he is listening.

"It's really fresh. She got it right off the boat."

"I used to sail," he says finally. "I had a friend, Charlie Melanson was his name..."

Charlie Melanson? Is that right?

"He had a boat, fibreglass, had a cabin that slept six or seven. He and his wife, and Catherine and I..." Andrew falls silent. *Who was Charlie's wife?*

"Does he still have the boat?" she asks.

"Who?"

"Mr. Melanson."

"*Doctor* Melanson," he corrects her. "What about him?"

Nadia tries to bring him back on track. "Where did you sail to?"

"Charlie used to get seasick. That's pretty funny, owned his own boat and got seasick whenever the wind came up. One time we were off St. Margaret's Bay, and the wind was coming up the coast so we had to tack all the way down. Rollers coming in, pitched the boat like a... Like a... Grant! Charlie *Grant* was his name. My best friend..."

He stumbles and sits down on a rock, favouring his right knee. Nadia sinks down beside him, her eyes intent upon his face, waiting for him to continue. When he doesn't, she finds a dried sea urchin and leans over to pick it up. A half crescent is broken out of its shell. She holds it up for him to see.

A half smile bends Andrew's mouth, and his eyes look through her and past her, clouded and unfocused.

"Want to take that back to show Mommie, sweetheart?"

Nadia draws back, frowning. She drops the shell and stares intently into his bewildered eyes.

"We have to go back now, Penny," he says lethargically. "Your mother will be worried about us."

He makes no move to get up, and his shoulders slump forward. Nadia reaches for his hand. It lies limply in her own as he gazes off over the ocean, seeming to forget she is there.

"Doc? Dr. Striker?" He ignores her and she sits in silence, still holding his flaccid upturned hand. She places her left hand on top and traces the lines in his palm, but he sits unresponsive and unaware. Long minutes pass.

"We had to put him off…"

Nadia snaps to attention. "Who?"

"Charlie. His face was green as grass. We put him off his own boat, took him ashore in St. Margaret's Bay and left him to find his own way down once he got over being sick. The three of us took the boat the rest of the way. His own boat!" Andrew laughs gently.

"Where were you going?"

"Didn't I tell you? Chester Basin. He rented a new mooring down there. He used to keep the boat at the Armdale Yacht Club, but we spent most of our time sailing down here among the islands, so he figured he'd find a place closer down along the shore."

"Does he still have the boat?"

He looks down. His hand rests between both of hers, and he stares at it in confusion. "Did something happen just now?" he asks.

She releases him. "Don't you remember?"

"I guess not." His expression is distracted and troubled.

"You were talking about your friend getting seasick, and then you just stopped for a while. Anyway, does your friend still have his boat at Chester Basin?"

"He keeps it… He kept it…" He pauses in dazed confusion. "Charlie is dead."

"I'm sorry."

He breathes deeply and straightens his back. "It was a long time ago." He looks around. "Where are we?"

"Almost back from Long Point. Dr. Striker, do you know who I am?"

"Of course I do, Nadia."

"You didn't before. I think you were talking to your daughter."

"That's ridiculous! Penny lives in Ottawa." He stands up abruptly and walks several paces away from her.

"I know, but…"

"Why aren't you working at the restaurant?"

"I had some time off, remember? I was going back now." She pauses, watching him closely. "You were walking me back."

"What?" *For Christ's sake! What's going on here?*

They skirt around the outcropping that separates the gravel from the public beach and come upon the bathers sunning themselves along the shore, young mothers mostly, a few teenagers, many children. Andrew feels suddenly very much out of place, an old, tired man in rumpled clothes, walking beside this lovely young woman, this girl in a swimsuit, this child… Child…

They pass a group of children making sand castles with their plastic pails. He slows and then stops to watch them. A tiny girl with strawberry blond hair looks up, and he smiles at her. He turns to go, then looks back again. "Penny…"

"That isn't Penny, Dr. Striker," Nadia says softly. He shakes his head as if to clear it, and she takes his hand and draws him away. After a half dozen steps he pulls up short and looks back.

"She shouldn't be out here alone," he says. "Jennie?" The children pause in their play and stare at him. Nadia tugs at his arm.

He turns to go with her, letting her lead him from the beach and onto the shoulder of the road. "That's Jennie," he says. "She comes to the beach sometimes. To play with Penny, I think."

He stops again and stares wildly around him in confusion. His eyes drift to Nadia's concerned face, and in one last lucid moment he recognizes her and understands what is happening. His face collapses, and tears pour out of his eyes.

*   *   *

Nadia is supporting his slumping form as he tries to climb over the low rock wall along the beach. She spots her mother coming across the road from the canteen.

"Mom, I need help!" she calls out.

Fran hurries forward and reaches out to grasp Andrew's elbow. "What happened?"

"Oh Mom, I don't know. Can we just get him inside?"

One on each side, the two women help him across the road and up the path to his cottage. Nadia finds his keys in his pocket and unlocks the door. They guide him into the living room.

Andrew sags into the armchair and closes his reddened eyes. Mother and daughter move to the far side of the room and talk in whispers.

"What's going on?" Fran asks.

"We were just walking on the beach, talking," Nadia replies. "He seemed fine most of the time, but every once in a while he called me Penny. He seemed to think I was his daughter. We got to talking about religion and stuff, and he got kind of upset."

"Maybe we should call nine-one-one."

Nadia looks over at his wilted form. "What's wrong with him, Mom?"

"Some kind of dementia, I think," Fran answers. "Maybe Alzheimer's disease. I've heard that in some people it sort of comes and goes."

"Just before you came, he was talking about somebody else. He had lunch with a little girl, her name was Jennie, I think, and he thought he saw her on the beach. Then he looked at me and his face all screwed up, and he started to cry."

Fran shook her head. "Didn't you tell me he was a college

professor?"

"That's what he said. At Acadia."

"He doesn't seem that old, either. It's sad…"

"Can't we do anything?"

"I think it's best just to let him sleep for right now," her mother says. "He's not like this all the time, is he?"

"No. Most of the time he seems okay."

"Then we'll wait until he's awake again, and if he knows where he is, we'll try to talk to him. Convince him to get some help."

Nadia moves over to Andrew's side, and Fran leaves the room and goes down the hall. Presently she returns with a blanket from his bed and places it over him. His eyes are closed, and his breathing is shallow but regular.

"Josh is all alone," Fran says quietly. "We have to get back to the canteen. He'll probably stay asleep. One of us can come back every so often to check on him."

"I'm scared to leave him," Nadia says. "He gets so confused sometimes."

"We'll do what we can, but we have our own responsibilities." Fran heads for the door, and Nadia returns Andrew's keys to his pocket. Then she follows her mother reluctantly. They go out into the warm afternoon.

*   *   *

Old Cat wanders out of the bedroom and paces down the hall. She enters the living room and drifts over beside Andrew's chair. She emits one of her distinctive yowls, and he opens his eyes in confusion. He discovers the blanket that covers him and wonders how it got there.

The cat jumps up on his lap. He strokes her head and she turns around three times and kneads the blanket. A lethargic peace settles over him, and he shifts in the chair to give her more room. Old Cat lies down and begins to wash and Andrew drifts off to sleep again, forgetting his promise to go to meet Jennie's mother that afternoon.

Running Away

Andrew pulled into the driveway and stopped in front of the garage door. The drive from the airport had taken just under an hour. He removed his suitcase from the trunk and went into the house through the front door.

A small pile of mail lay under the slot in the door. He leafed through it distractedly, noting how little that was addressed to him was of any importance: a few bills, several ads. The rest was for his wife.

Won't leave much of a void when I'm gone...

He had much to accomplish before Catherine's return. Thanks to the groundwork he had laid before going to Ottawa with her, all of the financial arrangements were in place. But the details of arranging his departure remained, as did hiding his destination from her, and finding for himself a place to live where no one would be likely to find him.

He knew that the kindest thing would be to spare his family the spectacle of the final and inevitable disintegration of his personality. No matter how painful his physical absence might be for them, it would be quick and final. The alternative, the gradual mental dissolution of all that made him dear to them, would be infinitely worse.

All he could do, all he *had* done, was insure that Catherine and the children would never know want because of his actions.

Finding no reason to delay further, he called the real estate agent in Bridgewater and confirmed his intention to rent, sight unseen, a small cottage that stood near to the waters of Green Bay. Then he set about dealing with the few personal possessions he planned to take with him. Once they were assembled he surveyed them sadly: clothing, some books, a few recordings of favourite music. They seemed a pitifully small summation of his life, no more than would fit in his car for a single journey away from what had gone before.

The most difficult part of his preparations, his letter to Catherine, he put off until the following day.

* * *

Arising early the next morning, Andrew packed the car with everything he would need at the cottage. Then he spent the next several hours bringing order to his library, his photographic equipment and his extensive collection of antique toy trains, all of which were to be left behind for Catherine to dispose of. Handling his beloved treasures, especially the exquisite model trains, filled him with joy at their beauty. Packing them away prompted an almost unbearable sadness as they disappeared from his sight, probably forever.

Shortly after noon everything was accounted for. He stacked the boxes in one corner of the basement and placed detailed inventory pages on top. He took one last reluctant look at them and debated selecting one locomotive, perhaps one complete train set, to take with him. He bent and began to reopen a box.

Then he shook his head sadly, thinking it better to have nothing to remind him of past pleasures. He replaced the lid on the box and stood up again. He made his way to the stairs and climbed back up to the first floor.

One task remained: the letter to Catherine. He walked down the hall to his office and sat at his desk, uncertain of how to begin.

Dearest Catherine, of course. And then what?

For nearly half an hour he attempted paragraph after paragraph, vainly searching for words to explain what he had to do, and why he was doing it. Some of the sentences were sterile, some uncomfortably maudlin, and none conveyed the agony he felt at leaving behind the essence of their life together. He could never explain it in words she could accept.

He crumpled and threw away page after page, sitting in frustrated despair. Finally he determined how it must be done, simply and with a minimum of explanation. He removed the discarded pages from the wastebasket and carried them to the fireplace and lit them with a match. He watched as they dissolved into ashes, those awkward and stillborn attempts at communication hidden forever from Catherine and the children. Then he returned to his desk and drew a fresh sheet of paper to him. This time the words flowed easily.

My dearest Catherine,

I am leaving. Words can never explain the reason, and so I trust to your love to accept that I do what I must.

All of our affairs are in order, and if you contact the bank, Trevor will explain the details to you. I know you can count on him to see that you and the children will be well provided for.

Please do not try to find me, as it will only cause both of us much unnecessary grief. And please believe that my absence represents no lack of love for you. It is instead because I love you too much.

Remember the good times, my dearest, every day of your life. You gave me so much, and I am forever grateful for your love.

Andrew

He folded the paper and placed it in an envelope. He wrote her name on the front and carried it with him into the kitchen. He placed it in the centre of the table. Without a backward glance he went into the garage, got in the car, and started the engine.

NINE...

Jennie sits expectantly by the window, hoping for Andrew to arrive before her mother arrives home. Every minute or so she glances at the clock that rests on the bookcase. Nearly four thirty. The minutes creep slowly by, and she wanders restlessly into the kitchen. She opens the refrigerator, looks inside, then closes it again. She stands indecisively in the middle of the floor, her arms crossed over her thin chest, hugging herself.

She hears the crunch of gravel on the east side of the house and runs to the window. Her mother is getting out of their car. Jennie watches as Elizabeth Horton opens the back door and releases her little sister from the car seat. Five-year-old Nancy tumbles out of the car and runs toward the house. Jennie goes to the door and opens it.

"Hi, Nance."

"Jennie, look what I've got!" Bouncing with excitement, Nancy thrusts a wrinkled manila page in front of her. The edges are ragged, torn from a bound colouring book, and the image is a black outline of a ballerina, gaily crayoned.

"Did you do this all by yourself?" Jennie examines the crayon marks, far more of them within the lines than in any of her little sister's previous efforts. Nancy beams proudly and nods. Their mother reaches the door, juggling her purse and two grocery bags.

"Hi, Mom. You're late." Jennie hands the picture back to her sister and reaches up to help, taking one of the bags from her mother's arms and carrying it toward the kitchen.

"I had to do the shopping." Elizabeth turns to her youngest daughter. "Run upstairs and change your clothes, sweetheart. You can wear those shorts again tomorrow."

Nancy runs for the stairs and Elizabeth turns and walks into the kitchen. Jennie is unloading the bag, placing the canned goods on the counter and the frozen things in the upper compartment of the refrigerator.

Her mother sets the second grocery bag down. "Where were you today?"

"Right here," Jennie says casually.

"I don't think so."

"You talked to me on the phone, remember? I called you back."

"What I remember is, you gave me a song and dance about being out in the yard and not hearing the phone. Then I waited for five minutes and called you back again, and no one answered."

Jennie's face turns ashen. She regards her mother silently. Elizabeth begins to unload the rest of the food, and Jennie carries the items to the cupboard and slowly and deliberately places them inside.

When they finish, Elizabeth says, "We have to talk about this." She beckons, and Jennie follows her into the living room. Music is coming from Nancy's tape recorder upstairs, and muffled thumps suggest she is trying to emulate her Crayola ballerina.

Mother and daughter sit side by side on the sofa. "It's time you told me what you've been up to."

"Nothing, Mom."

"I'm sorry, dear, but I don't believe you. You know it worries me to be leaving you home alone during the day, and if you don't answer the phone, I don't know what to think."

"Geez, I have to go to the bathroom sometimes! And you can't expect me to sit in the house all the time. Nothing's going to happen to me out in the yard."

"I let the phone ring twelve times today."

"I guess I just didn't hear it."

"Where did you go?"

Jennie fidgets and looks down at her hands. "I was just out back somewhere. Out in the woods by the stream."

"You could have heard the phone from there."

"Well, I didn't!"

Elizabeth regards her daughter's defiant face for several long moments. "If I can't trust you, we're going to have to make some other arrangements."

"Please, Mom," Jennie begs, "I haven't been doing anything wrong. Give me another chance."

Her mother stands up. "From now on, whenever I call, you have to be right here."

"I will. I promise!"

"All right, we'll see." She sits down again and gathers the child's hands up in her own. "Sweetheart, you and Nance are all I have in the whole world that's important to me. If anything happens to you…"

"I'm *fine*, Mom. Nothing's going to happen to me." Jennie's mind races over the past few days, her encounters with her new friend, her dangerous bike ride.

I can take care of myself.

Elizabeth's eyes linger on Jennie's anxious, pleading face, making the child uncomfortable and apprehensive. Then she gathers her into her arms. "After supper we'll go over the rules again, okay?"

"Okay! Thanks, Mom."

"You'd better not be scamming me."

"Who, me?" Jennie's mock indignation mixes with a sense of relief. But she knows she will have to be very, very careful from now on.

* * *

Catherine enters the house from the garage and sees the flashing light on the answering machine. She drops her purse on the counter and presses the play button. An official-sounding voice comes from the speaker.

"This is Corporal Jeffrey Comeau, Bridgewater Detachment of the RCMP. I'm calling about a gentleman named Andrew Striker, whose name is listed for this number."

Oh my God, something has happened to him.

"I spoke with Mr. Striker yesterday afternoon, and I'm trying to contact someone who knows him, a relative or a close friend. Please call me as soon as possible." He recites the telephone number of the Bridgewater RCMP detachment, and the recording ends.

He spoke with him. That means he's all right.

Catherine scribbles down the number and is about to punch it in when the answering machine begins to play a second message.

"This is Corporal Matt Burgess, New Minas RCMP. I'm calling for Mr. Andrew Striker or for anyone in his family, on behalf of Corporal Jeffrey Comeau."

Again an official request for a return call, and again a number to return the call, this time on the 681 New Minas exchange. Catherine writes it down and shuts the answering machine off.

Of the two choices she opts for the nearby New Minas Detachment and calls the number, asking for Corporal Burgess when the duty officer answers.

"May I tell him who is calling, please, and the nature of your business?"

"Catherine Striker, returning his call," she says impatiently, irritated at the delay.

"One moment."

Catherine fidgets as the line emits a series of clicks. The passing seconds seem to her to be hours, until finally another voice speaks to her.

"Matthew Burgess. Is this Mrs. Striker?"

"Yes. Is it about my husband?"

"You're married to Andrew Striker, ma'am?"

"Yes, yes!"

"We've been trying to reach you."

"I know," she snaps impatiently. "I was out of town for a few days, and I just got back. What is it?"

"A member of the Bridgewater Detachment relayed a message to us yesterday. He found Mr. Striker sitting in his car, somewhat confused, and helped him to find his way home. The officer thought some member of the family should know."

"Home? Did the officer bring him here?"

"I understand Mr. Striker is living in a cottage somewhere near LaHave."

Catherine fights down feelings of panic. She has found no trace of her husband in the year that he has been gone. The relief she feels at hearing where he may be is tempered by the fear that he could be in some sort of trouble.

"Do you have an address?" she asks.

"Not an exact one. You can get that from Corporal Comeau. His number is…"

"Never mind, I have it. Thank you very much, Corporal Burgess."

"My pleasure, Mrs. Striker. I hope everything works out well for you."

Catherine disconnects and calls the Bridgewater exchange number. "Corporal Comeau, please."

"I'm sorry, Corporal Comeau is out of the office. May I take a message?"

Catherine feels the panic begin to rise again. "He called me two days ago about my husband. He's been missing for over a year, and he found him, and he called me to tell me."

The repetitive pronouns confuse the issue, and the voice on the other end of the line prompts her to slow down. Trying to compose herself, Catherine starts over. As soon as she explains the problem, the officer promises to make contact with Comeau and call her back. Catherine relays her number and disconnects. Then she hangs up and sits nervously by the instrument, willing it to ring.

* * *

Jennie and Nancy help clear away the dishes after supper, and the younger child settles down to watch TV.

"Can I go outside for a while?" Jennie asks her mother.

"Where to?"

"Maybe down to see Michael."

"Okay, but no farther. And be back before it gets dark."

"I will." She heads for the front door and goes outside. She picks up her bicycle from beside the front steps and pedals out of the yard onto the road.

The evening is warm and the air almost still. She approaches the Bush Island bridge, stopping for a only a moment in front of her friend's house. She sees Michael in the distance, playing with two other children in the back yard, but she remounts the bike and starts off again, crossing the bridge and pedaling hard. She soon reaches the eastern end of Crescent Beach.

She can't understand why Andrew never appeared. He had seemed so intent on making her confess to her mother, and she had hoped that they could all reach some sort of understanding that would allow her to go to the beach without lying about it.

She wheels the bike off the road and into some bushes, concealing it from any casual passerby. She walks down onto the beach and starts off in the direction of the public bathing area. There are only a few cars on the sand, the closest one standing alone in front of the pilings and the others much farther off near the ramp that leads to Route 331. She looks to see if any of them might be Andrew's, but all are unfamiliar to her.

She can see just the roofs of several more vehicles above and to the left of the ramp, their bodies mostly hidden by the large, wave-smoothed rocks. She decides to see if Andrew has parked up there, and strides off purposefully.

Halfway down the beach she comes upon the solitary car on the sand. She can clearly see two male figures sitting inside. The one in the driver's seat is smoking; the glow from the tip of his cigarette flares brightly with each inhalation. The other is drinking beer from a can.

Instinctively she veers away from the car toward the water's edge. As she passes by, the sound of a horn startles her. She looks toward the car, and the passenger side window rolls down. A stubble-shadowed face peers out at her, stained teeth in a wet mouth, stringy black hair.

"Hello, little girl. Do you want some candy?"

Jennie lifts her chin and stalks off, followed by raucous laughter from inside the car. She increases her pace and soon comes abreast of the next vehicle, the first of four parked near the foot of the ramp. Although it is empty, she gives it a wide berth. A number of teenagers are down by the shore, just at the edge of the water. Two are tossing a football.

One car's engine starts up, and the driver pulls out of line and starts up the incline, leaving only two cars and a decrepit van remaining near the bottom of the ramp. She passes the last of them and makes her way up to where she can see those that are parked on the upper level. She is disappointed to find that Andrew's is not among them.

She climbs to the top of one of the rocks and sits down dejectedly. The air is damp and heavy and the sun hangs low in the sky, partially obscured by dense, patchy clouds. The atmosphere feels vaguely threatening: the first hint of rain to come, perhaps a wind storm overnight or the next day. The beach no longer seems welcoming.

She watches as the teenagers gather their blankets and stuff them in through the sliding door of the battered minivan. A child comes out of one of the portable toilets beside the road and hurries down the ramp to join his family. He helps his father collect his plastic toys, and they get into their car and drive off, followed closely by the teenagers in the van.

Why didn't he come to the house like he promised?

The sun is now dropping rapidly toward the horizon, and Jennie climbs reluctantly down from her perch. Another car leaves the lot, and the beach is now almost deserted. Thinking she had better be home before her mother starts to worry, she skips down the ramp and begins to jog eastward. Within a few minutes she tires, and settles for a fast walk.

She is shuffling among the seaweed along the high tide line, hoping to spot a starfish and paying little attention to her surroundings, when she hears the sound of a car door opening. She looks up and sees two figures emerging from the isolated car a hundred yards ahead.

Jennie continues on cautiously, watching as the two men amble slowly in the direction of the water. Both are shabbily dressed and carry beer cans. When they get to the tide line, they stop and take a long drink. They turn away from her, talking to each other, and she sidles left to pass between them and their car.

As she comes within range, one of the men spins abruptly and runs to cut her off. Panicked, she skids to a stop and looks around desperately for help. The only other car is far off down the beach behind her with no one near it. She whirls and sprints toward the water. The second man darts after her and catches the flapping tail of her tee shirt. His other hand clamps onto her upper arm.

Jennie screams and tries to hit him. The man grabs her wrist, and she drops her chin and sinks her teeth into the back of his hand. He howls and drops her arm, but hangs on to her tee shirt. She kicks out and connects with his shin, then spins and tries to run toward the water. Her tee shirt rips and she is free.

She reaches the surf line and runs east, and the first man sprints to cut her off. He reaches for her and she plunges into the surf, leaping over the shallow crests of the waves. He splashes after her. She throws herself forward and thrashes her arms, churning the water in a desperate but efficient crawl stroke.

The man wades in up to his waist as his companion reaches the edge of the surf, yelling to him.

"Get her! Go after her!"

"I can't swim, goddamnit!"

"Jesus! Neither can I!"

Jennie is now many yards out, swimming strongly. The men trot along the beach, keeping pace with her progress.

"Little bitch is some kind of fish."

"She's got to come out sometime."

Jennie keeps well offshore as she follows the curve of the beach where it narrows and recedes toward the islands. As the sand gives way to rough gravel, interspersed with larger rocks, the men are forced to pick their way along more slowly and carefully, and she is soon out of their sight. She swims around the end of a large glacial rock that lies embedded in the sea floor beyond the low tide line. She finds a shallow inlet, almost hidden from view of the beach.

She looks up and spots one of the men climbing the side of a nearby outcropping. She ducks low in the water and finds shelter beneath a rocky overhang. She hears him stumble and curse, and then the sound of the other man's rough voice as he joins his companion.

"Shit! She's drowned by now. Let's get out of here."

"What if she ain't? What if she calls the cops?"

"What can she say? We didn't do anything to her. And we stole the car, so even if she can describe it, it won't lead anybody to us. We'll just junk it somewhere and steal another. Let's go."

"I just want to get my hands on..."

"Forget it! Come on."

Jennie hears them scramble down off the rocks and swims from the inlet into the lee of a huge boulder where she can look toward the beach. She pulls herself halfway out of the water and listens carefully, but hears no sound other than the gentle wave action among the rocks. She sinks down and swims further back along the shore, finally finding a shallow area where she can see all the way to the men's car.

Keeping her head low, she strains to spot them. They are hurrying along the row of pilings that separate the beach from the road. She ducks down into the water again, her eyes and nose just barely above the surface, and watches as they approach the car, open the doors and get inside. The sound of the engine reaches her ears, and the car spurts forward, spraying the compacted sand and slewing sideways in their haste to be gone. The car reaches the ramp and disappears out onto the highway.

Jennie drags herself onto the shore, exhausted. She looks around the deserted beach to get her bearings and locates the clump of bushes where she has hidden her bicycle. She drags it out and climbs on for the ride back to Bush Island.

The sun has nearly set as she crosses the bridge and approaches her home. The evening air, her wet clothing and her fear all combine to chill her, and she pedals faster to try to warm up. She steers into the yard, leans the bike against the front steps, and enters the house.

The living room is empty. She can hear her mother in the

kitchen and calls out to her.

"Hi, Mom, I'm home."

Then she heads quickly for the staircase and runs up to her room. Nancy's tape recorder plays loudly inside her room, and Jennie passes by the open door unnoticed. She enters her own room and shuts the door, then quickly strips off her wet clothing and pulls on a robe.

She goes out into the hall and into the bathroom. Taking a large bath towel from the linen closet, she rubs her hair briskly to dry it as much as she can. She runs a comb through it and heads back to her room.

Her mother is standing inside the room next to the bed, looking down at the small heap of damp cloth on the floor. She looks up as Jennie comes in. "Well?"

"I fell in," Jennie says meekly.

"How could you fall in? You weren't supposed to go any farther than Michael's house." Jennie looks down at her toes. Her mother steps close and puts her fingers under her chin, tilting it upward so she can look into her eyes, and Jennie shrinks back, trembling.

"Now tell me what happened."

She wants to tell her mother everything, about the two men, about her friend Andrew and how she has been running away to the beach each morning, about how frightened she is. She bursts into tears, shaking all over, and her mother gathers her into her arms.

"You aren't hurt, are you?"

Jennie shakes her head.

"Okay, it can wait then. I think you need a warm shower first."

Jennie lets herself be steered out of the room and into the bathroom again, and Elizabeth turns on the water. "Be sure you get all the salt off," she says, "especially your hair. When you're ready, we'll talk about it some more."

Jennie watches her mother leave the room, then turns and steps into the shower. The warm water soon eases her trembling, and she sluices off the salt and scrubs herself clean. She lathers up her hair and stands for long minutes under the stinging spray, reluctant to face the interrogation she knows will soon come.

Finally unable to stall any longer, she turns off the water and steps out onto the centre of the bath mat. She is patting herself dry when her mother re-enters the bathroom.

"Feel better?" Elizabeth asks.

"I guess so."

"I'll get your peejays."

Jennie wraps the towel around herself and trails along as her Mom enters her bedroom and crosses to the dresser. Elizabeth opens one of the drawers and takes out a clean pair of lightweight summer pyjamas. She crosses over to the closet and finds the child's slippers, then turns around again.

Jennie stands just inside the door, her eyes downcast. Despite the hot shower she is shivering, and she hugs herself under the damp towel. Her mother puts down the slippers and takes the towel from her. She pops the pyjama top over the child's head and pulls it down. Then she hands her the bottoms, and Jennie steps into them.

"Want me to dry your hair?"

Not looking up, Jennie bobs her head in a slight nod. Her Mom walks back to the bathroom and takes the hair dryer from the linen closet. She carries it into the bedroom and plugs it in. She turns it on low, and gently combs the wet strands as she plays it left and right over the child's head. Jennie stands perfectly still.

Elizabeth sets the dryer aside and shapes Jennie's hair with a brush. Satisfied with the results, she places her fingertips gently on her daughter's cheeks and raises her face. Their eyes meet. "How about something to drink? Hot chocolate?"

"Okay."

They pass by Nancy's room. The younger girl is lying on the bed, engrossed in a picture book. She looks up and waves, then returns to the page. The music plays on.

"Want some hot chocolate?" her mother calls in.

"Sure!" Nancy jumps down off the bed and snaps off the tape player. She runs out to join them, and all three go down to the kitchen. Elizabeth takes milk out of the refrigerator while Jennie gets some mugs down off the shelf.

*   *   *

Andrew comes awake abruptly, disturbing Old Cat. He feels confused by his surroundings. He tries to remember how he got back to the cottage, but everything after mailing the letters is vague and shadowy. His head throbs painfully. He straightens up and Old Cat drops to the floor and stalks indignantly to the kitchen. She yowls.

He enters the kitchen and finds the cat standing before an empty dish. He takes a fresh can of her food from the cupboard and opens it. He scoops some into her bowl and also refills her water dish, and Old Cat settles down to eat.

Thoughts of Jennie and Nadia tease the borders of his memory, but his headache scrambles and muddles them.

Was there something I was supposed to do?

He gives up trying to sort things out and shuffles down the hall to his bedroom. He kicks off his shoes and falls across the bed.

The sun drops low behind the pines, slanting in against the bedroom wall in gently swaying patterns of russet and gold. Gradually the light fades and the shadows lose their colour. Old Cat comes into the room and jumps up on the bed. She kneads the covers and fashions a nest for herself, leaning her warmth against Andrew's back. He drifts into the limbo between consciousness and sleep.

*   *   *

Nancy is upstairs in bed. In the living room Jennie sits on the sofa, waiting apprehensively for her mother to finish rinsing the mugs in the kitchen. Finally Elizabeth enters the room and sits down next to her.

"Feeling better now?"

Jennie nods, her eyes on her hands, which are folded in her lap. She knows she is in deep trouble, and can't quite understand why her mother isn't more angry.

"Sweetheart, you scared me to death tonight."

Jennie looks up in wonder. Preoccupied with her own fright, it hasn't occurred to her to think how her mother might feel. "I didn't mean to."

"I'm sure you didn't, but that's what happened. And you

haven't been telling me the truth lately. That has to change. Did you go down to the beach?"

"Uh, huh."

"After I told you not to?" Jennie continues to stare morosely at her hands.

"How did your tee shirt get torn?"

Jennie shrugs.

"I'm not going to scold you," her mother continues, "but you have to tell me what's going on. Have you ever run off like this before?"

Jennie shakes her head. The lies are mounting up.

"Then why tonight?"

"I don't know. I just felt like it, I guess."

"And you just felt like going swimming, too? All by yourself? This isn't like you."

"I fell in."

"So you said. And that sounds like a fish story to me. You *were* by yourself, weren't you?"

Jennie doesn't answer. *If Andrew had come this afternoon like he promised, I wouldn't have been. And none of this would have happened.*

Elizabeth breaks the silence. "So what do you think I should do about this? What would you do if you were me?"

"I don't know."

"One last chance. Are you going to tell me what you've been up to?"

Jennie stirs nervously on the sofa. Without Andrew to back her up, she knows that anything she says will only make things worse. *If only he had come, then Mom could see how nice he is, and how he looks out for me...*

"Well?" Elizabeth prompts. Jennie shrugs.

"Okay. I love you very much, and I'm very worried about you, so I guess the only thing I can do is ground you. For the rest of the summer."

"Mom!"

"I'm sorry, dear, but you don't give me any choice. Unless you tell me what's been going on, you're not to go out of this house, except with me, until school starts. Understood?"

Jennie nods miserably.

"And can I trust you not to do it, or do I have to get a baby sitter for you?"

"Mom, for Pete's sake!"

"All right, but there won't be any more second chances. When I call you on the phone from work, you have exactly two rings to answer, no more. Bathroom or no bathroom."

"That'll be a pretty sight. Me running for the phone with my pants down."

Elizabeth grins and keeps silent. Jennie finally raises her eyes and sees her mother's amused expression. In spite of her misery, she breaks into a smile. Then she begins to giggle.

Elizabeth gives her a hug. "That's more like it. And someday I hope you'll feel like telling me what's been going on."

Jennie regards her solemnly. "I will. Honest. Maybe even tomorrow." *If Andrew ever comes.*

"Okay, we'll leave it at that. Still friends?"

"Sure."

"Even though you're grounded?"

Jennie sighs and hugs her. "Even though I'm grounded." But she is already thinking about how long she dares to be out of the house the next morning without risking getting caught.

*   *   *

Nadia collects payment from the last two customers of the evening and follows them to the canteen door. She closes and locks it behind them and moves to clear the table they were using.

She hears Josh singing to himself as he cleans the grill next to the takeout window. She gathers up the dirty plates and glasses and takes them into the kitchen. Her mother is separating the garbage from the compostables.

Nadia comes up beside her. "When we're done here, can we go check on Dr. Striker?"

"I think we should," her mother says. "Just in case he needs anything."

"He didn't have any supper."

"We can take him something. There's chowder left, and I think it's still pretty hot. We can put it in a takeout bowl."

"I'll make him a sandwich, too. Mom, can we do it right now? I'll finish cleaning up when we get back."

"Sure," Fran says. She moves to the stove and checks the heat under the leftover seafood chowder.

Nadia butters two slices of bread and takes lettuce, a tomato and sliced turkey out of the cooler. She assembles the sandwich and wraps it in waxed paper. "Any coffee left?"

"Not much, and what there is would rot the cup."

"That's okay. Maybe we can make some there. I saw a coffee maker in the kitchen."

Fran pours the chowder into a bowl and snaps a plastic lid on top. She reaches for a pasteboard takeout tray on an upper shelf. Nadia places the sandwich in the tray next to the bowl of chowder. She picks everything up and they head for the door. Josh looks up as they pass by.

"We'll just be a few minutes," Fran says to him. "You can lock up if you finish cleaning the grill before we get back." He grunts his acknowledgement, and they go out into the night.

It is full dark, and the sky is overcast and threatening rain as they make their way carefully around the end of the canteen and start up the narrow road. All of the windows in Andrew's cottage are dark. They climb up the front steps and Nadia is about to knock, but pauses. "Think he's still asleep?" she asks her mother.

"See if the door's unlocked."

Nadia opens the screen door and tries the knob. It turns in her hand and they enter the silent and empty living room. She turns on a table lamp.

"Do you think he went out again?"

"Let's look around first," Fran says quietly. They enter the kitchen and Nadia puts the tray of food on the counter. Then they walk down the hall toward the bedroom. The darkness is almost total, and Fran switches on the hall light before they enter the bedroom. It casts enough glow for them to be able to see the bed and the figure lying on it.

Andrew sprawls at an awkward angle, fully dressed except for his shoes. Old Cat lies curled up next to him, her back pressed tightly against his side. His head hangs down over the side of the bed.

"Is he okay?" Nadia whispers apprehensively.

Fran walks carefully around the end of the bed and touches his outstretched hand. He stirs and shifts position slightly.

"He'll have a stiff neck when he wakes up. Maybe we can straighten him out some." She slips her hands under his shoulders and levers him back toward the centre of the bed.

Nadia takes his feet, and together they manage to turn him until his head rests on the pillow. Old Cat utters a soft squeak of annoyance and stalks to the foot of the bed.

"He feels cold," Nadia says. She looks around for a blanket. Finding none, she goes into the bathroom and opens the linen closet. She takes a spare blanket from the top shelf and returns to the bedroom.

Old Cat reclaims her spot next to Andrew's back as soon as Nadia spreads the blanket over him. She looks at her mother helplessly. "Isn't there anything else we can do?"

"Let's just leave the food on the kitchen counter. He'll see it when he gets up."

"Suppose he's all confused, like before?"

"We can't do much about that tonight," Fran says. "If he isn't better in the morning, we can call somebody for some help."

Nadia looks down at the sleeping man in frustration. "I can't just leave him here like this. I was afraid he might get lost last night. Or hurt himself or something. I'm going to stay here, Mom."

"I don't think that's a good idea. He might not appreciate us butting into his business."

"I don't care. He's sick, and I can't just go off and leave him like this."

Fran takes a deep breath. "There's nowhere for you to sleep."

"I can use the sofa. There's one more blanket in the closet, and I can wad up a towel for a pillow. I'll be fine."

"And what will you do when he wakes up?"

"I don't know!" Frustration is building within her. "I'll try to get him to eat, I guess. And if he's still confused, I can at least keep him from trying to go outside and wandering away."

Fran backs up and lowers herself to the sofa. "Come over here and sit beside me for a minute." Nadia sighs and drops down onto the shabby cushion. Fran takes her hand. "You know what his problem is, don't you?"

"Something like Alzheimer's, I guess," Nadia says sadly.

"I think so, too. What I don't understand is, why he's out here on his own like this. Doesn't he have any family?"

"Not close by. That's why I have to stay! We have to find somebody to take care of him, but until we do, then *I* have to!"

"Why is it your responsibility?" her mother asks gently.

"Who else is there?"

Fran inhales deeply. "There's no cure for this, you know. It's the saddest disease I know of. People who have it just lose all their memories, even forget their families and friends. If they live long enough, they end up unable to do anything for themselves. They have to have constant care."

"Dr. Striker isn't like that, at least not yet. We've had long talks, and he's really intelligent. And you were right, the book that he wrote is beautiful."

"He wrote that many years ago."

"Right. But it's just one more reason why I have to look after him now, at least until we find his family. We owe him that."

Fran sighs and pats her hand. "I'm not sure I follow your line of reasoning, but I'm not going to argue. Promise me you'll come get me if you need me?"

"I will. Thanks, Mom. I'll help you finish cleaning up and come right back here."

Fran gets up off the sofa. "Never mind. If Josh is still there, he'll help me. If not, I can do it."

Nadia gives her a hug. "You're the best."

"And you're a nut. But I'm very proud of you." She kisses Nadia softly and turns to the door. "Remember, anything you can't handle, come and get me. Or call me. Even if it's late." She opens the door and goes out into the night.

A few drops of rain have started to fall. The wind is picking up across the bay, bringing the first cool intimations of autumn to the Nova Scotia coastline. Summer is short this far north, and shorter for some than for others.

Homecomings

Catherine Striker knew that something was wrong as soon as she entered the arrival area at Halifax International Airport. Andrew was nowhere in sight. As she stood by the luggage carousel and waited for her bags, a tall grey-haired man approached, wearing a light jacket with a company logo on the left side of his chest. He removed a peaked cap and addressed her by name.

"Mrs. Striker? Mrs. Catherine Striker?"

"Yes?" She regarded him closely. The cap suggested some sort of uniform, although he was otherwise conventionally dressed. Catherine estimated his age as late sixties.

"Oliver Diamond, ma'am, Annapolis Limousine Service. Your husband arranged for us to pick you up."

She was immediately concerned. "Has something happened to him?"

"Not so far as I know. The office didn't tell me anything more, just that I was to meet your flight and drive you back to Wolfville."

"May I see your identification, please, Mr. Diamond?"

The man extracted a leather folder from his inside coat pocket and flipped it open for her. It contained his chauffeur's license, prominently displayed in the left hand window, and a limo service ID card with his photo on the opposite side. She examined them carefully and handed the folder back.

"How did you know who I was?" she asked.

He extracted an envelope from another pocket. "Your husband left this photo for us." He took a print from the envelope and handed it to her. Her own face stared back at her, a picture from happier times, taken during their visit with Penny in Ottawa the previous summer.

"If you wish, you can give me your claim ticket and wait in

the car," he said, waving toward the automatic doors behind them. "It's just outside that door. How many bags do you have?"

"That's all right," she said distractedly. "I'll wait with you." Absently she placed the photo in her purse. She felt unaccountably anxious. She had eagerly anticipated seeing her husband again after their two-week separation. Now her old fears about his recent instability surged to the surface.

Oliver Diamond tried to initiate polite conversation, but Catherine seemed not to hear him and he abandoned the effort. The first of her bags appeared on the carousel and she gestured toward it. Diamond snatched it off the belt and set it down between them. The second one emerged shortly thereafter.

"That's all," she said. Diamond led her toward the exit and they left through the sliding doors. He walked to a white stretch Lincoln that sat close to the curb and triggered the electronic trunk release on his key chain. The lid snapped open and he lifted the luggage over the edge, then turned and opened the back door for her. She bent and climbed inside, and he hurried around to the driver's seat.

"Are you comfortable, Mrs. Striker?"

"I'm fine, thanks," she said, feeling anything but. As the big car pulled away from the curb and coasted down the incline toward the exit ramp, she sat in troubled silence.

With expert ease Diamond cruised along the perimeter of the airport parking lot to the main access road and turned right in the direction of the highway. Catherine hardly noticed as he took the right hand fork and entered Route 102, heading in the direction of Halifax. Once under way, he tried again to initiate conversation, but she put him off with her mumbled one-word responses, and he gave up to concentrate on his driving.

Exit four loomed up on the right, and Diamond took the ramp to the 101 highway at Sackville. They soon left the city traffic behind, and as they swept into the countryside for the remaining forty-five minute ride into Wolfville, Catherine gazed out the window in worried silence. Her heart pounded uncomfortably in her chest. Sending a limo to pick her up was something she knew her husband would never do. Aside from liking to drive, he would not have wanted to postpone seeing her. At least she thought so. Her tension mounted, and the drive seemed to her to go on forever.

At last they reached Wolfville and pulled into her driveway, and Oliver Diamond assisted her from the limousine and retrieved her bags from the trunk. He carried them to the front door and set them down on the porch.

"May I bring them inside for you?"

"No thank you. I can manage." She fumbled for her purse. "I'm sorry, I've never taken a limo before. May I offer you a tip?"

He touched his cap ceremoniously. "That's not necessary, ma'am. Your husband took care of everything."

"Well... Thank you very much, then."

"My pleasure." He backed away two steps, then turned and walked toward his car. Catherine stood uncertainly. She watched him drive off, then fitted her key in the lock and opened the front door. She peered inside uneasily, not sure what to expect. The foyer was exactly as she remembered it, and she carried her bags inside and set them down just inside the living room.

"Andrew?"

Stark empty silence greeted her. Although she could not have explained why, the familiar surroundings seemed somehow cold and forbidding. She left the bags and started down the hall toward the den.

Andrew's desk was unaccountably bare. Instead of the usual array of bills to be paid and projects underway, the blotter lay clean and uncluttered. Only his letter opener was in evidence. She entered the room and surveyed the bookshelves, noting a number of empty slots where once they had been crowded to overflowing with volumes and recordings.

Now thoroughly alarmed, she headed for the bedroom and went directly to his closet. His suits and sport jackets hung in their accustomed places, and she relaxed momentarily. Then she noticed that most of his casual wear was missing. In the rack on the floor, only his dress shoes remained. She turned to his chest and began pulling out drawers. Most were more than half empty.

She sat on the edge of the bed and looked around, confused and unable to understand what could have happened. The top of his dresser was almost as bare as his desk. His comb and brush were missing, although his engraved platinum pen, a retirement gift from his colleagues in the English Department, lay there abandoned. The pile of loose change he habitually dumped on top was gone. Other than the pen, there were no personal items at all.

He wouldn't leave me. He loves me. I know he does.

Distressed and anxious, Catherine stood up and started down the hall. She bypassed the living room and headed straight to the kitchen and the blinking answering machine. She pushed the button and a single message played, a brief call from Penny asking her to call and let her know when she arrived safely.

She turned from the counter and headed directly toward the garage. Her own car was in its regular place. Andrew's was gone.

She retraced her steps into the kitchen and spotted the envelope in the middle of the table. She seized it and tore it open. Without sitting down she read it through once, then collapsed into a chair and read it again through a torrent of hot, bitter tears. She read it a third time, then buried her head in her arms and sobbed uncontrollably.

When she had once again regained control, she went to the phone to call Penny and Donald.

* * *

Andrew picked up a key at the real estate office in Bridgewater and asked for directions to Green Bay. Upon arriving at the cottage he stepped out into the unkempt yard and surveyed the rundown building, its gutters sagging and bare wood beginning to show through the paint on the siding. He climbed the porch and slipped the key into the lock. The door swung back to reveal a shabby room, made more dingy by the fading evening light. He flipped a wall switch and a low-wattage bulb came on overhead, accentuating rather than alleviating the gloom.

He paced through the rest of the cottage and surveyed the meagre furniture. Then he went back out to his car and began unloading the trunk. It took only a few trips to get everything inside. Leaving the boxes and suitcases unopened, he entered the kitchen and sat at the battered table, looking out into the near darkness of the back lot. The

faint outlines of wind-stunted pines gradually faded as full darkness
descended. The overcast sky hid both stars and moon.

Home. Probably the last one I'll ever have.

* * *

After a long and tearful conversation with her daughter,
Catherine managed to bring things into perspective. By the time she
called Donald she had her emotions under control. Both son and
daughter offered to come and lend support, but she asked them to
wait, at least until she knew more. Then she began to focus on what to
do next.

First she called the New Minas RCMP Detachment to report
her husband missing. The officer who answered the phone began to
ask questions, and Catherine maintained rigid control over her emotions
as she relayed the evening's events. Sensing no immediate threat to
anyone's safety, the officer assured Catherine that an investigation
would begin as soon as possible, in an orderly fashion. They arranged
for someone to come to the house later that evening to interview her
for further information.

Next she picked up the phone and called Bob Melanson at
home. By then she had attained a numb serenity and was under tight
control, although the tone of her voice alerted the doctor that something
was very wrong.

"He's gone, Bob. The car, his clothes, everything. I've called
the RCMP…"

"It may not be what you think," he said reassuringly. "Tell me
exactly what happened."

"He didn't meet me at the airport. A limo picked me up. And
when I got home the place was empty, and I found a note."

"What does it say?"

Calmly she read Andrew's few lines into the phone. For several
long seconds Melanson didn't reply. Then he said, "I'll be right over.
Barbara too."

She drew in a deep, shuddering breath. "No, that's all right.
I'm sorry to be such a…"

"Never mind," he interrupted. "You don't need to be alone right now. Give us ten minutes." He disconnected and Catherine sat back, somewhat relieved. It would be good to have her friends beside her, someone to help her clarify her thoughts and decide what to do.

Fifteen minutes later she heard a car in the driveway and went to meet the Melansons at the door. Barbara embraced her. They stepped inside and went into the living room to sit down, Catherine on the sofa and the other two in separate chairs. She described her return from the airport and showed them Andrew's letter. For several moments they sat in silent reflection.

"Why would he do such a thing?" Catherine said at last.

"I think you know," Bob said.

"He always has to be so damn *strong*, has to do everything for himself. Always thinks he knows best…"

"Catherine…" Barbara began.

"You know it's true," she said softly. "I love him, but I'm not blind. He's had these memory lapses and probably thinks he's going senile, so he's built himself a fortress and shut me out. That's the kind of thing he's always done."

"It looks like he's been planning to leave for a while," Bob said, "probably since before he took retirement."

"Is it Alzheimer's?"

"That or something like it. He wouldn't let me finish the tests, and they wouldn't have been conclusive anyway, not at such an early stage of the disease."

"What does he think leaving me will solve?"

"You said it yourself," Melanson said kindly. "You know what he's like. He's a proud man, and he's lived his life by the power of his mind. To feel it deteriorating must be a terrible blow to him, but he fears your pity more."

"Pity! I wouldn't *pity* him! I *love* him!"

"I know you do. And he does, too. But I'm willing to bet he's researched this disease pretty thoroughly, and if it really is Alzheimer's, he knows how it will take everything away, his personality, his memories… Everything."

"It wouldn't matter to me."

"It would to him."

Catherine unfolded the letter again. " 'I trust to your love to accept that I do what I must,' " she read aloud. "Damn it, he's so *wrong!*"

She got up and paced angrily across the room. "He makes me so damn *mad!* This is when he needs me most!"

She stared out the window at the empty front lawn, struggling to regain her composure. Then she turned back to face her friends.

"Will you help me find him?"

"Of course we will," Barbara said quickly, but the doctor was more cautious.

"When you find out where he is," Bob said, "what will you do then?"

"Bring him back, of course! Take care of him! I love him!"

He smiled at her sadly. "Read his letter again. The last paragraph, I think."

She looked down at the page. " 'Remember the good times, my dearest, every day of your life. You gave me so much, and I am forever grateful for your love.' "

"No, before that."

" 'Please do not try to find me, as it will only cause both of us much unnecessary grief. And please believe that my absence represents no lack of love for you. It is because I love you too much.' "

She grimaced and let the paper flutter from her hand to the floor. She folded her arms tightly across her chest and turned toward the window again.

"You see?" Melanson said to her back. "He won't return willingly. Whatever is happening inside his mind, he's convinced himself that this is the right thing to do. It may be part of his illness."

"I can't just let him go! I won't!"

Barbara stood up and walked over to stand beside her. "Maybe it's the best thing to do, at least for now. Let him come to terms with this by himself. He'll resent you if you try to force the issue."

"But…"

"I know how hard that will be," Barbara continued, "but he'll be okay, at least for a while. He's always been able to take care of himself."

Catherine turned to Bob again. "What's likely to happen to him next?"

"Every case is different. He has a powerful intellect, and I think the deterioration will likely be fairly gradual. But as the disease develops, the periods of confusion will lengthen and increase. His feelings and emotions will probably change, too. We won't know for sure just how until it happens. He could become more accepting, more compliant. I wouldn't be surprised if loneliness and his love for you will drive him back here fairly quickly."

"But you don't know that for sure."

"You're right," he admitted. "I don't."

"What else could happen?" Barbara asked her husband gently. "I think she should hear whatever you think is possible."

"At worst he could become more unstable. Sometimes this sort of dementia takes the form of unreasonable anger."

"That's how he's been ever since this started." Catherine said. "Until the last few months, that is. He seemed to calm down, but now I think it's all been just an act, as if he's been putting up a front for me and hiding how he really feels." She stared miserably out the window. "I'm going to look for him. Something could happen to him."

"Catherine, you asked for my advice and I'm going to give it to you. Let him go for a while. Respect his wishes. You could send the Mounties out looking for him, and they'd no doubt run him down sooner or later. If he's still in the Province, it should be easy, although there's no guarantee of that. But if he doesn't want to come home, they can't make him."

"I can't just *sit* here…"

"Sure you can, at least for right now. He's not too sick to take care of himself. Look at all the planning that must have gone into this, his retirement, probably setting up his pension to take care of you… Isn't that what the note implies? Getting everything in order. My guess is that when you talk to the bank, you'll find every T crossed and every I dotted. That's how Andrew is."

"But he's sick!"

"He recognizes that, and he's doing what he thinks he has to.

It may not seem rational to us now, but to him it is. And his life isn't in danger. Leave him alone for a while. Let him try to come to terms with this himself, in his own way."

Catherine regarded him carefully, then turned to Barbara. "Is that the right thing to do?"

Barbara put her arms around her comfortingly. "I wish I knew. But I agree with Bob, we don't have to decide tonight. Andrew's okay for right now. I'm sure of that."

*   *   *

Summer gave way to fall, and fall to a bleak and lonely winter. Catherine went through the motions of her life, and as spring approached, still with no word from Andrew, she realized she had finally come to accept his absence.

How much longer should I wait? And if I do find him, who will he be?

TEN...

Andrew awakes to find the room dark and hears the sound of water dripping from the eaves outside the cottage. He lies beneath a blanket but cannot remember having crawled under it. He throws it off, burying Old Cat, and gets to his feet unsteadily.

The cat stirs and complains softly. She makes her way out from under, turns around twice and takes a few perfunctory licks down her flank, then curls up again and goes to sleep.

Andrew shuffles into the bathroom and relieves himself. He turns to the mirror and surveys his bloodshot eyes and rumpled clothes. He runs the water and splashes some on his face.

What do I have to do today?

He goes out through the living room and notices Penny asleep on the sofa. He walks over quietly to stand beside her, noting with confusion her unfamiliar dark hair. He reaches out to wake her, but hesitates. He pulls the blanket up gently over her shoulders and turns and walks quietly out of the room.

Nadia stirs slightly at his touch, sighs in her sleep, and settles back into the warmth of the sofa.

He enters the dark kitchen and makes out the vague shape of the takeout tray sitting on the table. He unwraps the sandwich and examines it, trying to remember when and where he got it. He puts it down and touches the cold soup container lightly. Then he turns toward the back door and opens it.

The rain has stopped, but the air is heavy with mist. Random drops splatter softly on the back steps from the small overhanging roof. The sound of dripping is starkly defined against the silent background of the woods.

Andrew goes outside and looks up at the overcast sky, starless and nearly black. He walks a few dozen paces through the wet grass toward the pine grove. He reaches the trees and turns to look back. He can no longer see the cottage and forgets where he has come from. He sets off along the tree line, skirting the property of the adjoining cottage, then the next one, and the one after that. Eventually he comes out onto a narrow dirt road and turns left. This takes him to the Green Bay road, and as if by instinct, he heads for Long Point.

The first few drops of a shower pelt down on his head and back. He has forgotten to put on a jacket, and his light cotton shirt becomes first damp, then increasingly soaked.

* * *

Jennie awakens to a grey day. The sun lies buried behind an overcast sky, and a light fog overhangs the summer-brown fields and roads of Bush Island. She looks at her bedside clock and is surprised to see the time: just after seven. On previous mornings her mother's departure for work had awakened her.

She gets up and finds the room chilly and damp, the fog seeming to seep in around the window frames. She goes to the closet for her robe, finds her slippers beneath the bed, and walks out into the hall. She sees a light on downstairs and hears noises coming from the kitchen. She goes down to find the others.

Nancy is sitting at the kitchen table, lazily poking at the Cheerios floating in her bowl, trying to make them sink. Her mother is washing the dishes from the previous evening's meal.

"How come you're still here?" Jennie asks as she comes into the room.

"Hi, sweetheart," her mother greets her. "You won't have to get your own breakfast today. What would you like?"

"Why aren't you at work?"

"I'm not on the early shift today. I don't have to be in until eleven, but I won't be home until after eight. You can get your own supper tonight. Or wait until I get home, and we'll have a late one together."

Jennie feels sudden panic. She has to go out to find Andrew, find out why he didn't come to her house yesterday, tell him about what almost happened to her with the two men on the beach last night. "When are you leaving?"

"A little before ten thirty. There won't be much traffic in Bridgewater then. Want some cereal?"

"I guess." She sits at the table, and her mother sets out a bowl and spoon.

"What kind?"

"Doesn't matter."

"A little grumpy this morning, are we?" Elizabeth takes three different brands out of the cupboard and sets them on the table. She goes to the refrigerator and returns with a carton of milk.

Jennie chooses Froot Loops and fills her bowl. She reaches for the milk. She pours it carefully, then plucks the spoon out of the sugar bowl.

"Go easy on the extra sugar," he mother says. "Dentists are expensive, and you're sweet enough already."

"Yeah, sure." She dips the spoon and sprinkles the granules over the cereal. She takes a bite, and then another. "Mom?" Her mother looks around inquiringly. "I'm not really grounded, am I?"

"I'm afraid so."

"But I can't be!" the child blurts out. "Not today!"

Elizabeth looks at her in surprise. "You know what we talked about last night. As long as you're keeping things from me, those are the rules. What's so special about today, anyway?"

Jennie stares morosely at her cereal, not eating. Her mother waits for an answer, then shrugs and turns back to washing the dishes in the sink.

"I have to go somewhere this morning," Jennie mutters quietly.

"Not today you don't."

She looks up. "It's really important, Mom."

"What is?"

Several minutes pass. Nancy finishes eating and squirms out of her chair.

"Hold it!" her mother says. "Haven't you forgotten something?"

Nancy skids to a halt. "Excuse me?"

"Excuse me, *please*."

"Excuse me, *please*." she mimics. "Can I watch TV before I get dressed?"

"That's *may* I. Okay, just for a little while." Nancy scampers out of the room and Elizabeth says to Jennie, "She thinks this is a special treat, not having to go to day care so early."

"I'm glad *she's* happy!" Jennie mutters. Elizabeth ignores her.

She picks at her meal. Finally she makes up her mind. "I have to go see Andrew," she says, barely audibly.

"What?"

"I have to go see *Andrew*."

Her mother turns from the sink, wiping her hands on a dish towel. "And Andrew is…?"

"My friend."

Elizabeth walks over and pulls out a chair. She sits down and places her elbows on the table, resting her chin between her palms. "Spill it!"

The words flow out in a rush. "I went to the beach on Monday morning, and there was this man there, and he told me all about starfish, and he said I shouldn't go to the beach all by myself, that it wasn't safe."

Her mother sits bolt upright. "And he was right! Didn't I tell you that you weren't to go there without me?"

"I know, but I was stuck here all alone, and I was bored. I can take care of myself."

"You think so? Jennie, I don't make up these rules just for fun. You're only eleven years old. Did you go in the water?"

"Not Monday…"

"Some other day, then. My God, child, you could have drowned! And you were talking to some strange man on the beach? What were you thinking!"

"He's nice, Mom," she says desperately. "He comes there every morning, and he said he'd come meet you so you could see he was an okay guy, and then maybe you'd let me go to the beach with him every morning while you're at work. Only he didn't come."

Elizabeth shakes her head. "I'm not surprised! You must *never* talk to strangers. You know that."

"He *isn't* a stranger. He has a cottage over at Green Bay, and he showed me this really neat book that has starfish and shells in it." She sees the fear and anger on her mother's face and hurries on. "He wrote a book, too. And he even took me to see Gram."

Her mother stares wide-eyed. "You've been riding with him in a car? *You know better!* How could I ever have thought it was safe to leave you here alone?"

Jennie frowns angrily. "You never let me make up my own mind about things. He's *nice!* He *likes* me!"

"You're only *eleven!* You don't *know…*" Her voice trails off, and Jennie looks up into her face apprehensively.

"Jennie, I'm very upset with you," Elizabeth says with icy calm, "but you're here now and you're safe, and we're going to sort this out right this minute. Start at the beginning. You have to tell me everything."

*   *   *

Catherine spends a restless night, waiting for some word from the RCMP officer in Bridgewater. Finally at a few minutes after five the telephone sounds, and she catches it on the second ring. "Hello?"

"Is this Mrs. Catherine Striker?"

"Yes. Corporal Comeau?"

"I'm sorry to be so slow in getting back to you, but I just got in from duty. The detachment called me last night about the address you wanted, but I didn't have it with me. I had to come back here and dig through my desk to find it."

"Where is he?" Catherine says impatiently. "My husband."

"I thought you should know, I found him in his car by the side of the highway. He seemed lost, and I checked his license and it had your address."

"Please, Corporal, where is he?"

"I'm sorry. I followed him back to a cottage in Green Bay. He seemed okay by that time, so I left him. He hadn't committed any traffic violations or anything."

"Where is he, exactly?"

"Do you know the area, ma'am?"

"Only a little. Is it somewhere near Bridgewater?"

"South of here," the officer says. "There's two ways to get there. On the map, it looks shorter to go through town here and take Route 331 down past LaHave, but that's really pretty slow, two lane traffic and all."

"What's the faster way?" she prompts, trying to hurry him along.

"You're coming from Wolfville, right?"

"Yes, yes!" *Get on with it, damn it!*

"You take Route 12 out of Kentville to Chester Basin and then get on the 102. Go all the way past Bridgewater to exit fifteen. It'll say Italy Cross." Catherine grabs a pencil and begins scribbling down the directions.

"Follow the signs to Petite Riviere," Comeau continues. "That's east. You go through Crousetown, and then about another five kilometres the road dead ends into Route 331. You getting all this?"

"Yes, go on."

"You go left on 331, and pretty soon you'll see a one-lane bridge. That's Petite Riviere."

"What do I do after I cross the bridge?"

"You don't. Turn right just before you come to the bridge. It's a paved road, but a little rough. Just keep going until you come out by the water. That's Green Bay."

Catherine scribbles down the last few instructions. "How do I find the right house?"

"You'll see the beach on your left and some cottages on the right. Some are year-round homes, too, good-sized ones. Then there's a little restaurant on the right, more like a canteen, and the road narrows down. There's more cottages beyond that, and his is one of those."

"Which one?"

"I can't remember exactly. I was only there once. But you know his car, don't you?"

"Yes."

"Just look for it, then. Or you can ask at the canteen. They open early for breakfast, and somebody there must know him."

"Thank you, Corporal."

"You're welcome, Mrs. Striker. If you have any problem finding him, just call the Detachment, and we'll send someone out to help you."

"You're very kind," she says, impatient to get going. "How long will it take me to get there?"

"It's a little more than a hundred kilometres from Wolfville to Bridgewater. Assuming you're a law-abiding citizen," he says with gentle humour, "figure an hour and a quarter to be safe. Then another thirty-five clicks beyond that, maybe? Something like that. Less than two hours total, easy."

She hangs up and hurries to the bedroom to dress. She skips breakfast and is on the highway before quarter to six.

* * *

Andrew huddles in the lee of two abutted boulders near Long Point, waiting out the shower. As the first signs of approaching dawn appear over the bay, the rain gives way to a gathering fog, cold to the point of discomfort. He stirs and pries himself out of the crevice, twisting his arthritic knee painfully.

He limps out onto the path and starts back toward the cottage. Now more fully awake, he recalls isolated periods of time from among the jumbled threads of the past two days: his encounter with Jennie's grandmother, the walk on the beach with Nadia. Then he remembers his promise to Jennie to meet her mother, but the time sequence escapes him.

When was I supposed to go?

His progress is slow on his weakened leg, and he reaches the cottage tired and cold. He turns to go up the driveway and twists his knee again, sending an agonizing stab of pain up his thigh. He stumbles to the side of his car and pulls the door open, falling awkwardly into the driver's seat. His breath labours in his chest, and he flexes his arms, feeling a vague tingling sensation in the left one, a slight numbness.

He considers the growing ache in his stomach. He tries to remember when he last had a meal. An image floats in his mind, a takeout tray with a sandwich and a covered Styrofoam soup bowl, sitting…

Sitting somewhere. He puts it out of his mind.

The fog lies low over the bay, but visibility along the road is good. He reaches into his pants pocket and finds his keys. He starts the engine and puts the car in reverse, not quite sure of where he is going, but vaguely aware that he has some obligation to meet.

Nadia? Jennie? Catherine?

He backs out into the road and coasts too far. The car strikes a two-foot-tall pine in the row of stunted trees that separates the edge of the road from the beach. The tree bends beneath the bumper and scrapes loudly along the undercarriage.

Andrew brakes and sits in shaken confusion. The accident sharpens his senses, and he shifts the transmission into drive and starts to move forward. The damaged tree protests noisily, then springs free. With fierce concentration he grips the wheel and steers slowly past the darkened canteen and on up the road toward Petite Riviere.

* * *

Catherine turns off Route 12 onto the 102 highway and heads southwest. As she passes the exit for Mahone Bay, the sudden blast of a horn jolts her. She has gone to sleep at the wheel and crossed the centre line. Whipping the wheel to the right, she narrowly misses an oncoming truck. She shakes her head to clear it, but her eyes flutter, slightly out of focus.

It won't do Andrew any good if I end up a statistic.

A sign announces the next exit, number eleven to Blockhouse. Afraid to continue, she takes the off ramp and spots a restaurant across the road. She enters the parking lot and parks clumsily, narrowly missing the bumper of an oversized pickup truck.

She checks her watch. Twenty minutes for coffee and something sweet to put sugar in her blood, and she can be back on the highway in time to make Green Bay before eight. She gets out and locks the door. The smell of fresh coffee welcomes her as she opens the door and finds a seat at one of the tables.

*   *   *

Nadia awakens to a cramp in her leg. She hops up and straightens it out, limping in small circles to work out the pain. A quick look out through the window tells her that she's probably overdue at the restaurant. Then she remembers the events that led her to sleep on Andrew's sofa.

She reaches down and kneads the knot out of her aching calf, then hurries down the hall. Andrew's bed is empty except for Old Cat, who comes to attention when Nadia enters the room. She yawns and stretches, then hops down off the bed and heads for the kitchen.

Nadia checks the bathroom, then goes back down the hall to the living room and through into the kitchen. Except for the cat, she is alone in the cottage. The takeout tray still stands on the table, the soup now congealed and the sandwich unwrapped but otherwise untouched. She returns to the living room and looks out the front window. The driveway is empty.

She hurries back to the kitchen and calls her home number. As she waits for it to be picked up, she searches the room for a clock. After the eighth ring she gives up.

Dad's gone to work, Mom's at the canteen by herself, and I'm probably in trouble.

She is about to call the canteen when she feels Old Cat nudging her ankles. She looks down just as the animal emits her piercing cry.

"My God, you're loud! What do you want?"

As if understanding the words, Old Cat sidles over to her dishes and meows pitifully. In spite of her worry over Andrew, Nadia laughs and bends to pick them up. The cat twines in and out between her legs.

"Water first, you pest." She refills the bowl from the tap and sets it down on the floor again. Then she opens the refrigerator door and looks inside.

"Nothing!" she says aloud. "No cat food, no people food, nothing!"

The discovery triggers her concern for Andrew, and she is anxious to begin the search for him. She opens the cupboard beside the sink and looks inside. She finds a few cans of cat food and takes one out, then searches in the drawers for the can opener.

Sensing impending breakfast, Old Cat takes up her post next to the water dish, and Nadia finds the opener and fills the other bowl. She sets it down on the floor and Old Cat buries her nose in it noisily. Nadia finds a scrap of foil wrap in a drawer to cover the half empty can and places it in the fridge. Then she returns to the phone and tries the restaurant number.

Fran's voice comes over the line. "Green Bay Canteen, good morning."

"It's me. I'm sorry, I just woke up."

"Take it easy," her mother says. "We won't get much business with the weather like it is, so you don't have to hurry. I can manage until you get here."

"Mom, he's gone! His car's gone. I thought for sure I would wake up before him, but I didn't, and now he's out there somewhere."

"Just relax. Maybe he only went for a ride. He probably didn't want to wake you."

"He didn't eat a thing. The stuff we brought is still sitting here, and he hasn't got anything else in the house. He's sick, I know it."

"I'm sorry, dear, but your dad's got the car, and he's already left. The only thing we can do is call nine-one-one. Are you sure you want to do that?"

Nadia is torn by indecision. "Did Josh bring his car?"

"I'll see." Fran puts the receiver down, and Nadia hears her muffled voice in the background. Then she comes back on the line. "He walked down."

"Ask him if I can walk up to his place and get it."

"Nadia, what good will it do? How will you find him? The man could be anywhere."

"Please?"

"Oh, all right. Get yourself down here, and I'll try to talk Josh into it."

"Thanks, Mom!" She drops the receiver in the cradle and goes hunting for her shoes. She finds them next to the sofa and pulls them on, not bothering with the laces. She starts for the door, then notices the corner of a piece of paper sticking out of the top shelf of the bookcase.

She hesitates with her hand on the knob. She walks over to the bookcase and slides the paper out from under the books and reads it. *All of the books on this shelf are to be given to…* She drops it in panic, flees out the door and runs toward the canteen.

* * *

Jennie sits across from her mother at the kitchen table, tears running down her face. "Please, Mom, don't do this. I have to go."

"From now on, I decide what you have to do, and I'm going to make sure you do it."

"But nothing bad happened to me," she says desperately. "I'm fine. I'm great!"

Elizabeth sits back, exasperation plain on her face. "Let's make a list. First you meet up with some stranger. Then you go riding your bike all the way to Green Bay without permission."

Jennie has left out the part about the truck nearly hitting her.

"Then you let this man, somebody I don't even know and who could be a criminal or something, drive you home. And you went with him to the nursing home, and last night you went to the beach without permission and nearly got yourself kidnapped or raped or something. Have I missed anything?"

Jennie sits morosely. It sounds so much worse spelled out that way. Then she brightens. "But that didn't happen, did it? I'm *fine*, and that proves that Andrew is a good guy, and that I can take care of myself."

"It doesn't prove a thing, except that you were very, very lucky this time. I taught you to have better sense. At least I thought I did. And the worst thing is the way you've been lying to me, with no regard for your own safety, or for how I'd feel if something happened to you."

"I'm sorry…"

"That isn't good enough any more."

Jennie is sobbing. "But I told you everything, just like you wanted!"

"Not until I pried it out of you. It's just too late now. The time to tell me was at the beginning, right after the first lie. Then we could maybe have been straight with each other. But now I know I can't trust you."

"It doesn't have to be too late. You can come with me to the beach, right now, and if Andrew's there, you can see how nice he is, and then I'll have somebody to look after me when you're at work."

"No, Jennie. This man, whoever he is, is still a stranger. Even if you have him sized up correctly, which I sincerely doubt, you can't expect him to take responsibility for you. That's *my* job. It used to be yours too, but from now on it's just mine."

Jennie drops her face onto her arms and cries quietly. *I'll never see Andrew again.*

Her mother looks at her watch. "I have to get your sister ready for day care, and you have to get yourself cleaned up and dressed, too. For today you'll have to stay at McDonald's with me. Get some books together so you'll have something to do."

Jennie lifts her head miserably. "I can't go there every day. They won't let me."

"You're probably right. But it gives me an extra day to figure something else out. Maybe you can help out at the day care. But you won't be staying by yourself. Not for a long time to come."

* * *

Andrew eases the car along the narrow road until he reaches the Mariner Gift Shop. The intersection confuses him in the dim morning light, and he turns left instead of continuing on to Petite Riviere. The road winds inland and finally ends at Route 331, and he turns south, heading toward Broad Cove. The turnoff to Italy Cross and the 102 highway lies behind him.

Intent upon staying on the road, he crawls along at less than half the speed limit. Several cars pass him by. One honks in annoyance, and he yanks the wheel to the right to give it clearance to pass. His car coasts onto the soft gravel of the shoulder, and he brakes to a stop and turns off the ignition.

Nothing around him seems familiar. There are few homes visible on this lonely stretch, and no other landmarks. His mind wanders back to the day he tried to go home from LaHave and ended up on the road to Bridgewater instead. Panic assails him, then subsides in a nebulous fog of tangled thoughts and memories. He lies back against the headrest and closes his eyes.

* * *

Driving too quickly, Catherine negotiates the twists and turns between Italy Cross and the coast, and finally comes out at the intersection with Route 331. She consults her notes and turns left. Shortly the bridge at Petite Riviere comes into view, and she slows for the turn that will take her to Green Bay.

There is no other traffic, and she bounces too fast along the rough pavement past the community hall on the left and the gift shop on the right. The road narrows, and she brakes for the sharp left turn that leads down to the shore.

The sky is a dark, flat grey, and a squall line is visible out over the bay. She pulls up and checks her notes again. The beach is to her left and a row of homes sits shrouded in fog on a gentle rise on the opposite side of the road.

This looks right.

She strains to see ahead down the road as the first few drops of rain strike the windshield. She switches on the wipers, puts the car back in gear, and starts off again.

Several hundred yards farther along, the road dips down and then crests over a small hill, and she can see a building ahead that might be the restaurant that Corporal Comeau described. She sees a slight figure come out of the door, pulling on a jacket and starting to run along the side of the road in her direction. She continues to drive forward, scanning the homes and cottages that dot the side of the low hill.

A few cars stand in their driveways, none of them Andrew's. She strains to peer through the gathering storm, trying to see if other cars sit among the cottages beyond the canteen. She turns on the headlights. The clouds erupt in a squall of sudden, wind-blown fury.

*   *   *

Slightly out of breath, Nadia slows to a fast walk and pulls the collar of her windbreaker up around her neck. The rain soaks her hair and her denim jeans. Josh Watson's home is just a few hundred yards farther along, and she can make out the shape of his old and battered Honda squatting beside his house. Clutching the keys, she begins to run again.

The blinding rain assaults her, slowing her down once more, and she shields her eyes with her forearm. A pair of headlights emerges from the gloom, and she hears the car's engine drop to an idle as it coasts toward her. She looks up and sees the near side window sliding downward, a figure leaning across the seat to call to her.

"Excuse me, do you know which house belongs to my husband? His name is Andrew Striker."

Nadia grasps the door handle and tumbles into the passenger seat of Catherine's car.

*   *   *

Andrew awakens to a blast from a horn behind him and opens

his eyes as a fast-moving cube van passes within inches. The wind from its wake makes his car sway. He raises his head and blinks in confusion. The past hour is lost to him, and he tries to orient himself. This time he recognizes his surroundings, the country highway between Petite Riviere and Broad Cove.

He starts the engine and manoeuvres onto the blacktop. At the first driveway he noses the car in, then backs out in the opposite direction. He drives on slowly, and several cars pull out to pass him.

As he nears the bridge at Petite Riviere, fat raindrops begin to splatter his windshield, and he turns the wipers on. Impelled by habit, he is intent on driving to Crescent Beach, in spite of the threatening dark clouds approaching from the southeast. He continues on at a slow and steady pace and finally reaches the turnoff. He leaves Route 331 and slows for the ramp, letting his car coast down onto the sand.

There are no other cars, and no one else in sight. The surf churns angrily, dark grey and clogged with seaweed and debris. White foam spatters from the crests of waves, and black clouds entwine and roil over the bay, driven toward the shore by a rising wind. There are no birds; even the hardy gulls that own the sand are sheltering inland.

Andrew stops the car and gets out. His thin shirt offers little protection against the cutting wind, but he doesn't notice. He lowers his head and plods off eastward, his gait awkward and uncertain. He stumbles along the surf line, soaking his shoes and the cuffs of his pants. His arms feel numb, stiff with the cold and something else.

He raises his head and looks off toward the far distant line of trees near Bush Island. Something catches his eye, some small anomaly on the flat, desolate sand. He squints. Someone is sitting on the beach, illuminated by a rigidly geometric circle of brilliant sunlight.

He bends his head once more against the storm and starts off again, angling inland above the high tide line to avoid the surf. He spots a starfish entangled in a strand of kelp and stoops to pick it up. It curls slowly around his finger.

See, Jennie? I told you it was alive.

Jennie!

He looks up again and she is there, a small figure sitting on the sand, her red pail between her knees, her busy hands digging and scooping. He tries to run toward her but stumbles and falls. Cold rain soaks his hair and runs down his neck inside his shirt.

He raises his head and sees the child turn to look at him, smiling broadly. Her eyes grow huge, shining brightly in the glow of her patch of sunlight. Her tapered starfish fingers wave in happy greeting.

His eyes drift out over the water to find a sparkling white boat, heeled over smartly and her sails full, gliding along a calm and sunlit sea. Charlie Grant stands at the helm, his broad face beaming in delight. Catherine stands beside him. She raises her hand in greeting, and her huge, sad and lovely eyes loom large before him. He tries to respond but cannot lift his arm, cannot even feel it.

The boom slams across the deck as Charlie spins the wheel, tacking off away from shore. Catherine's face seems to hang for an instant in midair, then turns abruptly away. Her back is straight, her long, beautiful hair cascades down and streams out in the wind, and she and Charlie and the boat dissolve in a violent crash of surf.

Andrew stiffens his arms and tries to rise. He can no longer feel his fingers, and it takes him several attempts to regain his feet. He still clutches the starfish, now bent and crushed in his numb grasp. His legs feel disconnected, and each halting step seems to bring him no closer to the smiling child and her bright red pail. She is farther off now, close to the end of the beach near the rocks.

He tries to run but his right knee collapses under him, spilling him once more to the sand. He sprawls face down. The mangled starfish drops from his hand. Sheets of rain lash the back of his neck and soak his shirt and pants.

Jennie bounces up and down in her bright yellow and blue bathing suit, waving to him joyfully from the far end of the beach. The red plastic pail swings back and forth in her hand. The sun shines from her hair, Penny's luminous copper hair, and he hears her calling to him.

He struggles to his feet. His knee protests but supports him, and he limps onward. Jennie is sitting on the sand again, this time at the very base of the distant rocks. She sifts through great clumps of seaweed, gleefully plucking dozens of starfish from among the strands and placing them in her bucket.

The squall line reaches the beach, its horizontal blasts of wind-driven rain fierce and drenching. Andrew doesn't notice. Intent on reaching the rocks, he places one foot carefully in front of the other. He stares down as if from a great height. Each step is someone else's. He can no longer feel his aching knee.

He looks up through the rain toward the brilliant patch of sunlight that now beams down upon the nearest rock, a huge outcropping wedding the sand and sea. Jennie sits far above on its highest point, waving to him merrily.

He struggles forward and finally reaches the gravel verge that surrounds the rock where she stands. He tries to climb and stretches out his left arm to steady himself. His hand rests against the face of the rock, but he cannot feel its surface.

His balance deserts him. Falling backward, he sits down hard and clutches his deadened left arm, now hanging as if severed from his body beneath his rain-soaked shirt. In confusion he struggles to raise it, and a searing white-hot pain lances across his chest, smashing the air from his lungs. He collapses backward, his head striking the rough gravel and scattering the covering layer of broken shells.

Rain falls upon his closed eyes. In the darkness of his mind, a single point of light, a bright and radiant, blue and yellow imp, waves her arm in a happy arc above her head.

"Where did you find your cat?" she calls out to him.

Who's going to feed Old Cat?

ABOUT THE AUTHOR

Educator, musician and author, Peter H. Riddle was born December 29, 1939, in Long Branch, New Jersey. He earned a Ph.D. degree from Southern Illinois University in 1974. He joined the faculty of Acadia University in 1969, and presently teaches at the rank of Full Professor. His specialties are Music Theatre, Theory and History. Dr. Riddle's publications include numerous musical compositions and arrangements, several novels, and eleven volumes about the history and technology of antique toy trains. He and his wife Gay make their home in Wolfville, Nova Scotia.